# THE OAKLAND QUARTET

By

Abby Mendelson

iUniverse, Inc.
Bloomington

# The Oakland Quartet

iUniverse books may be ordered through booksellers or by contacting:

iUniverse
1663 Liberty Drive
Bloomington, IN 47403
www.iuniverse.com
1-800-Authors (1-800-288-4677)

ISBN: 978-1-4759-4898-1 (sc)
ISBN: 978-1-4759-4899-8 (ebk)

Printed in the United States of America

iUniverse rev. date: 09/17/2012

# THE OAKLAND QUARTET

For the many friends who have inspired this book.
I graciously thank them all.

# Books by the Author

## Fiction

The Oakland Quartet
End of the Road: American Elegies
Ghost Dancer: 21 Stories
Scotch and Oranges
Paradise Boys

## Non-Fiction

Pittsburgh Prays: Thirty-Six Premier Houses of Worship
The Pittsburgh Steelers: Yesterday and Today
The Official History of the Pittsburgh Steelers
Pittsburgh: A Place in Time
Reckoning with Rainbows: The History of the Pressley Ridge Schools
A Century of Caring: This History of the Holy Family Institute
Pittsburgh Born, Pittsburgh Bred (Co-Author)
The Power of Pittsburgh (Contributor)
Pittsburgh Characters (Contributor)

# Contents

▼

I would be remiss if I did not express my sincerest gratitude to those helped create *The Oakland Quartet*:

Judy Mendelson, whose great faith, constant encouragement, and infinite patience made *The Oakland Quartet*—and all things—possible;

The many people whose stories I have shamelessly stolen, adapted, and recreated. I trust that I have represented them accurately. I humbly apologize for any errors.

Me miserable! which way shall I flie
Infinite wrauth, and infinite despaire?
Which way I flie is Hell; my self am Hell;
And in the lowest deep a lower deep
Still threatning to devour me opens wide,
To which the Hell I suffer seems a Heav'n.
O then at last relent: is there no place
Left for Repentance, none for Pardon left?

—John Milton, *Paradise Lost*

# PROLOGUE

▼

# BEEF

The tall, courtly man nearly whispered as spoke. "Get two," he said, flipping up the scarred baseball with his left hand, then slicing it to the shortstop, who fielded it cleanly, tossed it to the second baseman, who whirled and threw it to the first baseman, who threw it back to me.

The courtly man nodded, took a handkerchief out of his trouser pocket, wiped his brow, then accepted the ball.

"Deep in the hole," he barely said, then hit the ball just past the shortstop, who raced back for it, fielded it with both hands, set himself, then executed a long, accurate throw to first.

Forbes Field, called America's most beautiful ballpark when it was built in 1909, was a vast expanse of green hemmed in by a red brick wall. Over the ballpark's left shoulder stood Mr. Carnegie's Institute, the stone blackened by decades of mill smoke. Over the right shoulder, the vista of Mary Schenley's Park was a softly rolling green. As the older man batted the ball toward them, and the players scampered about the hard-packed infield, the bouncing ball sent up small poofs of dust. Wordlessly, running back and forth, sweating, stopping, reaching down with their worn leather gloves, the boys fielded flawlessly, spinning, turning, making the throws.

"Runner on third," the courtly man barely smiled, then chopped down on the ball, sending it bounding high to the second baseman, who looked hard at me, covering home, and at third, before flipping the ball to first.

"Good eyes," the courtly man smiled, then swung again. "Around the horn."

Everybody said it—they were the slickest infield Oakland ever saw. Pie Traynor himself said that, and we believed he was more than just being nice. Oh, he *was* a nice man, walked everywhere, always a good morning or a good word for everyone. He knew they played ball, knew they played for Central, so one morning, when the Pirates were out of town, he worked them out at Forbes Field. Beautiful morning it was, too, cool and clean, although we could feel the heat hanging in the distance; it'd get hot later in the day, we knew. But that morning, it was just fine.

They were always together, and they were all there, along with Duffy and me. Mongol at third—Mongol because of his slanty eyes. With his blond hair so fine and thin he was starting to lose it, he looked like something off the steppes of Central Asia. Not that his knuckles dragged along the ground, but he was hulking, bruising, big-shouldered and barrel-chested; a weight lifter. He had good range and could *fire* the ball to first. Pie Traynor liked that—he was a third-baseman, too, maybe the best ever, and he liked that. He didn't have to say it—I could see it from the glint in his eye and his little smile when he chopped the ball to Mongol, saying, "lefthander," in his soft Massachusetts drawl. "Lefthander" meant fast runner going down the line, and Mongol'd grab the ball and gun it to Stash, already standing in his stretch, knowing the ball was coming right to him, waiting patiently for it.

It was Stash at first, of course, ever since we were kids, seven or eight years old, Stash the tall one, thin as an ax handle, making the stretch at first. "Throw it *low*," he'd holler, "and I'll pick it." He could, too, really dig it out of the dirt, make just about any play you'd like to see. "Get two," Pie Traynor'd say, chopping it to Stash, who'd turn, throw to Whitey covering second, then slide like an ice skater back to first to take the return throw. "Three-six-three!" Pie Traynor'd say, "nothing sweeter!" And Stash'd grin and kick the dirt around the bag a little just like Gus Suhr used to do.

"In the hole," Pie Traynor said, and rapped it sharply between second and third, where Whitey ran back for it, snagged it, stopped himself, then threw to first. "Just in time," Pie Traynor smiled.

"Not bad for a guy too blind to see," I muttered to Duffy, but all he did was shake his head.

Sober enough in the morning sun, Whitey, like Paul Waner, could shake off an all-night drunk and play some ball.

Sober enough in the morning sun, Whitey was as steady a shortstop as Dick Groat. But how often did Whitey play in the morning?

"Make the pivot," Pie Traynor said, hitting the ball to Nig at second, who, like his hero Billy Maz, never seemed to touch the ball. Smooth as Jimmy O'Hara's bar top, Nig picked it up, turned, and fed it to Whitey, coming across the bag to throw it to Stash waiting at first, Nig chattering all the time.

"Behind the bag," Pie Traynor said, the ball scooting down the left field line. Chasing it, Mongol gloved it, bobbled it, tried to grab it, dropped it, picked it up, bobbled it again, dropped it again, then in frustration picked up the ball and heaved it into the stands above third.

"You're going to have to do something about that temper, son," Pie Traynor said gently. "It'll get you in trouble a'one of these days." He paused. "A ballplayer has to have a cool head. Especially," he smiled sadly, "if he's going to play the hot corner."

Mongol, red-faced, muttered that he was sorry.

Of course, the other teams knew that about him, too. Cool-headed, Mongol was the Colossus of Clout, as powerful a hitter as anyone in the City League. But get him angry about the slightest thing—both his parents were easy targets—and he'd be gripping the bat too tightly, pounding it, overswinging, striking out.

Working them out for a good hour, maybe more, tie tight to his neck, suit jacket resting insouciantly on a scarred wooden seat, Pie Traynor watched the four of them fielding and sweating in the late morning sun. When the Pirates were out of town, and with 59-year-old Pie Traynor in charge, neighborhood kids got a free pass to work out in Forbes Field. Having taken a liking to the four, *Mister* Traynor, to all of us, agreed to see if they had the tools for a real tryout.

He was that kind of man. Even though it'd been more than 20 years since he'd put on a uniform, he always had time to talk to people on the street, to answer questions about baseball, to give an autograph to a kid who'd never seen him play. And play he did. One of the all-time best third basemen, Pie Traynor anchored two World Series teams, 1925-27, later was the player-manager.

I never saw him, but my dad did. "Great reflexes," my dad liked to say, "well, you need 'em at third. Ol' Pie had 'em—had 'em strong. Quick hands—quickest I ever seen. Strong, accurate arm. Hell of a hitter, too, .338 in '22, .366 in 1930, .320 lifetime."

Pie Traynor liked the Central boys—there was no doubt about it. Maybe because they weren't big—and as a skinny teenager he was passed over by his hometown Boston Braves. Maybe because they were slick and fast. Tall, phlegmatic Stash at first; short, swarthy Nig at second; wiry, unfocused Whitey at short; heavily muscled, short-tempered Mongol at third. Me and Duffy—Beef, the backstop-sized catcher, Duffy, the rag-armed pitcher—may have come along for the ride, but we were never really in the running. As a ballplayer, I was like the Penn-Lincoln Parkway in the morning—heavy and slow—and Duffy, well, Duffy always thought he was better'n the rest of us, so he never really worked hard. "I'm a college man," he'd say, even though his shanty Irish old man hauled trash and washed dishes like everybody else.

Duffy'd been saying that since he was 10, and made good on it. Scheduled to start in the fall, he had graduated Central near the top of the class—the rest of us near the bottom. While Duffy was getting ready for what Nig called "all that high-class coed cooze," the rest of us were looking for something to do. It was 1958, a good time to stay out of the army—well, it's always a good time to stay out of the army. Likewise, it was always a good time to stay out of the mills—if you could find something better to do.

Baseball? For the Oakland Quartet—that's what everyone called them, from Jimmy O'Hara, who ran the neighborhood, to Regis Moran, who made sure everybody remembered that Jimmy O'Hara ran the neighborhood, to Father Dave, who celebrated mass and taught religion and civics at Central, to Bill Roland, just getting his start on City Council—it was a way off the street, a way out of the hustle of shining shoes and slinging hash, a way out of the mills. "All that travel," Mongol said. "All those bars," Whitey smiled. "All those endorsements," Stash grinned. "All that pussy," Nig laughed, then they all did.

Yes, they could field, but they were kids, short (except Stash) and skinny (except Mongol), who couldn't hit—or couldn't hit well enough to be considered anything more than low-minor scrubs.

Pie Traynor nodded to Duffy, who threw three bags of balls to them. *Crack*, single here. Double there. Pop up. Strike out. Duffy was groovin' 'em pretty good, but the Oakland Quartet wasn't doing much of anything. Finally, he threw a belt-high fastball to Stash who turned on it and really connected. I looked up into the sun. Going, going—to 20 feet short of the left field wall, where the ball thudded to earth, a long, loud, harmless out.

"OK, boys, nice work," Pie Traynor said, wiping his face with his handkerchief. "That's it for today."

"You work 'em out for a little bit, Beef," Pie Traynor said, handing the bat to me. "I'm going to sit for a minute in the dugout and fill out the scouting report."

Of course, we knew what it was. Four good-field, no-hit infielders, Duffy a rag-arm high-school pitcher, and me a slow-as-hardened-slag catcher whose knees were just starting to go bad.

"Thank you, Mr. Traynor," Stash said, and the others nodded and mumbled the same.

"Think nothing of it," Pie Traynor answered, his broad Boston accent flapping like Old Glory in the slight summer breeze. "Glad to take a look."

That was more than 40 years ago, when four boys from Oakland stuck their heads out of the smog for a hopeful look, like Icarus, then crashed back to earth again. I'm as old as Pie Traynor was that day, and I have two plastic knees to show for it, two plastic knees because of all the abuse I gave them as a catcher. I was mustered in and mustered out of the peace-time army. I went to college on the G.I. Bill. Now I live alone, above a bar; I make my living as a social worker. And I know this as well as I know my own name: your entire life can turn on a single, irrevocable instant. Accidents or active acts of will, I've seen it happen time and again.

But I've never seen it more than with the Oakland Quartet.

This is a story in black and white, like the year in which it takes place, 1958. It's a story about an old neighborhood, Oakland, with its sagging frame houses, broken sidewalks, trash-choked alleys. Like an old couch, Oakland had a crumpled, lived-in look, too many late nights, too many unwashed days.

It's a story about a steel mill neighborhood, where working-class families turned their backs on outsiders. Oakland had its own rules, minded its own business, expected you to do the same.

It's a story about gritty streets and mill smoke, about grim lives and grimy wash hanging in unweeded backyards. Most of all, it's a story about four flawed boys—young men of promise—wanting to play ball, learning to hustle, waiting on the army, dealing with the crime they committed, piecing together the rest of their lives.

It's a story of four boys who didn't understand limits, who didn't know when—or how—to stop.

Ultimately, it's a story about one act that destroyed their lives.

In Oakland, 1958, people stayed at home; people stayed in their village. They watched their black-and-white televisions; their ballplayers wore white uniforms at home, gray uniforms on the road.

Every man had his place to drink, and every man preferred to drink with his own kind. For us, for the Irish, we kept regular hours at public constabularies like Jimmy O'Hara's Emerald Lounge, after hours at private places like the Gaelic Club, which the dagos called the Garlic Club. Well, they would. At the Emerald and the Gaelic it wasn't just the old timers who remembered NINA—No Irish Need Apply—signs in store windows and on factory gates. We all did, and we all learned whom we could—and couldn't—trust. So when we didn't *have* to mix with dagos and niggers and hunkies, we stayed with the Irish. "At least a fellow can have a beer without the room turning into a punch palace," Regis Moran said. "Most of the time."

For all his toughness, Regis Moran epitomized that idea. He had the geniality—one might even say the gentility—that only a very big, very tough man can afford. More wont to laugh than fight, Regis Moran hadn't had to prove anything for a very long time. And everybody in Oakland knew it.

Like Regis Moran, when we drank, we didn't preen. We didn't parade. We didn't wear team gear. We didn't paste our service record on our bumpers and back windows. Our wives and girlfriends wore pony tails and earrings, and we wore our service jackets home—wore 'em 'til they wore out. Then we went shopping at Sears for civilian replacements.

The Oakland we grew up in was a neighborhood of veterans who never talked about it, never talked about what they saw or did, what they feared or hated. It was a neighborhood where every home had war souvenirs, uniforms and bayonets and helmets. One man brought his parachute home, then gave it to his kids as a backyard tent. They used it until it fell apart.

Our Oakland was a neighborhood where we didn't slap high fives, or low fives, or any fives at all. We didn't pound our chests like gorillas, or spike the ball, or take curtain calls for every sacrifice fly or ground-out. Instead, quiet was the order of the day. We dressed—and acted—like adults. We did our job, kept our mouths shut, and were grateful for what we had. Many people had less, we reminded ourselves, and they often lived right around the corner.

Oakland was a neighborhood where mothers wore housedresses, didn't drive, did their own laundry, and shopped for groceries every day. Whether they were regularly beaten, like Mongol's mother, or dazed and lost, like Whitey's, or tall and elegant, like Stash's, or hot-blooded, like Nig's, they were all quiet. If they talked to their neighbors, on the way to the market or hanging out wash, they spoke quietly, as if they were in a confessional, so that no one could overhear them. In Oakland, 1958, women knew their place.

Most important, though, living in Oakland meant taking care of our own. No questions asked, no quarter asked or given, we took care of our own.

The Oakland Quartet learned that lesson with their mothers' milk.

In the summer, the heat came early to Oakland and stayed, day and night, 'til fall. On the streets, broken bottles battled with cars for curb space. Behind them, the alleys stank with the smell of rotting vegetables and stale urine.

Forbes Avenue stirred sluggishly in the morning heat, like some animal struggling into consciousness, the moms 'n' pops rolling out their awnings and opening their stores. Gus Miller himself walked briskly down the street, looking for all the world like Connie Mack in his suit and high, starched collar, and opened his Wonder Store, ready to trade his treats for Oakland's pocket change.

Deliveries began. Battered kegs of beer rolled into Jimmy O'Hara's basement, along with loaves of bread, cartons of eggs, and boxes of frozen food. Cardboard boxes full of pretzels, Slim Jims, and Beer Nuts all slid down, too, like the hard-boiled eggs and Tabasco set on the bar, salty food to stir up thirst.

Dirty busses lumbered east and west, groggy men walked down the hill toward Eliza, scarred lunch buckets in hand, a surly goodbye waved to wives and sweethearts, parents and children.

Oakland was awake.

Stash noticed it first, that young City Councilman Bill Roland strutted around the neighborhood as if he owned it.

"Ah, he's shanty, just like the rest of us," Nig said one morning, watching Roland's figure retreating down Forbes Avenue. He passed a Lucky Strike to Whitey, who took a deep drag, then gave it to Stash. "My old man told me so."

"English," Mongol said, and spit, "not Irish. We got the same bastards over here."

"Yeah," Stash said, "but he started out shanty like the rest of us. Now he dresses in them fine suits like he was the laird of the manor."

"Jagoff," Nig said, reaching for the cigarette. "Laird of the fuckin' manure, if you ask me."

"Well, nobody did," Stash said, and they all laughed, even Nig, whose first impulse had been to take a swing at him, but didn't.

Although Oakland was Roland's political fiefdom, unless somebody tougher or smarter could take it away from him, he hated to be called Boss. "Don't call me Boss!" he'd thunder at even the most innocuous use of the term. For kids, of course, he was Mr. Roland. But for anyone of drinking age, he was Bill; later in life he was Old Bill, and he was still approachable. After he got himself elected Mayor, and made many friends, and a lot more enemies, Roland was surrounded by handlers and bodyguards, especially that snake Garth Childress, whom Father Dave—kind, decent, balding, round-faced Father David Reddy—simply considered Satan Incarnate. "It's harder and harder for a body to get next to him," an old hand complained, but no one, least of all Roland, seemed to be listening.

He's like a bank, Stash decided. You pay in, and you take out. He knows people, he gets people jobs, and he gets a piece of everything. He's just like Jimmy O'Hara, except there's more of him.

On an Oakland summer day, or night, you'd smell hot pavement, frying meat, sewage, gas and motor oil, bus exhaust, and human sweat. From the steel mills, from Eliza, there'd be the smells of sulfur, of burning coal; near the gin mills you'd smell beer, Iron and Duke, Fort Pitt and Stroh's, Stoney's and Straub's.

There was *always* soot on the window sills, no matter how many times a day a body cleaned them, but it was good soot, because it meant men working shifts, and that meant pockets full of money.

At night, when the windows were open and the air was still, you could hear them making steel in Eliza's iron belly, thumping like a muffled heart, thrumming like a distant dynamo.

Sure, the mills meant good paydays, but they were a better place to stay out of. "They're hot, dirty, and dangerous," Stash said one day.

"The mills or the women?" Nig laughed.

"I'll take 'em both," Mongol nodded.

Forbes Avenue had fine stores and good restaurants, traffic and toffs, swank and swells. But it was on the back streets—on Bouquet and Bates, Dawson and Oakland, Atwood and Meyran—that this story takes place. It takes place in the weary frame homes where the Oakland Quartet lived, the broken streets they walked, the dark, dank bars they drank in.

It takes place in the thick, overgrown park at the edge of the ravine.

It takes place in a time when baseball was still *the* game, when a tall, tough saloonkeeper named Jimmy O'Hara ran the neighborhood, at least the Irish part of it. Jimmy O'Hara—tall, square-shouldered, hint of a smile; it was Jimmy O'Hara's neighborhood, just like the Emerald was Jimmy O'Hara's bar, because he knew Bill Roland, and a lot of other people, and found work for people, and gave them money, too, if they needed it. Of course, they all *owed* Jimmy O'Hara; they all had to give him a little something every week for his favors. To his credit, Jimmy O'Hara was always nice about it, except once or twice when Regis Moran had to pay someone a visit. Everyone understood that having a job—having *something*—was better than having nothing.

The *something* often included all sorts of side hustles, for five or 10 guys at a time, a little of this, a little of that, you know, some of it legal, some of it not. On Pirate game days, it was all hands on deck, two dozen or more, everybody parking cars—in alleys, on sidewalks, all over lawns. Everybody selling souvenirs and hot dogs and wee pints of liquor. Of course, the cops had their hands out, too, and so didn't see anybody breaking any law, so never wrote any tickets, at least not in those places that were protected. Otherwise, it was a fine and a tow—and devil help you get your car back in less than three days! "That'll teach 'em a lesson," is all Jimmy O'Hara'd say. "And an easy one it is, too. If me brother Frank was here, he'd slash their tires good and proper."

But Jimmy O'Hara's brother Frank wasn't there. Frank was down the river, doing a dime in Western for armed robbery. "The damned fool," is all Jimmy O'Hara'd say. "He got himself in that fuckin' jackpot. Now let him get himself out of it."

Even without Frank to direct traffic, that's how it was on game days, Duffy and me waving cars in with hand-made signs and ping pong paddles, Stash and Nig and Mongol and Whitey fanned out across the neighborhood, parking cars in spaces you'd think were too small for roller skates much less Buicks and Oldsmobiles.

Pirate players were all around, current and retired, Pie Traynor and Frankie Gustine and many more. Even the great Paul Waner, a squinty-eyed little man they were afraid to talk to, and who Mongol most wanted to be 'cause he got so many hits.

"You got a Paul Waner bat?" Nig'd needle him.

"Nah," Mongol'd say, "I got a Gus Suhr bat. A real one. Ol' Gus gave it to my old man when my old man'd park his car down by Farmer's lawn. Parked it real good, too. Never no scratches or dings or nothin'."

"He ain't near as good as Paul Waner," Nig'd say. "Gus Suhr ain't no Hall of Famer."

"Should be," Mongol'd say. "Ain't no justice." Then he'd cross his arms, and stare off at Eliza's orange glow on the horizon.

They cribbed cigarettes, and when they couldn't get 'em, they bought Luckies from Gus Miller. Ol' Gus never seemed to care who smoked, or where or when. When they didn't have any money, they stole smokes from the Gaelic Club when Regis Moran wasn't looking, which he didn't, or not very often, anyway.

All of 'em born in 1940—although the running gag was that Mongol wasn't born, he was hatched—the Oakland Quartet had no living memory of World War II but plenty from Korea. They remembered how the mills seemed to burn hotter, and longer, and how many men weren't around. Still, they couldn't talk much about Korea, because Whitey's dad was shell-shocked there, and it hurt too much for him to speak about it.

"I'm livin' with strangers and other people's washing 'cause me dad ain't right," is all he'd say about it—about his mother taking in boarders and doing laundry to make ends meet—then change the subject.

All four of them were underage, but it never stopped 'em from drinking. Never stopped anybody, really, in Oakland, as long as you knew where to go, could see over the bar, and knew how to keep your mouth shut. Because the Oakland Quartet were ballplayers, and were with Jimmy O'Hara, they got served in a half-dozen Oakland bars, in Jimmy O'Hara's Emerald, of course, and Quinque's (the only dago joint on Bouquet Street), Cozy's and Frankie Gustine's (but only when Frankie wasn't around, 'cause he was funny that way about drinking, maybe 'cause he roomed with Paul Waner, and saw what drinking did to him and so many other ballplayers), the Oakland Cafe and the Fort Pitt Tavern (but only in the back room, which was fine with them 'cause it had a television, and only when the Liquor Control guys weren't around, which they weren't very often, 'cause they were lazy bastards when they weren't actually on the take).

There was Chief's, too, but that was all the way to the north end of Oakland, so far away it could have been in Ohio, and so why the fuck bother?

Then there was the Gaelic Club, when they mostly could get beers, Regis Moran being tough about it sometimes.

But even when Regis Moran—all six-foot-three and busted knuckles of him—was giving them heat, they all admired him. Honest, strong—"fucking

Chingachgook," Stash said, but as usual no one knew what he was talking about. "Stand-up guy," he translated, "a real brick," and they all murmured assent.

"Never did his friends no wrong," Nig answered.

"Never busted the wrong head," Mongol nodded sagely, for him the ultimate accolade.

"Fuck no," Whitey said.

"You need somebody to stand up," Stash said, "Regis Moran'll stand up for you."

To outsiders, though, Regis Moran was a fearsome man, a Central Casting enforcer. Big, burly man, big, meaty hands, biting the ends of his cigarettes, coughing and spitting—he actually looked worse than his well-earned reputation as a world-class bare-knuckles brawler.

"The idea," he told the Oakland Quartet one sultry afternoon, "is *not* to get into fights, but make the other fella think you will. Make him afraid of you, make him think twice before takin' a swing. That'll stop him cold a'fore he starts. Saves a lot of wear and tear that way," he'd pause, then wink. "But if a body's dead set on havin' a dust-up, I'm the guy to see."

It was Father Dave who put Regis Moran into perspective for the Oakland Quartet. Asked why the good padre put up with Regis Moran's carrying-ons, the priest shrugged and sighed. Eschewing the turn-the-other-cheek sermon, which never seemed to work in Oakland, Father Dave simply shrugged. "He's my cross," he said. "I have to bear him.

"When a person shows you who he is," Father Dave added, "believe him the first time."

Of course it used to test Father Dave unmercifully when Regis Moran, being who he was, used to rail about Jesus and Barabbas, saying that only a sap would take the rap for somebody else. "You stand up for your friends," Regis Moran'd say. "You don't fall down for them."

"Now, Regis," Father Dave would begin.

"Beggin' your pardon, Father," Regis Moran'd get all red and chew harder on the end of his cigarette, "but this is stupid. All this self-sacrifice shit. You stand up. You don't bring in the bagpipes, sing a couple of choruses of 'Danny Boy,' shed a few tears, and take a dive. Horse shit. Take your whippin' straight up and be done with it. And don't be expectin' anyone else to take it for you!"

"Regis," Father Dave, being a good priest, would try one more time.

"It's every man for himself on this ship, Father," Regis Moran'd answer, biting his cigarette. "None of this let-me-die-for-Barabbas or whoever-the-fuck happy horseshit. Look out for Number One, is all." He jerked a thumb at his chest, then pointed to the Oakland Quartet standing around him. "You all do that and the world will be a better place. Believe me."

Their drink of choice was Duquesne, which grandly called itself the Prince of Pilsners. "The *piss* of pilsners is more like it," Nig said, spitting, but for Whitey, who did not discriminate, it was just fine.

"It tastes like fuckin' barge traffic water from the river," Mongol said.

"So does your mother," Whitey said, but Mongol didn't get mad, 'cause it was Whitey, and who could get mad at him?

Sometimes they got liquor—often kid stuff, blackberry brandy and Jumping Jack, sometimes something harder—from Tommy the Sailor, hair greasy and lank, face all flat and pasty, who went in the Navy in '42 just fine but didn't come back that way. Tommy had to be taken home drunk from the machine shop two days out of five. When he was sufficiently sober, Tommy bought them whatever they wanted.

Misery, they tell me down at the office, does indeed love company.

Whatever they had, they drank together, taking pulls from bottles secured in paper bags, smoking Luckies, sitting under a tree in Schenley Park hard by Dawson Street. Passing bottles back and forth, Whitey always took the longest pulls, then stuck his finger in and licked it when they were done. "Another dead soldier," he'd say with deep solemnity, then laugh and pitch the bottle down the steep ravine, the four of them waiting until they heard the crash far below.

When they couldn't drink at will—meaning when Tommy the Sailor wasn't around—Whitey got winos to buy him bottles at the State Store; Mongol lifted weights; Stash ran every hustle he could, from parking cars to collecting pop bottles, or got kids to run them, Stash taking a piece of everything; Nig had sex—in the park, in parked cars, on porches, anywhere he could get a girl to drop trou.

Part of the reason that the Oakland Quartet wanted to be ballplayers was because ballplayers owned bars, or visited them, and generally drank for free. "Gus Suhr owns his own liquor store out of state," Mongol offered, "so he drinks for free, too."

"So do I," Whitey said.

So did neighbors, who shared with one and other, although race was the great, unspoken divider. Micks and dagos and niggers—everybody else, too—they all stayed on their side of the line, moving across gingerly and only with permission.

"There's nothing," Jimmy O'Hara used to say, "that a ball peen hammer can't fix."

Or Regis Moran.

The Oakland Quartet grew up in a time when trolleys still rumbled down Fifth Avenue, and you gave your seat to a woman, any woman. It was a time you were polite to women, all women. It was a time that Jimmy O'Hara ran the neighborhood, the same way that old man Cicero ran things south of Bates Street. It was a time that everyone in the neighborhood knew you, and your family, and all your business.

It was a time that every one of us knew at least one Forbes Field usher or groundskeeper who would sneak us in. That when we drank underage we were discreet about it, even if we were carrying cold beers through the streets or serving them in our small back yards to men sitting on plastic folding chairs, each sweating, long-neck bottle crowned with an upside down glass. That we might have worn a suit on a date but loafed on the stoop in our undershirts.

It was a time that we never got out of line, but when we did we answered, "yes, sir," or took a punch in the face for our pains.

It was a time that all of us, the Oakland Quartet included, lived south of Forbes—Bouquet Street, and Oakland; Atwood, Meyran, Semple—but north of Bates, where the *Groceria* marked the border.

That border also marked their first score as a group, when Nig brought over a giggling, fat Italian girl from Ward Street. She said her name was Gina, not that anybody cared; she was a couple of years older than they were, and she took 'em all on. They all took a turn, in his aunt's living room, on the couch, Mongol last, and he made everybody look away.

It was also Nig who found that wayward girls home, north of St. Paul's off Craig Street. He'd whistle, and the girls'd sneak out a back window, and they'd do it on top of the garbage cans. Nig said he thought he'd died and gone to heaven.

That's where you looked for girls, for that kind of girl, south and north, not where we lived, not our kind, never our kind, not then at least, because everyone of them had parents, and everyone knew someone else.

For Nig, those girls was the start of it. From time to time he showed up in a car, or in a house when no one was around, or in the back room of the

Fort Pitt Tavern, with some local talent, not pretty—*definitely* not pretty. Sometimes the Oakland Quartet'd have to kick in a buck or two, never as much as five; sometimes she took everyone free. One time, an old whore wanted five apiece, but they talked her into four for 10 bucks—and they swore she'd used the condoms before and washed them out.

Stash always handled the money, and Whitey and Nig and Mongol figured he took a piece for himself, the way he stole quarters out of the collection plate, rustling all the coins as if he were looking for change, but really palming a couple-three quarters while he dropped in a nickel or a dime.

"Small price to pay," Stash'd say.

Oakland, 1958: the neighborhood was flush after the war, two wars, really. People had jobs, folding green; "pockets," Regis Moran said, "got the mumps with money." I remember my mother telling me how people in the Depression, and even during the war, always wrote on both sides of a piece of paper, even scrap paper, even in the margins. That was the time that people used newspaper for everything—to clean themselves, to stuff under their clothes and into their shoes for warmth. They put it in cracks in walls and floors and used it instead of paint. People folded and saved waxed paper until it became so wrinkled that it fell apart—or became so transparent that it simply disappeared.

While most everybody in Oakland had running water, flush toilets, and hard-wood floors, not everybody could say that. North, and south, and east there were shanties, real shanties, with dirt floors, privies in the back, and buckets lined up by the door.

Some neighborhoods had open sewers in the streets. Nobody wants to remember that now.

Nobody had air conditioning in 1958, so on steamy summer nights people sat outside, in the hot, sulfur-thick air. Pirate games were on the radio, and lights and shouts from Forbes Field filled the night. Some people played music and danced. They drank the Prince of Pilsners, smoked Camels and Lucky Strikes, and called each other's parents Mr. and Mrs., or Sir and Ma'am, and stood up when they came in the room.

Sure, the skies may've been black from time to time, but they weren't as bad as they were before the war, before Smoke Control. Besides, soot never bothered anybody in Oakland. OK, sometimes it annoyed my mother, who had to clean the house twice a day, and the white-collar people, who had to bring an extra shirt to work. But for the rest of us, every kid knew that the mills meant money—and not only money for the steelworkers. For the whole neighborhood, for the grocers and the tailors and the beer gardens. They meant money for Jimmy O'Hara's, too, where the Irish went to drink.

Kids went in Jimmy O'Hara's before they could read, standing on a stool, playing the pinball machine before Jimmy O'Hara yanked it out of there and told the racket guy to take his machine and shove it up his dago ass.

Those kids didn't know then what they know now, that Jimmy O'Hara got out the vote, got people jobs, kept the peace, and while he was at it kept a piece of everything, too. "Employment agencies take a little bit off the top," he said one day, "why shouldn't I?"

That was all a long time ago, before Bill Roland, who was a young man then, turned his back on Oakland, before the 115-day steel strike took the wind out of Oakland's sails, before Eliza, at the neighborhood's south edge by the river, shut down for good. Eliza and her sisters all up and down the river closed and shuttered. They used to turn out hot rolled sheet 24 hours a day, seven days a week, and made the streets awash with money.

Teams visiting Forbes Field stayed at the Schenley Hotel, and before walking across the street to the ballpark, they'd hang around the lobby. The Oakland Quartet did, too, looking to run errands for tips or for an old, scuffed ball. This was Oakland; the players lived, ate, drank, and whored with everyone else.

Owners worked their own bars and restaurants and stores—Jimmy O'Hara and Anthony Quinque and Gus Miller; even old man Cicero—and gave work to their families. When the mills turned, money ran like water. But when the mills went on strike, the money stopped. Stopped for Stash's old man, who did fix-it and handy-man jobs, and Whitey's, who peddled scrap, and Nig's, who did carpentering and painting. It even stopped at Mongol's mom's rooming house—'cause who could afford to pay her, and what was she going to do? Throw her boarders out on the street? She already threw out her husband, who used to beat her something awful. Mongol swore he'd kill him one day, and we all knew he would.

Strikes meant hard times, times that everybody ate white bread and gravy and went to church regular, praying that the strike'd be over, and everybody'd get well again.

Winters were all overcoats and dirty snow and turned-up collars. But on summer nights, when everything was open, you'd hear the crack of pool balls above the firehouse, or above Jimmy O'Hara's. The Oakland Quartet'd play cards and bowl and bet on anything. But they stayed away from numbers 'cause Jimmy O'Hara said it was nigger business, and, besides, it was fixed.

It was Oakland, and like everybody else the Oakland Quartet grew up fast. The thinking was that if you were old enough to worry about going in the army, you were old enough to take care of yourself. "You make a mistake," Jimmy O'Hara'd say, apron stained, wiping down the bar with an old towel, "fix it. Don't be some fuckin' knucklehead. Don't be cryin' to somebody else. *You* fix it.

"In the late innings," he'd add, drawing himself a Duke, sending the bowl of hard-boiled eggs skittering down the bar to the Oakland Quartet, "don't let 'em hit anything down the line on you. Nothin' down the line. Hittin' the ball may bloody 'em, and that's good, but remember, it's defense wins the game."

If they managed to crib together a couple of bucks, they'd go for dinner at the Bamboo Garden, subgum chow mein a favorite. Afterward, they'd see what they could boost at Autenreith's, then stop by the Iroquois Apartments, to see if Dotty's husband was out of town. If he was, they'd all have at her, Nig leading the way as always, the other three sitting in the living room smoking, waiting, listening to Porky Chedwick on the radio.

Meals were taken at The Clock, *the* diner on Forbes, occasionally at Cicero's, when they wanted dago, spaghetti with lots of Parmesan and hot peppers. But it was eggs over easy and club sandwiches with Russian dressing at The Clock, endless cups of black coffee, and flirting with Helen, the youngest and prettiest waitress in Oakland.

Not the White Tower, *never* the White Tower, where the waitresses were old enough to be their grandmothers—and who wanted to look at *that* while you're eating?

No, it was The Clock, with its vinyl seats and linoleum tops, and Helen, who always seemed to be there, tall, brunette, pert, tight uniform top and short skirt, coffee pot in hand, Nig drooling and panting, begging for mercy, and Helen just laughing and shaking her head.

"No, no, no," Mongol'd say, "why would a high-class dame have anything to do with a lowlife mick like you?"

Later, the legend was that one night, bored and lonely, abandoned by her boyfriend and grateful for the attention, Helen gave Nig a tumble. But since Nig was Nig, and always bragged about sex he'd never had, no one believed that he'd actually bedded the legendary, unapproachable Helen.

Canter's for pastrami, Isaly's for ice cream, all the while dreaming about eating with the swells at the Park Schenley.

If they paid any attention, which they didn't, they'd know that in D.C. Ike was in the White House. In Texas, Elvis Presley, all of 23 years old, entered Fort Hood. In Oklahoma, a couple traded their baby for a truck. And back home, a fat little kid named John Kohle, Jr., shot and killed his father. "Give that boy a medal," Mongol said.

Scrounging empty bottles for the deposit pennies, hawking newspapers, and parking cars made them movie money, and in 1958 they saw *Vertigo*, *Bridge over the River Kwai*, *Paths of Glory*, and their favorite, *The Vikings*. "Hold out the hand that has defied me," Stash kept saying, then whacked whoever was closest with a stick. When Mongol'd say that he wanted to die with a sword in his hand, Whitey just giggled.

It was 1958 in Oakland, a time of open shirts and sweaty hands. A time when you heard 30 different languages on the street, but nobody seemed to mind or get in each other's way.

Miles Davis came to town that summer, and Billy Eckstine, and the Tommy Dorsey Orchestra (without the Sentimental Gentleman of Swing, of course, who had died two years earlier.) Gordon and Sheila MacRae made a stop, as did Dorothy Lamour and Tallulah Bankhead, *Circus Boy* Mickey Braddock and Nancy Walker. And the usual a parade of strippers.

The Oakland Quartet couldn't buy or bribe or talk their way in to see the girls, despite Nig saying how he was a grown man and dying, but they did sneak in all the time to see Bill Virdon, Bob Skinner, and Dick Groat; Big Klu, Bobby Clemente, and Billy Maz; Bob Friend, the Deacon, and Elroy Face.

By early June, Maz was hitting .323 (although he cooled off to .270 by August), and Dick Groat .309. The Steelers, under coach Buddy Parker, began early workouts, Willie McClung, Ernie Stautner, and not much of anybody else.

At the State Store, just up Forbes Avenue, Whitey could get Canadian Club for $6.44 a fifth.

*Butt time!*

It was usually Nig, but it could have been Whitey or Mongol or even Stash when the mood struck. They'd gather 'round, and Nig'd shake a Lucky from his pack, light it, and pass it around. When they were done, if they were in Schenley Park, they'd bury it, the way the soldiers did in war movies. If they were on the street, they'd flip the butt between the parked cars or in a high, long arch as far down the street as they could—five cars at a clip sometimes. At night, the sparks seemed to scatter to the moon.

It was 1958, and everybody smoked, everybody, everywhere. Even people who didn't smoke smoked.

Oakland ended with the Monongahela River and Eliza, dark and burning, a maelstrom at the water's edge.

Kids played stickball in the street until they couldn't see the ball in the dark—and could hear the sounds of furtive love.

There were beer bottles hurled and broken, doors slamming by wind or anger. It seemed that every night some drunk tried to start his car and ground the motor like a mixmaster. With the windows left open to the sulfur-laden air, and the soot of the mills, the sound woke everybody up. They stared groggily out of their windows, thinking of yelling, *it's flooded, jagoff*, but then thought better of it, and stumbled back to sleep on the clammy sheets.

In the morning they woke with the taste of the mills in their mouths and black grit on the tables.

In Oakland they lived with the sound of sirens, police and fire and ambulances, day and night. They lived with the sound of firefighters sitting outside the station, laughing, talking, playing cards. They lived with the sound of radios, pop music and pop flies, Patti Page and Pirate games on in every house, every stoop, every block.

In Oakland they lived with the sound of breaking glass, so much so that by the time of a kid's first communion, he knew a block away whether it was a long-necked beer bottle or a windshield that got broken.

In Oakland they loafed at the Strand, bowling all night, straggling down those steep stairs, sweaty and disheveled, shoulders and arms aching, even Mongol, blisters rising on their fingers and thumbs. They loafed at the Strand Theater, too, where they'd sit through movies two and three times, depending on their mood, depending on who was in the movie. Tyrone Power, sure—he died that November, and Mongol never got over it. Deborah Kerr, their ideal woman, pure, untouchable.

Marilyn was Marilyn, of course; no one could deny that, and Nig rubbed himself raw looking at her. And Janet Leigh.

But Deborah Kerr was special.

The Oakland they lived in, South Oakland, away from the museums and the mansions, was close to the hollow boom and sulfur smoke of the mills, the clack and moan of the freight trains running by the muddy river. In winter, slush turned black and stayed on the streets for days; on summer nights, sulfur clung to clothes and curtains like mildew.

They lived in small apartments, above stores, behind luncheonettes. They lived in a world of thin walls, where every lover's embrace, every mother's slap and scold was overhead, discussed, dissected with the same passion with which they poured over box scores, politics, possible mill strikes.

They lived where the street lights never seemed to eradicate the gloom, where every still and fleeting silence was punctured by Eliza's distant boom, more coal for her burning womb.

On summer nights, it got hot and stayed that way. Trying to sleep, they'd lay on sticky sheets, their breath laying on their chests like shrouds.

Like Duffy, I played ball with them; he pitched, I caught. I was big, barrel-chested; they called me Beef, and that was fine with me.

They all avoided the army that summer; beating the draft was easy when you had Jimmy O'Hara to stand up for you. Jimmy O'Hara was the man to see, and they saw him. He said he'd find something for them to do—and put in a word with Bill Roland, who made sure their numbers weren't called. Sole support of his mother here (Mongol), 4-F there (Whitey), a little of this for Nig, a little of that for Stash—there were plenty of ways around the peace-time army. But they'd all owe Jimmy O'Hara, and Bill Roland, and they knew it.

I didn't ask for Jimmy O'Hara's help and didn't expect it. Instead, I went in the army, the peace-time army, to Germany, working in military intelligence, listening to a radio for two years, drinking the local lager, fraternizing with the local *frauleins*, contracting the local gonorrhea. I had a grand time.

Like the Oakland Quartet, I did escape the gravitational drag of the mills. After the army, I worked around the country. When I came back, Uncle Sam paid for my social work degree. I stayed until my back went out and once again Uncle Sam stepped in, this time in the form of Social Security. I walk with a cane now. I did not succeed at anything of substance.

I didn't pitch in the minors or go to law school, the way Duffy did, or prison, the way Stash and Mongol did, and Whitey and Nig should have. I spent 20-odd years as a case worker, trying to understand people, mostly troubled teens, trying to help them, trying find the right round hole for the right round pegs. I often think about that; I often think that I did that to right a wrong, transferring my loyalties to deal with people like my teammates and their problems. Maybe I did that to keep other kids from wrecking their lives the way the Oakland Quartet did.

As a social worker, I learned that life is a matter of balances. Like being a ballplayer: you can't overswing, and you can't underswing. You have to hit the ball just right. Similarly, the trait that defines a person, that can make him great, can also destroy him. So it has to be handled just right. With each of them, each of the Oakland Quartet, those traits weren't. Left unguided and unchecked, their strengths ruined all of them.

Maybe that's why they bonded so strongly, were so loyal to each other, committed that crime that made no sense. Maybe the four of them together formed one whole misguided person. Maybe they all rose and fell—together.

Well. That's the fancy stuff. I'm a case worker, not a clinical psychologist; I try to deal in fact, not theory. I try to deal with things I can prove. And help.

However, I will say that while at first they complimented each other, as they grew older what bound them together was not the intersection of their personalities but instead their crime.

As a social worker, I think of their story as a kind of case study, an investigation into the lives of these young men—who they were, what went so terribly wrong.

It was their crime, which took on a life of its own. It was also the flaws in their personalities—the strengths that ruined them. Stash, too smart for his own good, thought he could skate through life on just brains and charm. Stash, always possessed of that great stillness, even as a teen, even as a child. Thinking, that ferocious depth of intelligence that commands, made Stash a leader, made him think too little and too much. Nig, too libidinous for anyone's good, could never think north of his navel; the few times he did, he got into trouble. Whitey, too sad and sensitive, developed a tragic sense of life which, transformed into a taste for the gargle, drowned him. Mongol, never thinking past brute force, had enormous strength—and a temper that ran away with him.

One died of drink. Two did terms in prison. The fourth is a shadow seldom seen.

These were not good lives—that never got past that summer.

It could have been any of them, but it was Nig who set out to do something nice, to help this shy, slow girl, and wound up sending everything straight downhill.

Proving that the road to hell is indeed paved with good intentions.

Proving that no good deed really does go unpunished.

And other sententia.

On a street of wooden porches—verandas, really, big old houses with wrap-around porches—Sally was a tough girl, a couple of years older than Nig, who smoked and spat and smacked the ball with the best of them. Standing on her porch, cigarette in hand, cocked on one hip, she'd smirk at us, then flip the burning butt into the street as slick as anyone.

"Ballplayers," she'd snort, hitch up the shoulders of her sleeveless blouse, then turn back into her house.

Now Sally didn't mean anything to the Oakland Quartet, not even Nig, who had the hots for anything that moved, or said he did. But Sally was different. Not only was she farm-hand tough, she was also related somehow to Jimmy O'Hara, meaning that she was untouchable. But Sally had a slow cousin named Mary Margaret, a nice girl that they all liked as a little sister. For the Oakland Quartet, and especially for Nig, she became a kind of a mascot, a gentle joke. They'd kid her, and laugh a little, and Sally'd get red-faced, and clench her hands into fists, and threaten to cut the balls off anyone who hurt her cousin, and they'd all laugh, and say, "no offense meant, Sal, no offense, Sally, no offense meant at all. Mary Margaret's a good kid, isn't she? Isn't she?"

And they'd laugh about it, Mary Margaret—slow and slender and just 16—most of all.

Every rule has its exception, and for Nig it was Mary Margaret. According to him, girls were on this Earth for only one thing, except Mary Margaret. Nig treated her as if she were Deborah Kerr. Swore he'd never let nothing bad happen to her.

"Hey," Mongol said one night, loafing on a cool stone stoop on Dawson Street, "why not put it to Mary Margaret? She's yours for the taking, you know."

Stash and Whitey, sharing a Lucky Strike, said, "yeah, sure, why not?"

Pausing, actually thinking, Nig searched for the right word. "It would be—unholy," he said.

They wanted to laugh—and nearly did—but didn't, because Nig was being so serious and all.

That anomaly silenced the other three. Because for Nig, the only thing he was ever serious about was chasing girls. That and playing baseball.

That, in a roundabout way, is how he got his nickname. Nig's real name was Henry O'Donnell, but he'd been called Nig from the time he stepped on a baseball field. Dark-skinned, dark-eyed, dark-haired, he barely looked Irish at all, although all four of his grandparents came over on the boat. "Black Irish," he'd always say.

"Black Irish, my ass," some yokel answered. "There's a nigger in your woodshed somewhere. Looks like your mother did the dirty deed with some coon. Or your grandmother with some stevedore on the boat."

Need I tell you that the guy barely got out the last part before Nig was all over him, Stash dragging him off the guy before Nig killed him, Mongol similarly giving the fellow a few upside the head before politely instructing him that the stranger's opinions about his friend's lineage were really not welcome and that perhaps the gentleman should take his theories—not to mention his sorry ass—somewhere else before they *really* had to teach him a lesson.

Nevertheless, that idea stuck about Nig's hidden lineage, and to get under his already thin skin some of the other City League players started calling him Nig. Of course, Nig wanted to fight everybody about that, and Stash tried to stop him by telling Nig that was what they called Babe Ruth because of his wide, flat nose and thick features. Nig *still* wanted to fight about it, except that Stash finally convinced him that, by and large, *they* are hung like horses, and Nig, being Nig, shut up after that. Turned out, he liked the name. It even went so far that if he was asked in a roundabout way if the rumors were true, he'd say, "well, you know what they say," and smile.

"Where there's smoke, there's fire," Stash would always add sagely.

Certainly could have been, because for Nig, it was all girls. Liquor, money, fighting—none of that mattered. From the time he was 11 or 12, it was all skirts. He'd lean against a car, spitting a good 10 feet, flicking cigarettes across the street, and look the girls up and down as they passed—giggled, looked away from him, then looked back again. The joke about Nig became that he scored so much he kept Trojans in business. "You oughta buy one that don't wear out," Mongol said one day, and they all laughed.

Nig's old man was a carpenter and painter, and when he wasn't home he was drinking, down to the way south end of Oakland, down to Lasek's, with all them hunkie friends of his. "Good riddance," is all Nig'd say about him.

Nig's mother was a short, stumpy sow who seemed to pop one out every year. They were all fair-skinned and light-haired, 'cept Nig. Like I said, there was talk. As Regis Moran'd say, cigarette between his teeth, "you pays your money and you takes your choice."

Nig's old lady was silent, overwhelmed, and Nig had too many brothers and sisters to count. They lived in a four-room apartment on Oakland Avenue, sleeping two to a bed, some even sleeping on the floor. After he was 14, and was experienced with women, Nig spent as little time at home as possible.

With Mongol it was all about muscles, all about rolled up T-shirts, flashing and feeling his biceps, talking about lats and reps. That would have been fine, but he had that temper. Duffy thought it was because his father beat him a lot as a kid, but I wasn't so sure. "Reminds me of his mother," I'd say, thinking of the big-hipped, blue-eyed woman they called Wild Irish Rose because you could hear her shrieks for two blocks. Mostly, she shrieked at Mongol's five brothers and sisters, who caught more hell, Regis Moran said, than Satan on Judgment Day.

But Mongol was always in it, too. There was that trouble he got into at Central—nearly killed a kid in a lunchroom brawl, but Jimmy O'Hara managed to get him off the hook. At CYO boxing he fractured the skull of a boy who'd accidentally bloodied his nose. Even Regis Moran, the biggest, baddest brawler of them all, said that Mongol'd have to calm down a bit or he'd pay a fearsome price. (For that matter, Mongol was fearsome with a tire iron, too, vandalizing cars, doing damage all over South Oakland—broken windows, curbside doors scored like hams.)

Speaking of price, Whitey never seemed to have the price of a drink, but that never stopped him—or even slowed him down. Whitey never met a drink—of any kind—he didn't like. Introduced to wine as a 10-year-old altar boy, by a terminally stupid priest who felt that a little taste wouldn't hurt the boy, Whitey loved the headiness of it, the funny feeling it gave him in the pit of his stomach.

And he wanted more. Whatever he could get, wherever he could get served—or not. When he was 14 Whitey figured out that if he swept the floor and hauled trash at the Gaelic Club, he could crib whatever he could carry.

Where was his mother when Whitey came home drunk? Generally asleep. Taking in wash and boarders, she did everything she could to keep the little Atwood Street house going. Korea had ruined Whitey's father, who couldn't do much—when he could anything at all. Whitey's older sister Dolores worked as an upholsterer at Goodwill until she was about 20, when some railroad men took her. One day a car horn honked, and, cardboard suitcase in hand, she was gone. No one ever saw her again.

Now you'd think that Stash'd go his own way. 'Cause with Stash it was all money. That was all he was ever interested in—money and baseball. Not girls, although he took his turns like the rest of them. Not liquor, although he took a drink now and then. Not fighting. Just money.

Stash was smart, too. A fix-it/handyman's older son, Stash was raised as royalty. Cleanly dressed, smart, tall, Jimmy O'Hara said that Stash could've done just about anything he wanted to—doctor, lawyer, anything—'cause he was that smart. Old Bill Roland—well, he wasn't *old* back then, just a pup, just a young councilman that Mayor Lawrence carried like a fob on his watch chain—said so, too. Could do anything he wanted.

'Cept that Stash liked easy money, quick money. Loved to see the dollars—wet, dry, didn't matter—cross the bar at the Emerald. Loved to see how much the vendors made at Forbes Field. Loved to figure the skim and the vig and the shy on a thousand Oakland hustles, from loan-sharking to front-lawn parking. Loved to watch the cards games at the Gaelic, all those dollar bills piling up like so much New Year's confetti. He looked at those the way Nig looked at women.

Maybe even more.

"My all-time hero," Stash'd like to say, "the guy I think makes the Hall of Fame? The chink or the dago or the rabbi—whoever it was that invented vigorish. The vig—*that* makes the Hall of Fame."

Now, Duffy and I weren't part of the Oakland Quartet. We loafed with them regular, sure. But the Oakland Quartet was the infield. Duffy pitched—he called himself a rag arm, but he pretty good at it. Not big, 'bout the size of Roy Face. Got by with good location, not much more. Kept the ball down, kept it away—good enough for Central, good enough for a look-see from the scouts. Nothing fast, nothing tricky, nothing that would fool anybody, but good enough for a look.

Duffy knew it, too, knew that baseball wasn't his future. Maybe because of that, maybe because the Oakland Quartet always talked baseball, and nothing else, Duffy looked at them as if they were some sort of lower humanity. He'd often call them sub-humans, or cretins, as in, "hey, Beef, we workin' out with 'em cretins today?" and everybody'd laugh.

We'd all be on the corner, leanin' on cars, splittin' smokes, but Duffy'd be up in his room, crackin' the books. "Lawyer," he'd say. "I'm gonna be a lawyer." "Sure, Duff," we'd all laugh, Nig the hardest. "Sure." But I knew it was true.

As good as he was a student, maybe Duffy should've been a bookie or a horse player, 'cause he could spot a winner down the block and around the corner. He spotted Bill Roland as a comer—as *the* comer—when he wasn't doing much more than caddying for the Mayor, running errands, fixing things. You should've seen Duffy's eyes light up when he met Roland the first time. I was there, watching Helen, having breakfast at The Clock, and Roland—dressed well as always, a three-piece suit, rep tie, watch chain across his middle—came in for a cup of coffee. You would have thought it was Bob Feller or Robin Roberts. Duffy introduced himself, and they talked. After that morning, it never surprised me that as Roland rose in politics, so did Duffy—some called him the most ambitious assistant DA in the city's history. "I'll be DA and more," he bragged, "a little mick from South Oakland." No one was dumb enough to bet against him.

Me, I was always tagged to be a catcher. I think I was tagged to be a catcher hanging on my mother's tit. Squat, low center of gravity, I could stand my ground, block the plate. Some loud mouth called me Fats once, and after I decked him, he switched to Beef, which I liked, and which stuck.

I could play back then—we all could, good enough for that Pirate look-see, good enough for all-city scholastic ball. I caught a lot, emulated Smoky Burgess—another short, squat, singles-hitting catcher—developed bad knees.

*If Ernie Lombardi can win batting titles*, they'd holler at me, *you can, too.* That was fun, and I'd laugh, but I wasn't even close.

That Central team had an outfield, too, although those guys didn't loaf with us at all. There was Jimmy Carlin in left, tall and dark and very impressed with himself. Always wore a tie; always had perfectly creased pants. Quick kid, no arm but could run down anything; batted lead-off or two-hole, depending. If he were a major leaguer, the scouting report on him would be quiet, steady, forgettable. Mama's boy; carried groceries home every day after school.

There was Billy Touhy in center, blond, skinny, the legendary Billy the Car. Anything that moved, anything on wheels, he could boost it, no sweat.

Finally, there was Chester Jenkins, a colored boy from the Hill, in right. Chester was a nice boy, quiet, round face, easy smile, never took offense, which was good, because a lot of people had something to say to him—a *lot*. I didn't go for that stuff, and neither did the Oakland Quartet, and maybe that's why Chester could take it so well. He was a good hitter, mostly singles to the opposite field, which was fine, because once he was on base, he was gone. "It's a game about hitting and running," Coach Casey always said, and nobody proved that more'n Chester. Played in right, had an arm like his hero Roberto Clemente. Well, not like Clemente; nobody had an arm like Clemente. Not then, not ever. But Chester had an arm.

Chester went in the army and moved away. Carlin's around somewhere. And Billy the Car did two terms in prison. Since we played nobody much has kept in shape, although Mongol is probably the best. A life term in prison—lucky it wasn't death row—and the weight room to keep the ass-grabbers at bay will do that for you. Whitey, well, he was a wreck before he died, and Nig and Stash are working hard to become old fat guys. Me, with two knees replaced and having eaten enough cheese cake for a banana republic, I'm not beating out any infield grounders any time soon, either.

In Oakland, everybody knew somebody, and the Oakland Quartet not only knew the Forbes Field groundskeepers, who let them come early and practice, but also knew the ticket takers, who let them in for free, and the ushers, who found them good seats.

After all, they were ballplayers and so deserved a little largesse.

At first they came for home-run king Ralph Kiner. After he was traded, in 1953 they watched what they called the all-Irish infield, the O'Brien twins. Eddie and Johnny, along with Danny O'Connell and Paul Smith—who could've been Irish, they said. They came early to see that 1958 infield—Big Klu at first, Frank Thomas at third, Dick Groat at short—all good players. Like scouts, the Oakland Quartet dissected their plays and discussed their merits. On one thing they all agreed, the kid second baseman, Billy Maz, was without peer. Great range, fabulous hands, smooth pivot, quickest release in the majors. "Best there ever was," Nig said. "Best there ever will be."

No one argued. No one even joked.

"Baseball," Mr. Traynor said to them one day, sitting in the seats behind first base, "is an unforgiving game that's impossible to play well."

"But you played well," Nig said. "You were one of the best."

"*The* best," Stash added in his distracted way, as if he'd heard the conversation before and was editing it. "No question about it."

"Be that as it may," Pie Traynor smiled, obviously pleased, "or may not, I was lucky. I played for a good team, good owners. They let me be." He paused. "You can't overestimate that in the life of a man."

He waved at a man in the outfield cutting the grass.

"Baseball is a long game," he said, "and a longer season. You boys are as good a novice infield as I've ever seen." He nodded to each of them in turn, acknowledging them. "But you tend to lose focus. The dropped balls. The wild throws. Then," he smiled sadly, "there's hitting."

That's all he said. That's all he needed to say.

Pie Traynor had been in Oakland nearly 40 years, but they could still hear the Boston in his voice, the open vowels, the drawled syllables. He was always generous with playing tips—"*slide* that right foot along the bag when you make that pivot," to Nig at second. "*Set* your knees first when you make that backhand stop on the line," to Mongol behind third. "Give your man a target *before* he throws," to Stash at first. "Cheat right, cheat left, depending on the *hitter* more than the pitch or the pitcher," to Whitey at short.

They memorized his words, practiced his advice on the field, on the street, in their rooms at home. In games, they felt his presence all around them. The Oakland Quartet didn't care who was pitching, who was at the plate. They *dared* all comers to get the ball by them. Mongol, all muscle at third, could knock anything down and get the ball to first. Whitey, drunk or sober, covered more ground at short than Dick Groat—or nearly. Nig, at second, undersized, scrappy, of the Billy Martin, Leo Durocher, Pepper Martin school, over-compensating, belligerent, looked like a dark crab scuttling about the dusty field, picking the ball, getting rid of it almost as fast as Mazeroski. And of course Stash at first—all legs and arms, a telephone pole swaying on the field. There was *nothing* he couldn't pick out of the dirt. Nothing.

They came out of the showers, out of Forbes Field onto Bouquet Street, hair still wet, into the sounds and the smells of the city. They were embraced by the aromas of fried chicken and grilled meat, of baking bread and fresh laundry, of cigarettes and late-morning coffee, of hot metal and mill sulfur. They raised their voices over the sounds of buses and trolleys, of mothers calling out of windows after their children, of idle chatter and the clack of high heels.

They were the sons of the working-class Irish, American athletes a half-step away from the steel mills. They dressed the part, T-shirts, tight pants.

A truck pulled up to the traffic light. "Little Debbie," the sign read, "has a snack for you."

"I'll bet," Nig snickered, then grabbed his crotch. "And I got one for her right here."

It was an early morning at the Gaelic, and the Oakland Quartet were exhausted from waiting tables, clearing empties, and sweeping the floors all night. Stretched out on wooden folding chairs, half-asleep, they listened as Regis Moran told them war stories—the fights with the dagos, where he had to knock heads and dodge knives, the fights with the niggers, where he had to figure out who was coming heavy and take him first. "There wasn't no problem in takin' any of 'em," he said, laughing, coughing, chewing on the end of his smoke, "it was just takin' 'em in the right order."

The Oakland Quartet laughed.

"That was before Jimmy O'Hara made the peace," Regis Moran nodded. "That was five years ago. More. Smartest thing he ever done. Now everybody's got their territory, and a man can walk around his own neighborhood without having to worry about bustin' nobody's head or nothin'."

He paused to light another Lucky Strike. "Course, sometimes what's gotta get done's gotta get done. Y'understand, boys?"

They all murmured assent.

"Another thing," Regis Moran said, standing, stretching, coughing, spitting into his handkerchief. "If keeping the peace has taught me nothin' else, it's taught me that there are some lines, you cross 'em, you can't come back."

The Oakland Quartet was silent.

"You remember that, now, boys." He raised a long finger. "There are some lines, you cross 'em, you can't come back." He dropped his cigarette to the floor and stepped on in it. "Take it from a guy who's crossed more than one line in his life. There are some lines, you cross 'em, you can't come back."

I keep thinking back about that, about that summer. I keep thinking that it all would have been fine, all baseball and girls, at least that summer, and maybe forever—maybe, like a lot of tough kids, Stash and Nig and Mongol and

Whitey would have turned out all right. But that damn dago just wouldn't let Mary Margaret alone.

And so their fates were cast that summer night when they were 18, looking to skate on the army, looking to protect a little girl.

That was the debate I had with Father Dave over the years, whether it was the crime that ruined them, or was it some flaw in their characters that the times and the neighborhood made worse. I guess it was the difference between a social worker and a priest, the different outlooks on life. For the Father, a round, ruddy man with a ready smile and a chilled six-pack of Ringnes, man, or Man, was a sinful creature whose inherent flaws, if left unchecked, would lead him to the kind of perdition the Oakland Quartet faced—alcoholism, penury, and institutions of one kind or another, hospitals, poor houses, prison, "even the work farm," the Father'd chuckle, "if we still had it."

As a social worker with a more progressive view of life than the good padre, I felt that they would have been fine, over time, life's standard socialization process straightening out most people. But the crime, with its long shadow, and the guilt that settled in their bones like cancer, ruined their lives forever.

We also asked the question: is there free will? Was this destined to happen? Was there some tragic flaw implanted in these four young men that would ruin their lives. Or was it the blind luck of one terrible incident that changed them forever? Was it nothing more personal, or planned, than a car skidding off an icy road? Was it something as blind as cancer—and as deadly?

Some say that our personalities are formed *in utero*, or least as we are raised, so that by age 10 it's as if everything we will ever do has been written down. Others say no, that personality—or fate, if you will—is more fluid, that we are shaped and formed by times and events as they go forward.

Either way, a single catastrophic event can alter lives forever.

Either way, between Father Dave and me there was no convincing and no conclusion, so this became an ongoing debate we had over many a long night.

"They're good boys, Father," I'd always protest.

"Yes," Father Dave would answer. "Good like you."

I'd laugh.

But the Father wouldn't.

It was that unsettled summer, when they were out of high school, too young to drink—legally, anyway; too young to think about getting married or getting a real job with the army staring at them. Some members of our class enlisted while in high school, even wore their uniforms to graduation.

It was peace time, and for the Oakland Quartet there didn't seem to be much purpose in going to an army base to loaf for two years. So Jimmy O'Hara and Bill Roland worked on deferments. "It ain't the Battle of Midway," I heard Jimmy O'Hara saying on the phone one day, so I knew he was speaking on their behalf, which was his way if you were one of his guys.

If not the army, a lot of Central boys went right to work in the steel mills—the pay was good, and the work was steady. But not the Oakland Quartet. "Prime directive," Stash'd say, "stay the hell out of the mills."

No mills—no Eliza, on Oakland's southern edge, none of her sisters, strung like Chinese lanterns all along the rivers. No Dorothy in Duquesne, no Homestead Steel, no Clairton Coke Works.

That summer, like many before it, they had baseball, parking cars, running errands for Jimmy O'Hara and the Gaelic Club, and whatever girls Nig could scare up.

But that summer had something else, too. That summer was special. That summer had murder.

# CHAPTER ONE

▼

# STASH

Nig, loafing in Jimmy O'Hara's doorway, saw him first. "Rufus alert," he sang out, ducking in out of the sun.

Stash and Mongol, playing gin rummy in the corner, didn't bother to look up. But Jimmy O'Hara did. Looking at the bank calendar hanging over the bar, he nodded slightly, then moved to the end of the bar, all the better to greet Mr. Taliaferro.

Heavy, sweating, mopping his face with a large white handkerchief, the big black man walked into the Emerald, glanced around warily, grunted, then walked over to Jimmy O'Hara. As the two men smiled at each other and shook hands, Jimmy O'Hara served him a large draft, always on the house. And he always took a sealed envelope from under the bar and handed it to Mr. Taliaferro, which the black man took without acknowledgement, passing it into the inside pocket of his three-piece suit.

"Scorcher today, isn't it?" Jimmy O'Hara said genially.

"Nice and cool in here, though," Mr. Taliaferro answered, drinking. "Makes a man feel welcome to be here."

"We always aim to please," Jimmy O'Hara smiled.

"Some men aim," Mr. Taliaferro cocked his head, "but you, Mr. O'Hara, always hit the mark."

Jimmy O'Hara nodded his appreciation.

"A pleasure, sir," Mr. Taliaferro put out his hand.

"It was all mine," Jimmy O'Hara said, took the hand, and smiled until Mr. Taliaferro was out the door.

"Duffy should've been here to see this," Jimmy O'Hara said to Stash.

"And why is that?" Stash asked.

"Because that shanty-Irish little mick thinks he's white folks," Jimmy O'Hara said. "Wait'll he finds the pig shit on *his* doorstep. Wait'll he finds out that somebody else owns the game."

"Every neighborhood has a boss," Jimmy O'Hara leaned against the bar. "In this part of Oakland I'm it. You know that."

Stash nodded.

"Well, every part of the city has a boss, and then the whole city has a boss."

"Stands to reason," Stash said.

They had locked the door of the Emerald, and Stash had finished sweeping up and carrying out the trash into the alley. Jimmy O'Hara was enjoyed a rare, late-night smoke, and offered one to Stash, who took it.

"Somebody who runs the numbers, and the sports book, and the vig. Who it is doesn't matter. But everybody pays for his territory. Everybody pays for his taste. Everybody kicks up."

"Even Art Rooney?" Stash asked.

"Let Mr. Arthur J. Rooney and all his sons and all his brothers stay over on the North Side where they belong," Jimmy O'Hara said. "And whatever they do there, or don't do, is none of my business. Oakland is *my* neighborhood, not his."

"But he comes over here for football," Stash objected.

"And leaves just as fast. If he's smart, the little pugilist'll keep it that way."

Jimmy O'Hara paused to take off his apron. "Whatever anybody does, he kicks up." He paused. "Even Gus kicked up."

"Greenlee?" Stash asked.

"Absolutely," Jimmy O'Hara nodded. "Knew him well. Fine man. His word was gold."

"Ran numbers," Stash protested, "didn't he? And you always said—"

"That numbers was nigger business," Jimmy O'Hara nodded. "That's right. It is. I don't have nothin' to do with 'em. Never did. Ol' Gus did, sure. And plenty more. Ran a hell of a ball team, too. The Crawfords. You'd'a loved 'em."

"Coloreds, weren't they?" Stash asked.

"The best," Jimmy O'Hara said. "Satchel Paige—great pitcher. Cool Papa Bell—fastest man I ever saw on a ballfield. Oscar Charleston—tough,

tough ballplayer. Josh Gibson—he could hit 'em like Babe Ruth. Every one of them was an all-star. Coulda played with anybody, white or black, didn't matter. Used to go see 'em—ol' Gus built his own ballpark up there in the Hill. Figured, why pay the white man for *his* ballpark when he could have one of his own?"

Stash smiled.

"He was a smart man. Very successful. Anyway, he kicked up. Inky kicks up. Everybody kicks up. That's the way the game is. We're lucky down here at the Emerald Lounge that we got our own little piece."

"Mr. Taliaferro," Stash said.

"Don't miss much, do you, Mr. Peter Andrew Kelly?"

Stash smiled. "Is he it?"

"Hardly," Jimmy O'Hara nearly laughed. "He's just a big black errand boy. Workin' man, like you and me." He paused. "In this racket, the shit flows uphill."

"To Roland?" Stash paused. "To Lawrence?"

It made perfect sense to Stash, but, still, all those pious civics classes at Central, all that reverence, all those hands folded in prayer.

Jimmy O'Hara smiled, sadly, the way a man does when a favorite son has come to learn some rare and forbidden knowledge. "Now I'm not saying it's him, and I'm not saying it isn't. You're too young to know something like that, Kelly. Let's just say that everything costs something. There's a price to be paid for things to continue the way they are. It's insurance, a little tribute to keep the peace. You could call it the business privilege tax. Mr. Taliaferro collects it."

There were other lessons to be learned, lessons that both amused and frightened Stash. Simply put, he'd grown up thinking that what was his was his, and always would be, and so didn't like the idea of sharing it—any of it.

But what Stash learned—and what drove him from considering succeeding Jimmy O'Hara, as rock-solid as his position and the Emerald were—was that the vigorish was a fact of life, as solid as Oakland Avenue beneath your feet, or Eliza burning the sky at night. You borrow money, you lose a bet, you run a game, you pay the vigorish. Like the heat baking the asphalt streets, like mill smoke settling on everything like a widow's black shawl, it was always there.

In Oakland, like a lot of places, they liked to humanize it—make the payments a little more personal. When Jimmy O'Hara ran the Emerald, and the neighborhood around it, he said a man has to pay the Chinaman—the Chinaman being the catch-all for the man who kept the books, or made the collections. It was even the name used for the percentage—the vigorish itself, depending.

"Me sainted Irish grandfather used to say, 'ye got to eat a peck o' dirt before ye die,'" Jimmy O'Hara liked to say, meaning there are things in life that you don't want to do but which you have to put up with. As a man of the world Jimmy O'Hara could shrug and pay the Chinaman.

Stash couldn't, couldn't bear the thought of giving up anything he made, or stole, or skimmed off the top.

Of course, Stash wasn't alone, just as the Chinaman wasn't always the most popular guy around. Sometimes, people took a great dislike to the Chinaman, because not only did he take things from them, he also reminded them of their failures. So sometimes being the Chinaman wasn't the safest job in the neighborhood.

So much so that every Chinaman needed a friend.

Mr. Taliaferro's waited outside.

The Mayor always had bodyguards. And Bill Roland's were never far away.

And everyone who dealt with the Chinaman had a friend, too. Jimmy O'Hara's was Regis Moran—everybody knew that.

Stash decided that if he ever got in the business—not that he would, you understand, but just in case—he'd have Mongol.

Who else?

Taliaferro aside, Stash knew that Jimmy O'Hara wasn't always this genial with his darker brothers-in-Christ. Was a time, when he was younger, and his vinegar a bit more binding, that Jimmy O'Hara wouldn't have anything to do with them—all of them, all on general principals. Ran a speakeasy back then, even after Prohibition, to avoid taxes and the blue laws. Paid off enough guys to make it jake, of course. Had a little place, first floor of a row house on Mawhinney Street. Kept the front door locked; everyone knew you had to go in through the back.

"OK," old man Higgins asked one hot afternoon, blowing foam through his ample gray mustache, "I'll bite. How's come the front door's locked?"

"Keeps the niggers out," Jimmy O'Hara said, wiping a glass.

As Father Dave would say, you never know what's going to stick with a young man—and what will affect the rest of his life. For Stash, it was a chance conversation with Regis Moran that confirmed who he was.

"What you want," Regis Moran told Stash early one morning, when the two were cleaning up the Gaelic, sweeping the butts off the floor, carrying the empties into the alley, "is to have some jack in your kick."

Stash nodded.

"You understand what I'm saying to you, Aloysius?" Regis Moran asked.

Stash nodded.

"'Cause then you're your own man. It takes more than these"—Regis Moran held up two ham-sized fists—"to make you independent. Sure, there's more to life than folding green. But that's where it starts. You remember that now, Aloysius."

Sweating under a scarred wooden case of empties, Stash assured him that he would.

The fat man limped into the Emerald, leaning on his cane. Enormous, sweating, his shirt pasted to his chest, he stood at the edge of the bar waiting to be recognized. "He never speaks first," Stash told Mongol, over gin rummy. Mongol turned his chair around to see. "That's his style. He waits."

"Big fuckin' tub of lard," Mongol said. "Who the fuck is this jagoff?"

"Just wait," Stash said.

Looking up, Jimmy O'Hara carefully folded his rag, set it on the bar, and walked over to the fat man, nodding, but nothing more. Finally, Jimmy O'Hara said, "how's it going?"

"Oh, you know," the fat man said genially, "a little of this, a little of that."

"That means they have business to discuss," Stash said. "If it was just a social call, he'd say 'passing well.'"

"What the fuck is all this shit about?" Mongol said.

"Be patient," Stash answered. "Learn something. It might save your life one day."

Because it was business, Jimmy O'Hara bent over the bar to hear better, making certain that the fat man didn't spray his words all over the room. Although Stash couldn't hear everything, the gist was there was a message from Connor, a dispute over payouts or territory, Stash wasn't certain.

"Who the fuck're they talking about?" Mongol demanded.

"Somebody owes something to Connor," Stash said. "I can't hear much else."

"Connor?" Mongol asked. "Irish?"

"Nah," Stash said, "dago. Connor's just a nickname. Lives up the river. Owns most of the valley. He's a big one—so big that when his mom died last year the Mayor went to pay his respects. In public. Broad fucking daylight."

"Holy shit," Mongol said, taking another look at the fat man.

"Holy shit is right," Stash said.

"But this ain't up the river," Mongol said. "What's he want here?"

Although Jimmy O'Hara never talked about it, Stash knew that every month a dozen or so new micks showed up in town, all coming to the Emerald, all coming to see Jimmy O'Hara for jobs, in the mills, on the railroads, in construction, even Downtown, if Bill Roland made enough money from it and was in the mood to give them a hug and kiss.

It was always Regis Moran sent to the Pennsylvania Railroad station to pick 'em up, fair-skinned and weary-looking, hopeful and disoriented. Jimmy O'Hara took care of 'em, and like any good employment service got a piece of everything they made for two years—"until the iron pickles," he'd say. If there was a problem—and there rarely was, for these were good boys, all vetted back home by Jimmy O'Hara's partner—INS always seemed to find a reason to ship 'em back, generally before the lad knew what had hit him, or could hire a lawyer to fight the deportation.

If any lawyer would take a case against Jimmy O'Hara.

In this case, Stash figured either some of the new lot had gotten out of line, or hadn't remembered who ran their construction jobs upriver. They had earned themselves a little chat, which might get rough. So for Jimmy O'Hara it was both a courtesy call and a reminder that if these men didn't square things with Connor, he'd have to.

Now Stash could have told all that to Mongol, but he didn't. Because Mongol didn't have the brains he was born with. Mongol'd get the story wrong, Stash knew, and somehow fuck it up. So the little Mongol knew, the better.

"Dunno," Stash shrugged. "Must be something big, though."

"You know," the fat man said, "I try to keep things nice. Nice and peaceful." He spread out his pudgy fingers. "Easy."

"I know you do," Jimmy O'Hara nodded, putting both his hands on the fat man's soft, wet right hand, "and I appreciate that. Don't think I don't. Tell that to Connor, too. Tell him I appreciate the courtesy. And I won't forget it."

As the fat man nodded to Jimmy O'Hara and turned to go, Whitey staggered in, eyes bloodshot, clothes askew. Looking at Jimmy O'Hara, the fat man said to Whitey, "you're a young man. You ought to watch that dissipating."

A place like the Emerald—any neighborhood tavern, really, in 1958—had a virtual license to print money, both above and below the line. How much money do you turn over? Impossible to calculate—too many small bills passing back and forth. So you skim off the top and pocket it—no taxes, taxes being another word for Uncle's vigorish. You pay off the cops and the liquor control boys not to come around too often—meaning you can serve underage kids and stay open after hours. OK, every so often you have to make it look good for the cameras. But they always let you know when you have to.

Stash loved the Emerald, everything from the worn wooden floor to the pressed tin ceiling, the antique fans to the beat-down beer odor that would never come out of the walls. While there was nowhere he'd rather be—except a ballfield—he also knew that his future wasn't there. Nig—he was the one who could keep all this running. He had the personality for it, as well as the head for small deals.

"The Emerald," Nig liked to say, "runs right at you, and it runs well."

For his part, Stash wanted a bigger game. He also wanted off the street.

"Puttin' on airs," Jimmy O'Hara said. "Lace curtain not shanty Irish."

Stash never saw it, and neither did Jimmy O'Hara. It took me years to realize that Stash, being a hybrid between genius and the gutter, did not really belong to either world, and so failed at both.

It was his own intellect, and his own shortsightedness when it came to consequences, that cursed him.

Like Cain, he was cursed. Like Cain, he wandered.

Although Jimmy O'Hara was fundamentally honest, honest included the occasional deal that was too good to pass up. For instance, if some things just happened to fall out of a freight car, or off the back of a truck, and said items just happened to make their way to the Emerald, Jimmy O'Hara'd sell 'em right over the bar. Watches, radios, leather jackets, anything to help a body make ends meet. "A little more for the poor box this week," Jimmy O'Hara'd say to Bishop Wright at mass, and the bishop would smile and nod.

It wasn't only the church that benefitted from the Emerald. It seemed to Stash that he had always seen Crazy Paddy there. Stash never remembered going in without Paddy sitting at a table by the wall, gesturing madly, babbling to himself. For some reason, Crazy Paddy could have as much beer as he wanted, always on the house.

One day Stash asked Jimmy O'Hara why.

"Really got a good fucking in the war," Jimmy O'Hara nodded at Paddy. "He used to be a machinist, you know, and a damn good one." Jimmy O'Hara shrugged. "If you can't take care of your own, what kind of man are you? Especially when nobody else wants to take care of your own.

"There's one thing you've got to learn," Jimmy O'Hara told Stash, loafing in the Emerald on a slow day. "You ain't got no trump, and you ain't got no clout. Not here, not Downtown. Nowhere."

Stash looked quizzical, but said nothing.

"'Cause you got nothing. You got nothing to pay, and nothing to trade."

Stash shrugged.

"You got to be worth something to them," Jimmy O'Hara nodded in the direction of Downtown. "I see you've set your eyes on Bill Roland. If so, that's fine. But unlike here," he pointed to the bar for emphasis, and Stash took it to mean the entire neighborhood as well, "if you lose your worth, he'll cut you off in a heartbeat. Sacrifice you for someone, or something, that means more to him."

Stash started to say something, but Jimmy O'Hara waved him off.

"Don't say nothin'. You've been warned. You stick with me, Mr. Peter Andrew Kelly, you and your whole infield. The four of you. Even that worthless rummy friend of yours. I took care of Paddy," Jimmy O'Hara pointed a finger to where Crazy Paddy sat, "and I'll take care of him. You stay out of trouble, and I'll take care of all of you."

Stash nodded.

"Now get them three other knuckleheads in here," Jimmy O'Hara said, tossing his dead cigar into the trash. "I got things for you to do."

How did a pureblood Irish lad name of Peter Andrew Kelly become Stash, for Stanislaus, a name as Polish as you can get? Stash was tall, with a broad forehead, and tight, slick hair, somehow seeming more Eastern European than Irish. Slovak. Slovenian. Stash.

Stash's silent, sullen father—all work, black tea, and hand-rolled cigarettes—had a small fix-it shop on Meyran Avenue, where Stash, his younger brother Patrick, and his parents lived in three rooms in back. Stash learned early to stay out of the shop—there was junk everywhere, mountains of it, all set to fall on poor, unwitting Stash and his baby brother. There were booby-traps, too, or so it seemed to Stash. Just ask the woman—a heavy-set mother of nine named O'Hanrahan—who ventured in too far, looking for her broken toaster, and wound up walking into a carving knife, which came right through her wool coat and dress, and opened up a two-inch gash in her arm.

Stash's mother—given to green print dresses and daily mass—got their clothes at the Thrift Shop and Salvation Army when she wasn't cadging hand-me-downs from her cousins in Johnstown and Altoona. Meals were largely potatoes, cabbage, the worst, toughest cuts of meat, and oatmeal, depending on the time of day. "Tough way to make a living," Jimmy O'Hara said about the Kelly family, "tough way to live."

For some, their earliest memory is something odd or pleasant—moving to a new house, say, or grandma's home-baked brownies. For Stash, it wasn't those, or St. Paul's, with its intoxicating aromas of incense and candles, or baseball on the field, with its exhilaration and emotion. (His father had no use for either St. Paul's or Forbes Field.) Instead, Stash's earliest memory was standing outside a Forbes Avenue jewelry store, holding his mother's hand, admiring all the shiny, sparkling things in the window.

Unlike Whitey, who was morbidly allergic to work of any kind, Stash never minded hustling for money. Shading crews at construction sites, he collected return bottles for pennies and nickels—enough to buy his next bottle of pop and maybe a couple of smokes. Carrying groceries, running errands, making drugstore deliveries, he talked about *moola*—typical teenage braggadocio. Canny, a wise striver in the way of Bill Roland, who never stated his agenda, Stash stopped mentioning money altogether. But that's all he thought about; everybody knew that.

Hawking the *Sun-Tele* at street corners, he often cribbed another boy's stack—and kept all the money. "Everything in life is resale," he'd shrug.

He'd shovel snow from people's walks, wash cars, work the Gaelic for tips. Polite, energetic, light-fingered, larcenous, Stash always had his eye out for a big, then a bigger score.

He always found a way to crib something somewhere. As a supermarket cashier, he knew that all the drawers were counted, so he couldn't skim anything out of there. Two dollars or more missing, the clerk had to make it right out of his own pocket.

But one store always rang up the taxable items last, especially cartons of cigarettes. So a couple of times a day Stash would tally the customer's groceries, but deliberately forget to include the smokes. When the customer would remind Stash, he'd open the register drawer, take the money, make change, and shut the drawer. Then, when it came time to tally the drawer, he'd make sure to lift the extra cigarette money. The drawer came out right, and no one was ever the wiser.

That was Stash: it was a great hustle, and nobody ever caught him at it.

Stash's first big idea was to become a ballplayer, slugging his way out of Oakland's back alleys, away from the mills, all the way to the Park Schenley and the Schenley Hotel. When Mr. Traynor made it clear that that wouldn't work, Stash switched to Plan B, working connections up the chain. First, of course, was Jimmy O'Hara.

Neither Joe nor Eloise Kelly approved of Jimmy O'Hara and his antics. They wanted nothing to do with him, would take nothing from him, wanted their boys to stay away from him. For Patrick, the pious one, that was no challenge. But for his brother Peter, who felt the real sting of poverty, who hated wearing other people's clothes, the lure of easy money was too hard to resist.

At least he had sufficient filial piety to make a separate peace with his parents: he never mentioned Jimmy O'Hara, and they never asked.

But Stash quickly tired of Jimmy O'Hara. Despite all the loose money, he didn't want unnamed, off-site people running his life. Or at least taking some of his money. So when Stash crossed Jimmy O'Hara off the list, next in line was Bill Roland.

That made perfect sense. Because Bill Roland meant more than money, more than merely the skim or the vig or kiting bar receipts. Bill Roland saw that Stash was smart, noticeably smart, quick at math, bored in school. Predictably, the nuns mistook him for a slacker and sought to beat the Deadly Sin of Sloth out of him—when they should have been searching for Avarice. (Of course, they found the other five Sins in the Oakland Quartet, especially Lust, Anger, and Gluttony.) Predictably, all the sisters' ministrations simply served to turn Stash inward and away, dreaming about easy money and the ways to acquire it.

Stash liked to hook his thumbs into his belt, throw his shoulders back, strut about as if he owned the world and the rest of humanity just paid rent. When he had his own cigarette Stash didn't so much smoke it as chew on the end like Regis Moran, waggling it back and forth, a gesture that indicated power and control. Duffy hated it, but as the Oakland Quartet's leader it was Stash's prerogative.

There was nobility in Stash, and he knew it. The way they say DiMaggio or Clemente knew it in their teens, too—other kids in North Beach would carry Joe D's shoes just to be near him. Unlike Nig, Stash never spoke a lot—silent, like his father, like the Yankee Clipper, Stash was presumed to be all the more intelligent the more he kept his mouth shut. But when he did speak, Stash spoke as if he expected to be heard. He'd open his pants—no matter where he was, on the street corner, in the living room, it didn't matter—and re-tuck his shirt. That, and a brief square of the shoulders, and he was set.

Now Stash liked women as much as the next fellow—as long as the next fellow wasn't Nig, whose appetite and imagination were both insatiable. Stash even had a few girlfriends in school. One, a shy redhead named Bernice, had him hooked for a bit. But a man cannot serve two mistresses, and Stash really fell in love with the vig. "The art," he said sententiously, as if mastering the sums of schoolboys, "is taking your cut off the top—and making the other guy glad to give it up. That's what separates the vig from mere thievery. *That's* the art.

"Jimmy O'Hara," Stash said one night, splitting a beer on a Dawson Street stoop, "he's no jagoff, he works for his money. But Old Bill—" to the Oakland Quartet he was Old Bill even then, as a young man, as he would later become Old Bill for the rest of the city—"he don't do nothin' for it. Makes introductions. That's the way to do it. That's the way to make money without working."

"Politics?" Nig said incredulously, with the same tone of voice he'd have used to say sanitation worker. "Being nice to all them—" not being possessed of an overly rich vocabulary, Nig did not have an apt descriptive for people whom he considered sub-humans. Finally, he reverted to the general case—"jagoffs?"

"Nah," Stash said, drained the bottle, and pitched it neatly over a wire fence onto a little lawn, where it fell with a minimum of sound and no breakage. "Just anything that beats workin' for a livin' an' 'at. Nothin' more."

"Whew," Nig said, "for a minute there I thought you was goin' soft on us."

Then he grabbed at Stash's crotch, and they all laughed.

"You know, Kelly," Jimmy O'Hara said one night near closing time, "I'm going to need someone to deal the cards for me. You're a smart lad. I think you can do it. What do you think?"

Stash, in his usual silent way, shrugged.

"Stout lad," Jimmy O'Hara smiled. "You know that we take bets on such things, as the Irish people are wont to do."

Stash nodded.

"And when we do we expect to be paid. Most of the time, we are. When we're not, we pay a visit to a fellow, to demonstrate to him that it's in his best interest to pay. Are you following me here, Kelly?"

Stash nodded.

"That's when you bring your friend Mr. Hannigan. Is that right, Kelly?"

Stash nodded.

"Stout lad," Jimmy O'Hara smiled. "Because if it got known around town that Jimmy O'Hara could be beat on a two-bit card game, then Jimmy O'Hara'd have to break every Irish kneecap in Oakland. Are you following me so far?"

Stash nodded, smiling now.

"I used to use Jocko over there," Jimmy O'Hara nodded at a small, smacked down man sitting in the corner. Rumpled suit, tie askew, stingy fedora crushed on his head, he looked like the stock newspaper rummy—Thomas Mitchell in *Mr. Smith Goes to Washington*. Except that at one time Jocko was one of the best street fighters in Oakland. A great protector of the Irish people and their interests, Jocko, even for his diminutive size, had stone fists and a fast punch. Cold cock you before you could see it coming. As kids the Oakland Quartet used to steal his hat, just to see him get mad and threaten them, but it was all a game.

"But Jocko," Jimmy O'Hara shook his head, "got old, and started feeling sorry for himself, and had too big a taste for the sauce. So," Jimmy O'Hara folded his rag and laid it on top of the bar, "time to move on."

"Regis Moran?" Stash asked.

"The obvious choice," Jimmy O'Hara nodded. "He'd scare the bejesus—and the money—out of anybody. But Regis Moran's good minding the door at the Gaelic. And I want some new blood there. Are you and your friend up to it?"

Stash just smiled.

"If you're going to get caught," Jimmy O'Hara slapped him on across the face, "don't let it be for nickels and dimes."

Bill Roland was still the goal, but Stash became a good card player, very good, good at counting cards, good at reading other players—who was holding, who was bluffing. He began dressing like Roland, in three-piece suits; like professional card players, Stash kept his nails cut and polished. Although he flirted with the girls at the nail clinic, Stash was always too full of himself to be bothered with what he called "shop girls." He went for the wives and daughters and dowagers of Schenley Farms; Stash always knew where the money was.

Working the Gaelic, he became an expert dealer—smooth, effortless, like his play at first base. It seemed that his hands barely moved as a dealt the cards, and when he snapped them, calling out their values, narrating the game, people started paying good money to sit at his table. The winners' tips, it was said, were sizeable.

"Go out to Vegas," Regis Moran told him, "make some real money."

But Stash refused. For him, like the rest, Oakland was his home, and he meant to stay there.

Hot night at the Gaelic; Stash snapped a card. "Three of clubs. Going low.

"Five of hearts. All red.

"Queen of diamonds. Another little lady." A pause. "Ladies talk."

The men around the table—ties loose, sleeves rolled up, bottles of beer before them—sweated, mumbled, looked at their cards, flicked ashes off their cigars, then looked again.

"Five hundred," a heavy, lank-haired man said thickly, tossing five blue poker chips in the center of the table.

"See and raise," an unshaven blond man answered, gently sliding a stack of chips into the center.

"Too rich for my blood," a man with an iron-gray crewcut shook his head.

"Fold," a man in a club tie said disgustedly, flipping over his cards.

Stash was at work.

Maybe things would have turned out differently if Stash actually liked playing cards. Maybe if he'd had more at stake he would have been able to stop the others from killing that dago. But the irony was that the better he did at cards, the less Stash liked it. Oh, Stash liked to deal well enough, but only to see how each man at the table thought, how he bet, how he was loose or tight with his money. Above all, he liked to deal because the dealer always made money, sometimes big money, if one of the players had a good night, was in a generous mood, and was a big tipper.

But as he was in school, by and large Stash was bored.

One of the Gaelic players—name of Delaney, somehow connected with Jimmy O'Hara in construction—liked Stash, lived in Schenley Farms, had him over to deal. "Never seen nothin' like it," Stash told the Oakland Quartet. "It was something offa TV. Fuckin' antiques in the living room. Wood-paneled basement. Wet bar. Felt-topped card table."

Stash, I heard later, was smooth and easy the whole night. Never made a mistake. Absolutely flawless.

I found out even later that Jimmy O'Hara had set it up, supplying all the necessities, liquor, cards, set-ups, even the occasional extra-curricular for those players who needed a little something during the breaks.

That was all fine. But when Bill Roland came around, Stash smelled real money. He made sure to run errands for Roland, including driving him from time to time, Roland never having gotten a license. There were messages to be given, and received; envelopes to be taken, and returned; people who needed to be noticed. Jimmy O'Hara himself had recommended Stash out of the Oakland Quartet, out of all the boys in the neighborhood, because Stash was noticeably smart and noticeably knew how to keep his mouth shut.

Stash leaned with his back to the bar. "Need-to-know basis," Jimmy O'Hara said to him around his cigar one day, and he knew that Stash knew what he meant. "Need to know."

Stash nodded. He never turned around.

As a sitting City Councilman Roland had an office Downtown, but he was never in it. Roland's real office was the streets of Oakland, and he was there all hours of the day and night, doing favors, collecting tribute, insuring votes. It might be that Stash liked that part of Roland's job most of all—that he never had to be anywhere regularly. He could hustle, make money, and just *be*.

Put another way, somebody always needed something done, and Bill Roland would find a way to do it—for a nominal fee, of course.

So while Stash was no arch-criminal, at least not at first, he did want to take the easy way to follow Regis Moran's dictum, to get more jack in his kick. To develop clout, to acquire trump. That's what he found so attractive in Bill Roland: as long as there was the skim, the vig, the pot of gold at the end of every day, life was sweet and worth living.

Later, as things went well, and they nearly forgot about Mary Margaret and the dago killing, Stash went to work, did his job, came home, ate his dinner, dandled his children on his knee, took his bath, watched TV comedies, made love to his wife, and went to sleep. He thought about nothing but the money he was making, above and below the line—which may explain why he never pursued Mary when she collected the kids and left him.

Stash was enviable: he felt nothing

Until, of course, he did.

Like all City Councilmen in 1958, Bill Roland was elected at-large, meaning that he had no district, no constituents to serve *per se*. Having said that, he was Lawrence's man in Oakland and certain points south and east. Roland passed packets along to the boss, kept some for himself, made certain that everything went smoothly, that the right people got the right jobs, and that certain problems got fixed the right way.

No different from any other big-city mayor, Lawrence abhorred political messes, hated looking bad publicly. So it was Roland's job to take care of Oakland's problems before the stain spread anywhere near the boss.

After all, one never succeeds by bringing the boss problems. One succeeds by bringing solutions. The last thing one wants to hear is the boss snarling, "fix it!" Bill Roland knew that and so performed his job superbly.

Like any good actor, Roland stood on his mark, found his light, and spoke the lines that were written for him. For this, he was richly rewarded, respected, beloved, even. It was the sweetest con job I have ever seen.

Even I wept when Roland died.

Of course Jimmy O'Hara held no official position of any kind, other than as a saloonkeeper. But as head of the Irish community, if anyone had a beef, they came to Jimmy O'Hara first. If Jimmy O'Hara needed something done, something he couldn't handle himself, he went to Bill Roland, which he did not do very often. Because Jimmy O'Hara felt that in Oakland they should handle their own affairs. And because he didn't want to owe anybody anything, especially not Bill Roland, especially not David Lawrence. Instead, Jimmy O'Hara wanted people to owe him.

Bill Roland knew that and respected Jimmy O'Hara for it. He respected a man who took care of his own, ran things with precision, cleaned up his own messes, and, most important, kept everything out of the newspapers.

Because sure as the sun rises every morning, even over smoky South Oakland, whatever happened in Oakland would sooner or later wind up on the Mayor's desk. Meaning that it would be Bill Roland's problem—double problem, really, the problem itself and the fact that the Mayor would be asked about it.

So Bill Roland appreciated Jimmy O'Hara, both his punctilio and punctuality, and tended to listen carefully when the Irish barkeep spoke.

On the rare occasion when Jimmy O'Hara asked for a favor from Downtown, Roland knew it was special and so he listened well. More often than not, Roland made it happen. In part because Roland was good at his job. In part because Jimmy O'Hara was too smart to ask for things that couldn't be done, and couldn't be done easily by the people who had the clout to do them.

So, reminding Roland of a few favors that he'd done for him, Jimmy O'Hara asked him to scare up draft deferments for the Oakland Quartet. "I could use these boys in my work," Jimmy O'Hara said, wiping down the bar, all in white as usual, white shirt open at the collar, white ducks, white apron tied at the waist.

"Now your work is runnin' a saloon," Roland asked, leaning his foot on the scuffed brass rail, drinking a beer, and peeling a hard-boiled egg, "is it not?"

Jimmy O'Hara shrugged and nodded. "Some of it, anyway," he said.

"And these boys are underage in this man's Commonwealth," Roland continued, "am I right?"

"Right you are, Councilman," Jimmy O'Hara nodded, "right you are."

"So what, if you don't mind my asking, are you going to do with four underage lads in what is undoubtedly Oakland's premier neighborhood tavern?"

"You're not actually askin' me that now, are you, Councilman?" Jimmy O'Hara smiled. Roland must have been bored that hot, sunny afternoon, and decided to have a bit of fun. Because asking Jimmy O'Hara—anyone, really—why he wanted certain people on his crew, well, it simply wasn't done. Of course, Roland knew that.

"No," Roland smiled back, "I never ask a man about his people."

Then why start now, Jimmy O'Hara nearly said but thought better of it.

"But I am curious," Roland, added. "So let me think a minute."

"Think all you want to," Jimmy O'Hara said, moving down the bar. "Thinking's as free as that beer you're drinking, Councilman."

Eating his egg, brushing a few crumbs off his vest, watching Jimmy O'Hara take care of two dusty truck drivers at the far end of the bar, Roland considered.

Nig: for all the scrappy little ass chaser's stupidity, to Jimmy O'Hara he was a kind of surrogate son. Fiercely loyal, ready to do anything, he was a good hustler, a good procurer for the odd gang-bang the straight-laced Jimmy O'Hara threw at the Gaelic. Cunt hounds, Roland smiled to himself, are born, not made.

As for Stash, it was apparent to anyone that the tall first baseman was good with numbers, made a good impression, was a good man to have around. Things were getting more respectable these days—Lawrence was seeing to that—and if Jimmy O'Hara wanted to keep pace, wanted to keep his piece of the action, he'd need somebody young and loyal and trainable to stand up for him. The bright, highly ambitious Stash was perfect—maybe for both of them.

Mongol—well, everybody needs muscle now and again. People have to be kept in line, have to remember who's boss—and who's not. Despite what those fools the newsies wrote, and Sweet Jesus did they write a lot of tripe, everybody needs to remember a little physical culture. Now Regis Moran is apt and able—perhaps the best all-time ass-kicker Oakland had ever seen. And he was as loyal to Jimmy O'Hara as the sunny summer day is hot and long—maybe even moreso. But guys like Regis Moran don't last forever. So bringing a young one up through the ranks isn't such a bad idea.

But Whitey? At one time, Jimmy O'Hara thought he could be a good mechanic. But Whitey was his father's son, with all of the old man weaknesses. Bill Roland shrugged.

A real dimwit on his way to becoming a hopeless drunk? Roland didn't see the worth in Whitey, and so asked.

As far as Jimmy O'Hara was concerned, no one needed to know a damn thing about anything he did, especially not Bill Roland, who could only be trusted so far, even though he was doing them a big favor by talking to the draft board. Still, Jimmy O'Hara didn't feel like telling Roland something the Councilman should have seen, that the Oakland Quartet were still boys, still had that Hollywood-inspired, post-adolescent sense of loyalty about them. Sure, time—and Jimmy O'Hara himself—would dissuade them of such foolish notions. But right now, nothing would seal the deal better—cement their loyalty to him—than getting Whitey that deferment, too.

Simply bringing Whitey would bring the other three, not that they needed much encouragement. But Jimmy O'Hara'd be damned if he'd tell the likes of Councilman Bill Roland that.

"I need an infield," he shrugged and drew Roland another beer.

Now this was a little thing, and it wasn't. Peacetime army deferments were a dime-a-dozen, sure, but it was the army, and if word got out that the local pols were tampering with Uncle Sam's Selective Service, things might not be taken so lightly. So it needed the right way to ask, which Jimmy O'Hara did, and the right touch to make it work, which Roland, round belly, three-piece suit and all, had.

The deferments were for the Oakland Quartet, all four of them. Although Jimmy O'Hara knew that Whitey would amount to nothing, as a man who made a living selling liquor he could hardly complain about Whitey. Still, Whitey was too much an unknown. And Mongol—he had his doubts about his stability as well. Sure, everyone needed muscle—Jimmy O'Hara couldn't argue with that. But this one, Jimmy O'Hara shook his head. A bit too rambunctious for his own good. For *my* good.

With Stash getting as much information as he could to make the cases better, Bill Roland found ways to plead the Oakland Quartet's cause. Mongol was easy—he was the sole support of his mother, more or less. Whitey, well, Roland could get him out on a medical. Nig and Stash were harder, but a wink and nod to the Selective Service board, and the four would stay out of the army—as long as they kept out of trouble and stayed in Jimmy O'Hara's good graces.

Of course, that summer they failed at both.

Stash was just the way Bill Roland liked his people—complacent, competent, completely invisible. "You've got to have a man you can turn your back on," he'd say, moving up Stash at light speed.

Sure, Roland had some qualms about Stash over the dago killing, but the more he observed the young man, the more Roland convinced himself that the murder was a childish prank gone awry. "After all," he'd say, drinking his VO neat, "everybody has a past they'd rather forget."

And of course it didn't hurt that Jimmy O'Hara kept pushing Stash's candidacy, hoping to have one of his own on the inside.

So after the dago killing went away, and everyone calmed down, Roland felt that Stash wouldn't betray him, wouldn't embarrass him if and when. Of course he was wrong in the long run, but when the time came Roland got Stash a job with city purchasing. No heavy lifting: Stash oversaw a few accounts. If something got lost here or there, or overpaid, that would be fine.

As long as the right envelopes got passed to the right hands.

Affable, able, deferential, Stash fit in well—a little too well, as it turned out. Seeing everyone else play the vig, he began running his own price-fixing and big-rigging schemes. At first it was small, just a couple of hundred for the right bid here or there.

Then, Stash being Stash, it just growed. Pretty soon, Stash was running his own operation out of the purchasing office.

To give him his due, Stash liked, even admired, all of them. As much as he emulated Bill Roland, and reflected being trained by Jimmy O'Hara, there was a lot of Regis Moran in him. Well, Stash looked up to Regis Moran, as we all did. It was hard not to.

There was a certain geniality to Regis Moran, born, I think, of being a big man who from a very young age was great with his fists. Unlike Mongol, whose anger always got the better of him, Regis was a chain-smoking survivor because he didn't *have* to fight—and when he did, he was so sure of the outcome he never lost his temper. He'd just dust the guy, then go back to whatever it was he was doing—gin rummy, Lucky Strikes, and a 12-ounce Duke, more'n likely.

"It's as if," Jimmy O'Hara said, "he's already seen the game film."

Unlike Jimmy O'Hara, who could have doubled for Father Dave for the number of times he gave the temperance lecture to the Oakland Quartet, Regis Moran felt that one or two loosened up the blood. "Help you jangle nice and easy," he'd say.

"Have a drink," he'd push one on Stash, "you'll be a new man."

Dutifully, Stash'd down it.

"Now that you're a new man, Aloysius," Regis Moran'd slide over a second glass, "have another."

Thinking back on it, Stash was a lot like Regis Moran—smarter and quieter, sure, but he had the same kind of stance, the same kind of self-assured power that comes from being a big man. Mongol's temper aside, the big man is never crazy in a fight. That's Nig—the little guy, who's got something to prove. Stash was quiet, considered; he got his licks in, sure, but only when the opening, the opportunity was right.

"Never get in a fight you can lose," Stash'd say.

Which wasn't Nig's way at all. Nig wanted to make a statement. Stash just wanted to win.

Which, for Stash, made the whole Mary Margaret business—that senseless dago killing—that much more confusing and out of character.

The question is why did Stash go for it? Unlike Nig, he had no skin in the game, no stake in the matter, as ethereal as Nig's stake was. Unlike Mongol, he didn't like beating on people. Unlike Whitey, he knew better.

And Stash could have stopped it right away. But he didn't.

Why not?

Stash always liked the idea of his own troops—it was his secret and his strength. The Oakland Quartet against the world.

Although they were always looking to boost things, it was Stash who came up with the way to boost stuff from stores. Stash, more personable, more articulate, would distract the clerk—even ol' Gus Miller himself, who knew all the scams—while Nig, with the fastest hands, would scoop up something—candy, comics, something they could eat, trade, or sell—then pass it to Mongol or Whitey standing behind him.

Well, maybe not Whitey, who was too shaky for such fine motor work, even back then.

Then, before the clerk could turn around, Stash was in place, Nig's hands were at his sides and his pockets were empty, and Mongol or Whitey was out the door. It was the damn slickest thing I'd ever seen—better, even, than their double plays. They never got caught. Not once.

But the Mary Margaret thing—that was more than getting over on the world. I used to go to the Museum of Natural History with Stash. He'd stand for what seemed like hours before the diorama of Jules Verreaux's *Arab Courier Attacked by Lions*, in which a camel rider fights off a pair of Barbary lions with a scimitar and a rifle. It's a study in mutual destruction—the man and the beasts are both fierce and frightening. Both are killing and being killed. Both are dying.

Then as now, it seems to me a symbol of Stash's life. Of what gave him so much power, of what caused his downfall.

Because in his heart, for all his good fellowship, Stash was incapable of feeling much of anything. On top of that, he had the oldest indigenous American instinct, as old as Daniel Boone and Huck Finn, as deep-seated as Francis Phelan and Dean Moriarty. It's the desire to run away—from danger, from trouble, from responsibility, from anything that can bind you. Cut your losses—cut your victories, even—and *run!* From friends. From family. From anything dear or sacred.

Stash's quixotic desire to escape everything he had created in Oakland, his insane embrace of Nig's mad, misguided, murderous scheme, was another American tragedy in the making.

That the idea of rough justice was easily sold to the Oakland Quartet is not as odd as it might seem today. After all, they lived at a time when people took care of their own. Stash's parents might have ignored all that, in their desperate attempt to become silent Americans, but it was as real as the cracked sidewalk outside their shop or the trash cans in the alley behind it. If such things didn't happen more often, it was because they didn't need to. Only when somebody really screwed up—broke into the wrong house or beat up somebody's nephew—did he found himself stapled to a roof, if he wasn't already thrown off it. In Oakland, circa 1958, there wasn't any rehab for rapists or child molesters—they were simply hurled from a bridge. Somehow, the people who took care of such things were never found.

This was the milieu of Stash and the Oakland Quartet, this was their world. At age 18, when young men constitutionally do stupid things, Stash felt old enough to take charge.

For Stash, the Mary Margaret thing meant a great leap forward—at an enormous price.

In the end, Jimmy O'Hara was right—Stash should never have things get out of hand. He should never have let a hot-head like Nig talk them into that mess—stirring up Mongol like that, then letting him loose. Stash should have known better, and, in that fatal slip, caused Jimmy O'Hara to lose confidence in him. Once a man like Jimmy O'Hara turns his back on anyone, there's no return.

Roland should have learned from that, but he didn't. He liked Stash—well, who didn't? Smart, smiling, presumably loyal, he was the kind of guy Bill Roland liked to have around—and so he wrongly presumed that Stash's judgment was sound. Of course, that was a mistake, which Roland later regretted—big time.

In fact, that error in judgment nearly cost Roland his mayoralty. Ultimately, it didn't because a man like Bill Roland never takes the fall. So when it was all over, Stash was ruined for life, not the Mayor.

When it was over—after the lengthy investigation, the painful, public arrest, the endless indictment, the minutiae-laden trial, the harsh sentencing, all during which Mayor Roland steadfastly maintained Stash's honesty and innocence, saying no finer man ever worked for City government, claiming the trial was entirely motivated by politics, that they had gone after a fine family man like Peter Kelly just to get at Bill Roland—when Stash was pressed in a private moment by a glaring Bill Roland as to why he would so betray his patron, all Stash did was smile, shrug, rattle his handcuffs, and say, "it was worth a try."

They never spoke again.

Father Dave was tall, like Stash and Jimmy O'Hara, an easy-going fellow with an quick laugh and a taste for a cold one. A former collegiate ballplayer at St. Vincent's, novice David Reddy pitched, played centerfield, and coached the freshman team. More than that, though, in Oakland he was Jimmy O'Hara's bookend. Jimmy O'Hara could get you what you needed on the street. But

Father Dave could fetch you all the rest, anything from a hot meal to absolution, whether you were a part of his parish or not. Somehow, he was always around, day or night, in church or out, and while he never seemed to talk more than a minute or two with much of anyone, he knew everything that was going on.

Like Jimmy O'Hara, Father Dave knew Bill Roland—and a lot of other people Downtown. You wanted your street fixed—and didn't want to be beholden to Jimmy O'Hara? See the Father. You wanted a stop sign at the corner because the kids played stickball and the cars went too fast? See the Father. So much so that when Bill Roland, thumbs stuck in the vest pockets of his three-piece suit, came to see Jimmy O'Hara, he always saw Father Dave first—and everyone knew it.

Now Bill Roland, and everyone else, knew that the Father never asked a favor unless it was absolutely necessary. And the Father knew how to return a favor. And the Father knew how to get out the vote. "Don't forget who's helping us Downtown," he'd say, helping his ailing and elderly parishioners to the polls on Election Day. "Without Bill Roland going to bat for us, they'd forget the poor people in the poor end of town. The shanty Irish," he'd shake his head, and his pensioners would nod gravely, "so let's not forget."

So when Bill Roland came to St. Paul's to ask Father Dave about this young fellow Peter Kelly, and the Father gave him a thumbs up, the deal was set.

Politically, at least, Stash had received absolution for the dago killing.

"You're slow making that pivot," Father Dave'd needle Nig, bumping the little fellow with his shoulder. "Me old grandmother from County Kilkenny can make it faster than that. And she's 95."

"Ah, Father," Nig'd say, while the others laughed, Whitey the hardest because he had the greatest faith in Father Dave.

So when it came to the war council about Mary Margaret, Whitey protested. Whitey wanted to see the priest first.

"The Father can do anything," Whitey protested. Whitey the simplest of them all. Whitey the rummy shortstop with the greatest faith.

"Nah," Nig spat, and stubbed out his Lucky with his shoe. "I think we're beyond the Father. I think we're way beyond that."

"Amen to that, brother," Stash said, while Mongol simply glowered and threw rocks into the darkening creek below.

# CHAPTER TWO

▼

# NIG

There he was, just as he had promised, parked on Fifth Avenue outside Central, honking the horn. It was a navy blue '48 Dodge, push button starter, three on the tree—no automatic transmission for Nig. He liked to feel that shift when he drove. Dashboard lights that turned different colors with different speeds. Upholstered seats, just like a couch. Just right for screwing. Stash, looking out of the second-floor window, nodded, then motioned to Whitey and Mongol.

Running down the stairs they were too excited to speak. There, at the curb, stood Nig, the Dodge's back door open, a big, buxom girl inside, with the hard, rounded behind that Nig had promised. With her plaid skirt and yellow sweater both pulled halfway up, she was smiling and waiting.

"Step right up, gents," Nig grinned. "My treat."

Just as you'd expect, Stash pushed the others aside and went in first, slamming the door behind him.

Undersized, dark-skinned, spitting and cursing, calling everyone a jagoff, Nig was always jerking somebody's chain, always pushing people just this side of a fight. Some sailor home on leave, having a smoke on the street? "Hey, admiral," Nig'd yell at him, "how 'bout throwin' some of 'em smokes over here?"

The acknowledged king of mother jibes—"your mother rides shotgun on a garbage truck" was a favorite—he often ended an argument by saying, "your mother!", turning around, and walking away. Nig always figured someone—Mongol, say—would have his back, which he always did.

Nig, who'd wet toilet paper and chuck it up on the ceiling, where it would stick in a soggy mass. Who'd unscrew the tops of restaurant salt and pepper shakers, so that anyone who tried to use them would ruin his meal. Who, in the chink chop-suey joint up the street, buried a cigarette in the little dish of mustard, where it was sure to be discovered by some future, disgusted patron.

When he rode shotgun in his cousin Paul's old Chevy, he'd drop firecrackers through the hole rusted in the floor. No car behind him ever crashed, but drivers wondered what had blown up under their chassis.

Male or female, Nig was the fastest goose in Oakland, fastest to move on any female of any age, fastest to dodge a restaurant check. Sometimes Mongol'd sit on Nig's chest and make him pay his share, and Nig would act all sacred, and they'd all laugh. But Nig would always pay up.

That Nig attached himself to Jimmy O'Hara like black soot on white drapes made perfect sense. Jimmy O'Hara was the most successful mick in Oakland, and everybody wanted to be like him. Or at least to sit in his shade on a hot summer day.

What was Jimmy O'Hara's interest in Nig? Nig reminded Jimmy O'Hara of a younger, smaller, darker, far more profane version of himself. Not as devious, certainly not as calculating, but those necessary character traits would come with time. And, sure, Jimmy O'Hara admitted to himself, Nig spent far too much time thinking with his dick. But he was young yet. He'd settle down. Jimmy O'Hara would see to that.

Nig also had something the others didn't—energy, commitment, desire to be responsible. When Nig said something would happen, you lay money on the bartop, Jimmy O'Hara knew. It would happen.

Stash was a better thinker, more careful, and that meant he'd always play the safe odds, go with the status quo. But Nig saw the future, took the long odds, got things done. He's a lad to bet on, Jimmy O'Hara told the man in the shaving mirror one humid summer morning, when everything from his shirt to the curtains was damp and limp. He's the rock upon which I will build my church.

Later, when it was all over, Jimmy O'Hara asked himself how he could have been so wrong. A father will do this about his own son, shake his head and wonder. But for someone else's bastard?

Nig's mom was short like Nig, but not dark; fair, with hazel eyes. The rumor was that she'd been a part-time prostitute, and maybe still was, and that Nig's real father was a Negro ironworker, but no one could prove that. They were nothing more than back-pew whispers at St. Paul's. All anyone knew now was that Edith O'Donnell—fat, fading, friendless—took the street car east every morning, presumably to work as a domestic in one of the big East End houses.

There was the thought that Edith O'Donnell had kept up some of her old ways, and on occasion snuck men—to whom she had not been properly introduced—to her room for the purposes of illicit commerce.

She had a temper, had Edith O'Donnell, and had no compunction about meting out corporal punishment, beating Nig with a strap or whatever else was handy, the offenses never catalogued. Nig took it, or didn't, ran away, or didn't, depending on time and tide.

In either event, Nig sometimes slept out of the Oakland Avenue apartment, away from the little room, third-floor rear, sometimes at the Gaelic after sweeping up, sometimes in the groundskeepers room at Forbes Field, sometimes behind the Emerald bar, if Jimmy O'Hara wasn't on that night.

"I never have to hustle pool," Nig said calmly, not bragging. "They all know I'm the big gun. I'm Kirk Douglas at the O.K. Corral. They come to play *me*." He smiled. "And lose."

As naturally gifted at the pool table as he was in the infield, Nig'd been hustling pool since he could barely see over the table. Backed by a bet-on-anything Oakland tout named Arnie MacDevitt, who wore a diamond stick pin in his tie and took 50 percent for putting up the money, Nig never lost. "Hell of a touch," Jimmy O'Hara himself said one night, watching Nig shave an impossible shot into the side pocket, squirreling the cue around his left thumb to breathe on the cue-ball, which barely nudged the eight-ball to sink it. "Golden hands."

"Gentlemen," Nig said, wiggling his fingers toward the crowd, and to a man they all paid up, shaking their heads, reaching in their pockets, peeling off bills, putting them on the pool table or in Nig's outstretched hand.

"'Gonna buy me a Merc'ry,'" Nig strutted, singing, "'gonna cruise up an' down the road.'"

Nig was playing pool one night when Bill Roland came around. Nig, clearing the table, singing "I'm a Man," was clearly showing off.

"'I'm going back down,'" he danced around the side, "'to Kansas, too.' Two-ball across the yard in the corner pocket." Crack, sunk. "'Bring back a little girl,' six-ball kisses her cousin and falls in the far corner, 'just like you.'"

Although none of the others would admit it, Nig was the best pool player of the Oakland Quartet. "Bing bang boom," he'd announce, as he hit a three-cushion shot to sink the four-ball in the side pocket. He only played eight-ball, rarely straight pool, and had a real knack for annoying everyone else.

"Five-ball," he sighted over his cue, "Santa Clara's gone aground." Snap, thud, two strangers making side bets on another impossible shot.

"Where'd he get the *patois*?" Roland asked Stash, leaning against the wall, cue in his hand as a prop, because, in truth, Stash, for all his height and hand skills, was a poor pool player. "Probably the same place he got his last dose of the crabs," Stash shrugged.

"Three-ball cuddles her neighbor," Nig'd say, lining up his shot, "and drops in for a visit." Sinking it—he always did—Nig'd say *oh!* as if he were surprised.

"One-ball," Nig pointed with his stick. "'If you can't come around,'" pop, bang, "'then please, *please* telephone. Don't be cruel,'" the seven, a long shot down the table, "'to a heart that's true.'

"And now," Nig'd say with great drama, carefully chalking his cue, "for the *coup de grace*, eight-ball around the horn in the far corner."

"Hot dog," Mongol'd shake his head.

"Jealous," Nig'd answer.

"I don't mind you hustling a little pool," Jimmy O'Hara'd say, arms folded across his chest, "just don't drive any of my paying customers away."

There was always a bit of a madcap in Nig, who was always doing something for a laugh. Like the time he found a cigar butt in the snow along Atwood Street, fired it up, and started smoking it.

Or the time he showed up wearing a green eye shade at a Gaelic card game—then proceeded to run the table.

Or the time he jumped onto Forbes Field during the National Anthem and sang with the All-Slovak Barbershop Quartet—four squares in crew cuts, bow ties, and plaid jackets, and Nig in his T-shirt and blue jeans. He got bounced for that, but, man, what a hoot!

Or the time he whipped three steelworkers at pool—shooting everything behind his back.

Stash and Mongol and Whitey laughed themselves silly, but Jimmy O'Hara just shook his head. "Someday," he said, "somebody's going to break that boy's thumbs if he's not careful."

Nig even liked to fool with Father Dave. "How do you make holy water, Father?" he asked the priest after mass one Sunday.

Standing in the doorway, nodding at his parishioners, Father Dave smiled and shrugged amicably.

"You boil the hell out of it," Nig grinned.

The Oakland Quartet laughed mightily at the joke.

Father Dave did, too. "A good one, boys," he laughed. "A good one."

Then he didn't. He just smiled and said, "But ye might do well to remember that in the days and years to come. About boiling and hell."

"Aw, Father," Nig began to protest, but Father Dave had gone inside. Like the Cheshire Cat, all that was left was his smile.

They'd talk about what they were going to do, Mongol and Whitey never getting past Jimmy O'Hara, playing ball, running errands, playing cards, and drinking. Nig was more mindful of the future, saying he'd like to do something that didn't involve working. "Tending bar, maybe," he said.

"Nah," Stash countered. "Tending bar is working, too. Owning the bar—that's a license to print money. That's what Jimmy O'Hara has. A goddamn license to print money."

Sitting in the shade of a building on Meyran Avenue, splitting a Lucky, the Oakland Quartet discussed how most of the neighborhood made a living, subset Jones & Laughlin Steel.

"Got to be a better way," Nig said, watching a middle-aged woman struggle with two oversized grocery bags.

"You make good money in the mill," Mongol shrugged.

"Yeah, but you got to work for it," Stash objected.

"That's a sobering thought," Whitey shivered. "Don't want none of that."

None of them did. The sons of laundresses and laborers, waitresses and construction workers, they wanted the next rung on the ladder. Not to be a machinist or a junk dealer, but something with more panache, more standing, "something," Nig'd say, "where I can wear nice clothes."

Education? Not part of the equation. For Duffy, maybe, but not for the Oakland Quartet. Baseball was a good living—"and plenty of broads,"

Nig'd say. "More broads than you can handle." If not that, then a "beer distributorship," Nig'd say, "next best thing to owning a bar."

For Nig, Jimmy O'Hara *was* the American Dream.

"Never pay retail," Stash said, "take the five-finger discount." So the Oakland Quartet boosted everything they could—meals, beer, smokes—especially smokes. Sometimes they could only shake one out of the pack that Regis Moran left by the cash register, or boost at the Gaelic, or bum off the Forbes Field grounds crew or ticket takers. Gus Miller—Ol' Gus himself—would sell 'em smokes, along with the Forbes Avenue drug stores—but there was always a way to find a spare butt.

For whatever reason, Nig was the least tolerant of the Oakland Quartet. For Stash and Whitey, even Mongol, a separate peace with everyone else in Oakland—Italians, Blacks, Poles, Slavs—was *de rigueur*, something they could live with. *Had* to live with, because their patron and protector, Jimmy O'Hara, lived with it. Since it was Jimmy O'Hara's neighborhood, they had to as well.

But that didn't stop Nig from barking under his breath—or complaining outright.

Like the evening, showered and dressed, they came into the Emerald, and Whitey asked where they could go for dinner.

"We could go down Bouquet Street," Mongol said, "for Italian hoagies."

"Goddamn guineas," Nig spat on the wooden floor.

"Or not," Stash said easily, as always trying to keep the peace.

"Anywhere they serve beer," Whitey said.

It's said that by the time a man achieves his majority he has already experienced his defining moment. Each member of the Oakland Quartet had one; Nig's, he claimed, was being introduced to carnality at age 10 by an older cousin. The other three discounted this tale, knowing the cousin, figuring instead that it was at that high school dance in the Central gym when they were all 14. An older girl showed up with a flask, and, after nipping with Nig and Billy Touhy, she went outside with both of them, Nig's hand proudly—proprietaredly—on her ass. They had her—perhaps it was the other way around—in the shadows behind the gym.

There was always the chatter afterward—because to Nig the story mattered almost as much as the act itself. Big ones, little ones, skinny ones, fat ones—doubleheaders were a specialty, as were friends and sisters. All while swearing eternal love, mind you, sneaking back for a taste of little sis, or a best friend visiting from Ohio. Seems like the ladies passed him around like an after-school malted milk. For his part, Nig had to let everybody know it.

"Every so often," Stash said, "he's got to take it out and show it to us."

There were times that Nig copped his mother's Dodge—his great-aunt's, really, who died and left it to Nig's mom, who used it only to visit cemeteries and her maiden aunt in Blaw-Knox, and who left it in the garage behind the building.

Nig's mom didn't like him using the car, but he knew when she wouldn't be there, and knew how to get it back into the garage just the way she did, so he wouldn't get caught.

"I only use it in cases of extreme necessity," he'd say, meaning he'd found some girl who'd put out, generally for more than one guy at a time.

"I don't know where he finds these girls," Mongol scratched his crewcut in wonder, "but I'm glad he does."

By the time he was 16, Nig had a small army of girls who found him irresistible; chief of them was a skinny little blonde named Sharon—whom Nig, in his typically indelicate way, dubbed Little Sharon Sure-Fuck, and she did, at least for him, anywhere, anytime, in cars, in alleys, on her parents' couch when no one was home. Never without suitable female accompaniment, Sharon or not, Nig never went more than a few hours without some kind of encounter.

"Too bad you can't charge for your services," Stash said to him one day, staring down the barrel of another losing pool game, "you'd make a fortune."

Smiling, Nig realized that he didn't know if Stash was kidding or not.

As intolerant as he was, when it came to women Nig never discriminated—white, black, nothing mattered to him. As long as it was female. One time, years later, he strutted into the Emerald with the most stunning black woman they'd ever seen—tall, shapely, regal. As he walked by Whitey he whispered, "I *like* my hot chocolate!"

Perhaps it was his naked sexuality that made him a favorite of women—at least a certain kind of women. No finesse. No *savoir faire*. As Stash said, put Nig in the middle of the Gobi Desert and he'd find someone to shack up with.

He even got some college girl to give him head in Schenley Park. "She says we're real," he'd say, then laugh. Often, after a night of pool, or smokes in the park, he'd announce proudly, "I'm going to get my dick sucked," and strut off.

"I bet she doesn't even exist," Whitey said.

"Why don't we follow him?" Mongol asked.

"Not worth the effort," Stash shrugged. "Unless she'll do us, too."

Of course Nig knew which Italian girls undressed in front of which windows and when. Of course he knew when all the girls had their periods so he could enter unwrapped and not risk pregnancy. "I'd rather have a little blood," he'd dance around, "than have to leave town."

Of course for Nig it was any time, any place. Like the time they were in Quinque's, across the street from Forbes Field, near quitting time. Sure, it was a dago place, but ol' Cheech made great hoagies, provolone melted on fresh rolls toasted in the oven, and every so often the Oakland Quartet had to have one. One night in walked an old whore, fat and drunk and sagging all over the place. Stash and Whitey and Mongol all started laughing, but not Nig. Nig went right over, whispered something to her, motioned to Cheech, who brought a couple of Buds, and they hoisted them.

The other three went back to talking infield—how far your feet have to be from the bag to make the double play, making the stretch at first, playing the ball not the man—when they realized Nig wasn't there anymore. Puzzled, they started looking around. Then Mongol—it had to be Mongol—said, "hey, I gotta take a piss," and went past the tables for the tiny rest room in the corner.

It wasn't 15 seconds before he came back, laughing so hard, then coughing, they thought he'd swallowed something. "He's in there," Mongol wheezed, "Nig's in there. He's dropped trou. He's got that old whore—Rosie, Posie, whatever the fuck her name is—up on the commode, legs in the air, and he's puttin' it to her. Right fuckin' there!"

Whitey and Stash started to laugh, then Stash said, "right fuckin' there is about right."

Five minutes later Nig came back, swaggering a little, but giving no sign that anything special had happened.

"Oatmeal in a bag?" Mongol said, then they all laughed.

"Probably smelled worse," Whitey said.

"Listen, you jagoffs," Nig gave them all the finger, "what are you going to do tonight? Go home and pull the pud? Why bother if you can get real pussy?"

Whitey shrugged and looked away.

"Look," Nig shook his head, "Oakland's got all this quim all over the place. It's fallin' out of the fuckin' trees. All you got to know is where to pick it up."

"Suppose you teach us," Mongol challenged him.

"Suppose you get fucked," Nig answered, and they all laughed.

As straight-laced as Jimmy O'Hara was, he wasn't above staging the occasional Gaelic gang-bang for the troops' comfort and entertainment. While it was easy enough to procure local talent for such events, the task fell naturally to Nig, who always seemed to have the knack of turning up something value-added in the mix—a stretch-marked Lebanese belly dancer, say, or Pocahontas complete with feathers and war whoops.

Generally, though, it was some nervous, wild-eyed girl who thought it'd be fun to take on everybody. While Jimmy O'Hara was never present for such carryings-on—they always took place on the ratty green couch in the back, fifteen or twenty guys standing around, having a smoke, waiting their turns—he did have two inviolable rules. First, nobody ever got rough with the girl. Second, everybody went in wrapped. Regis Moran himself—and later Nig—passed out condoms and made everybody use them. "We don't want no bastards," Jimmy O'Hara used to say. "And we don't want no abortions. That's a mortal sin," he always added piously. "That's murder."

One time, Stash came after it was over, and Nig asked him to walk home the talent, a wisp of a girl named Doris, skinny little chain-smoker with short black hair and a white T-shirt over a red bra.

Walking along Bates Street toward the river, Stash asked her why she did it. "I like getting fucked," she shrugged. "A lot. Besides, it beats gutting fish in the Strip District." She laughed until she coughed and spat in the gutter. "I may smell bad now, but not as bad as that."

Upon being told this, Nig, predictably, found it hilarious. "Two things smell like fish," he snorted, "and only one of 'em is fish."

Nig seemed to collect girls—and stories—like that. One time he drove the Dodge to an uncle's cabin near the Allegheny National Forest. Was going to spend the weekend fishing, he told everyone.

Across the street from the cabin was a Dairy Queen. And in the Dairy Queen worked a high-school girl, off for the summer.

He looked at her, she looked at him, and, to make a long story short, they spent the entire weekend in the rack. He never even unpacked his fishing gear.

"One rod for another," he laughed when he told the story.

Another time he drove with a cousin to Wildwood. Along the way, they picked up a couple of hitchhiking girls, who, it turned out, had no money. Could they stay with Nig and Cousin Charlie in their cabin?

"Sure," Nig said, "but you have to sleep with us."

"Do we really?" the girl asked, not so sure.

"Absolutely," he said, "or we put you out right here."

"Oh, OK," she said.

By Nig's count they made it eight times that night.

Cousin Charlie didn't complain, either.

In his most notorious case, some years later, one afternoon Nig went to the Iroquois Apartments, putting it to some woman whose husband was supposed to be out of town. Of course, the husband came home, caught the two of them. There just happened to be a gun there—the ownership is still in question—and the husband just happened to get shot. Four times, in fact. For a while it looked bad for Nig, who claimed innocence, 'til Duffy worked his magic and got him off.

Of course, Nig bragged about it all over Oakland—how he iced that jagoff, then fucked his wife 'til she was raw. It got back to Duffy, who was mightily pissed—after all, if Nig perjured himself, and if anyone even suspected that Duffy had suborned perjury, well, by that time he'd made so many political enemies that they'd likely disbar him for three lifetimes.

Deciding it would be best for him never to have anything to do with Nig again, Duffy put out the word that he and Nig were not to speak to each other, not even to be in the same room together.

And he held to it. God bless him, Duffy held to it. Except that one time, at Whitey's funeral, when it couldn't be helped, Duffy cut Nig out of his life.

He knew that time didn't make Nig any less crazy, and Duffy was scared.

In Oakland, sooner or later everybody came to the Emerald. Roland, of course; even Lawrence. Ballplayers. Celebrities.

One brilliant afternoon, as Nig was wiping off the tables, in from the bright sunlight strode a muscular man, new double-breasted suit, tie with collar pin, big smile, thick head of curly black hair, nose spread a little too wide across his face.

Before anyone could say anything, Jimmy O'Hara strode out from behind the bar. Seeing that, Nig stopped in mid-wipe. Jimmy O'Hara never came out from behind the bar for anyone—not Roland. Not Pie Traynor or Father Dave. Not even Mayor Lawrence when he stopped by for a snort and a short dog.

Broad smile, meaty hand outstretched, Jimmy O'Hara swooped down for a shake. "Hiya, Kid," he beamed.

"Hiya, Jimmy," the young man smiled. "Whaddaya know?"

"Enough to keep my left up," Jimmy O'Hara lifted his left hand as if to protect his face, and everyone laughed. "What can I give you, Kid?"

By that time, the entire room had stood up—Tommy the Sailor, Crazy Paddy, Mongol and Whitey and the rest, broad-backed millworkers and cement finishers and carpenters and bricklayers having an afternoon off. Forming a respectful circle, they greeted Billy Conn, the Flower of the Monongahela, who came *this close* to knocking out the great Joe Louis himself.

"Hiya, fellas," the Kid beamed. "Jimmy treatin' you right? 'Cause if he ain't, I might have to come back and teach him a lesson or two."

Quickly assuming his boxing stance, Conn moved his feet and shuffled both hands. "A tutorial," he laughed, "in the sweet science."

As they all laughed, an older, red-nosed man named Kelly raised his glass from the far end of the bar. "Here's to you, Kid!"

"You, too, pal," Conn called back, waving a hand.

"Good to see you, Kid," another man said. Broad in the chest, union jacket over his knit shirt, Timmy Regan stood to shake Conn's hand.

"Good to see you, too," Conn smiled, shaking the man's hand. "Good to be remembered."

"Oh, it ain't that long ago," Regan said. "And you're still in good shape. You look like you could go a dozen rounds right now."

"Make it fifteen and you're on," Conn laughed, feinting back and forth.

"What brings you here, Kid?" a third man asked. Wiry, scarred, Joe Dugan looked like he'd done some boxing himself.

"Got to see Jimmy," Conn winked and turned to go.

"Hey, Kid," Dugan added, "how d'you like my stance?"

Hunching over, Dugan held his right hand high, left hand low.

"Keep that left up," Conn said, moving Dugan's hands. "And don't forget to back off." Conn paused and smiled again. "That's what I tried to tell Joe Louis, but he wouldn't listen."

As everyone laughed, Conn followed Jimmy O'Hara to his office, closing the door behind him.

"Joe Louis, my ass," Nig said, wiping down his last linoleum-topped table, then getting the broom for the floor. "Shitty way to lose."

Jimmy O'Hara didn't merely tend his bar, he presided over it—broad shoulders back, belly sticking out, white shirt, white apron tied around his waist, bemused expression on his ruddy face. While Jimmy O'Hara didn't have much to say to civilians, because he didn't have to and didn't want to, he was never afraid to stand up to Roland or anyone else. "You're handing me a load of crap, boyo," he'd look down at Roland, "but let's get on with it because it's good for business, good for the neighborhood. And what's good for the neighborhood is good for Jimmy O'Hara."

He was in charge—there was no doubt about that. All he had to do was nod and point, and things moved.

Like everybody else, he had his rules.

"Guy's a fuckin' jagoff," Nig snapped at the bar one steamy afternoon.

"Hey," Jimmy O'Hara said, "there's no need for that kind of talk. Using language like that doesn't make you more of a man."

Nig scowled but nodded assent.

Straight-laced about many things, Jimmy O'Hara was especially strict about religion. One time, Nig tripped on a bar stool and swore. "Jesus," he said.

"We'll have none of that here," Jimmy O'Hara said quickly. "There's no need to blaspheme."

As a punishment, he kept Nig out of the Emerald—and the pool hall upstairs—for a week.

Sometimes Nig's mouth did get the better of him. Like the time he put in a whole Sunday cleaning out the Gaelic. Supervised by Regis Moran, he swept the floor, washed the dishes, took out the empties, scrubbed the toilets, and hauled the trash. When he was done, Jimmy O'Hara came by, inspected, nodded, and gave Nig a five-dollar bill.

After Jimmy O'Hara had gone, Nig exploded. "I worked all fuckin' day for a fuckin' fin."

Regis Moran shrugged.

"He's a fuckin' jagoff."

Faster than anything Nig had ever seen, Regis Moran was out of his chair and smacked Nig so hard across the mouth that he fell over.

"That's Jimmy O'Hara you're talkin' about," Regis Moran said, standing above him, pointing his finger.

Another time, Nig, loafing in the Emerald's doorway, saw Art McKennan rolling down Oakland Avenue in his wheelchair. "Well," he jerked a thumb at the Pirate public-address announcer, "there goes the neighborhood."

That was the only time I ever saw Jimmy O'Hara hit someone. Slapping Nig across the face, he began, "don't you *ever*," then stopped, took a deep breath, and spoke an octave lower. "That man," he pointed at McKennan's retreating figure, "has done more for baseball, and Oakland, then you *ever* will. So when you see Mr. McKennan, you'd do well to keep a civil tongue in your head. And don't be belittling those less fortunate than you."

Had he been asked, Nig would have answered that, yes, he wanted to be Jimmy O'Hara, wanted Jimmy O'Hara's crown, wanted his control of the neighborhood. Jimmy O'Hara understood that. He also knew, as everyone else did, that Nig thought too much with his dick. He's a boy yet, Jimmy O'Hara reasoned, and that behavior may decrease with time.

Despite that behavior, Jimmy O'Hara liked Nig's instincts, his unwillingness to back away from a fight, his embarrassingly naked ambition. Jimmy O'Hara needed a son and heir—everybody knew that. He knew Nig wanted it; he just wasn't sure if he wanted Nig. Something about his demeanor, like a guy overswinging in baseball, or jumping offsides in football, was wrong. Nig never had failures in nerve; what he had were failures in judgment.

And without the right judgment that would complement the toughness Jimmy O'Hara knew Nig had, Nig'd never develop the clout or the confidence to control the neighborhood the way he'd have to. The dagos and the niggers—not to mention Roland and all those political sharks—would eat him for lunch.

It was a kind of extended trial: Jimmy O'Hara kept Nig around, used him for certain things, especially those he didn't want too closely associated with either the Emerald or the Gaelic.

One day Nig came in the Emerald, nodded all around, then stood in front of Jimmy O'Hara, who was talking with a stranger. The man, noticeably big, with a round, flat face, tan suit and dark tie, and wavy hair smelling of Wildroot, looked down at Nig. "Who's this jagoff," he demanded.

"He's Henry O'Donnell," Jimmy O'Hara said easily, "and he's a man of many talents. You'll find he's very useful."

"Yeah?" the man said, then turned to face Nig. "Well, asswipe, let's see how useful you are. Let's see you useful me up some poontang."

Nig thought for a moment about cutting out this jagoff's heart and eating it, just to teach him a lesson, then thought better of it. This man, who was obviously important to Jimmy O'Hara, could wait for his lesson. So Nig smiled.

"Poontang?" He smiled again. "Yes, sir, that's my specialty. One poontang, sir, coming right up."

As the big man grunted, Nig noticed an angry glint in his eyes. The girl would be in for a rough time, he thought. Well, it's her lookout, he thought.

"Good lad," Jimmy O'Hara said, then moved away.

Jimmy O'Hara was never known to crack heads or anything of the sort—in part because there was always Regis Moran if he needed muscle. But Regis Moran wasn't always around, at least not at the Emerald. And sometimes a civilian'd get a mite frisky.

Like the time some dago punk decided he was going to stick up the place. Skinny kid, skinnier mustache, yellow windbreaker, pegged pants, stingy fedora pushed low over his eyes. Put his hand in his pocket like he had a gun and told Jimmy O'Hara to empty the register. "Nice and easy like," the kid said.

Jimmy O'Hara paused, looked deeply into the kid's eyes, and said calmly, "Son, I want you to think about this. I want you to look at something, and I want you to think."

Never taking his eyes off the kid's, Jimmy O'Hara reached under the bar, pulled out a six-inch Colt Python, and put it gently on the bar.

Now it's obvious that the kid—whose eyes swelled to the size of door knobs—had never seen anything so big in his life. With its gleaming chrome barrel and enormous cylinder, the gun seemed to dwarf the room.

Never taking his eyes off the kid's eyes, Jimmy O'Hara explained calmly—in the same tone of voice he would use if he were discussing planting tomatoes in a garden—what was on the bar.

"Look at it," Jimmy O'Hara said softly.

The boy looked down at the gun on the bar.

"Touch it," Jimmy O'Hara said. Sensing the boy's hesitation, he prodded. "Go ahead, touch it."

Gingerly, as if the gun were hot, the boy brushed his fingers across it.

"It's a Colt Python," Jimmy O'Hara explained. "Six-shot, three-fifty-seven magnum, six-inch barrel. At this range," he bent his head slightly to indicate his deep understanding of the subject, "it'd take a piece out the back of your head the size of a dinner plate." Jimmy O'Hara paused, never taking his eyes off the boy. "Do you understand?"

The boy nodded.

"You don't nod in the confessional, now, do you?" Jimmy O'Hara asked. "So let's hear it from you, son, your whole body and soul."

"I understand," the boy said. "I swear to God, I understand."

"You wouldn't be takin' the Lord's name in vain, now, would ye?" Jimmy O'Hara prodded.

"No, I'm not," the boy shook his head. "I swear I'm not. I'm sorry."

"Good lad," Jimmy O'Hara smiled, picked up the gun, and put it back under the bar. "Just so we understand each other. Now take your hand out of your pocket and walk out the door this fine summer afternoon. And don't ever let me see you in here again."

Soundlessly, the boy turned to go.

Waiting for him to leave, Nig asked Jimmy O'Hara about the oft-stated dictum that if you take a gun out you'd better be prepared to use it.

"Oh, but I was," Jimmy O'Hara laughed—a rarity. "You don't have to use violence all the time," he added. "Success means knowing when to use it and when not. When to show them the gun and when to open fire. When to chase them away and when to dump them in the river." Jimmy O'Hara shrugged. "Success means watching and listening and keeping your mouth shut."

Nig nodded.

"For close work," Jimmy O'Hara said, talking a two-inch Colt out of his pocket, "you don't need anything bigger than this. To scare 'em off, speak softly," he smiled broadly, "and heavy up with the Python."

Nobody ever saw Jimmy O'Hara drunk—drinking to excess was for civilians and amateurs. A man, a good Irishman, ought to know how to hold his liquor. For all that Jimmy O'Hara drank all day—"I'll take another, Jimmy, and pour one for yourself while you're at it;" which he always did, and charged the guy for it, too—nobody ever saw him slur his speech or stagger to the men's room. Not even when his brother went in the can. Not even when his mother died. Never.

Except one time. It had been a particularly cold and snowy St. Patrick's Day—one of those miserable March blizzards that tied Oakland in knots. The crowds were there, though, at the Emerald, and later, after hours at the Gaelic, drinking shots 'n' beers, singing songs, lying about how much they remembered the Old Country, Jimmy O'Hara among them.

When everyone had gone—all the scarves tied around their necks, and the watch caps pulled down to their eyes—Jimmy O'Hara poured himself a good stiff dram of Irish whiskey, downed it, and let the tears well in his eyes.

"Nobody speaks Gaelic anymore," he said, to no one in particular, although Nig and Stash and Mongol, there to sweep the floors, clear the bottles away, and take out the trash, were listening intently. As was Regis Moran, who, mercifully, passed St. Patrick's Day without having to break anyone's head. "It's all gone," Jimmy O'Hara said. "The Irish over there are more English than the damn English. And here we're more American than the Americans."

No one said anything, knowing, as they did, that you didn't interrupt Jimmy O'Hara, not when he was like this.

Hanging his head, shaking it back and forth, he wept for a full five minutes. Then, as if nothing had happened, he straightened up, smiled, and said, "come on, boys, let's clean up and get home."

"Right, Jimmy," Regis Moran said, and raising his hands to the other three, got up and began covering the tables and putting chairs against the wall.

It was the kind of hot day when shirts stick to the skin and Jimmy O'Hara had the door open. Standing behind the bar, sweating, he was distractedly wiping a glass. Nig hung up the pay phone and asked for a glass of water.

Jimmy O'Hara served him, then leaned back, nestling in the bottles of Irish and Canadian whiskey.

"You own it all, Jimmy," Nig said. "What d'ye have to tend bar for?"

"Well, I don't own it all, now, do I, Mr. Henry O'Donnell?" Jimmy looked at him. "That's a great whoppin' exaggeration. A big 'un, if I ever heard it. But even if I did, which I don't, I'd still tend bar. I like to *see* people. I like to take their pulse. I can't do that sittin' behind a desk and hidin' somewhere. Or fishin' in them Florida Keys. Or runnin' whores in and out of some nite club. You have to know people. You have to see them. You have to be *there*."

"You can be there without doing this," Nig objected. "You're still standing behind a bar as if you just got off the boat."

"Let me tell you something," Jimmy O'Hara jacked a finger in Nig's face. "And I want you to remember this. This is Oakland. *Oakland*. It's not Dublin. Or even New York. You never, *never*, act like a big shot. Never. Understood?"

Nig's eyes never left Jimmy O'Hara. "Understood."

"Good," Jimmy O'Hara said. "What's more, if you want to keep your business—*your* business, what's rightfully yours—you need to stay close to the action, close to the street. *This*"—he gestured around him—"is perfect for that. Because there's only so much a messenger can tell you and get it right. You got to feel it yourself."

"Right," Nig said after a moment. "Right."

"Now you're starting to think," Jimmy O'Hara answered.

There were a handful of guys who loafed at the Emerald, and more often than not Jimmy O'Hara had to find a way for them to get home. Widowers and World War II vets and played-out mill hands, the scales had tipped against them: they were long on drinking and short on sense.

So at last call, or what passed for it, Jimmy O'Hara depended on Nig, and a couple of others, to make sure that the old gents found their way safely. "If they piss themselves," Jimmy O'Hara'd say, "that's OK. Just so long as they don't fall, or wind up sleeping on the stoop or in the gutter."

One guy assigned to Nig was Tommy the Sailor. "Poor Tommy," Jimmy O'Hara'd say, "he could get lost going down a fire escape."

"When he's near-sober," Nig'd say, "he talks about how hard it is for him to sleep because of his nightmares."

"Stands to reason," Jimmy O'Hara nodded. "He was at the Battle of Midway. His ship was sunk, all hands lost, 'cept Tommy. They put him in the VA, and Tommy'd wake up screaming, so they'd shoot him full of something. Made him into a living statue. At least here he's among friends and friendly faces." Jimmy O'Hara paused. "It's something."

Tommy favored white T-shirts stretched too tight across his beer belly. He had gone into the navy at 20, but now with thinning hair and pasty skin, he was three sheets past alcoholism. Favoring Camels, he'd fire 'em up with a Zippo lighter with an anchor—brother to the one tattooed on his forearm—he had soldered on in the machine shop.

On bad days, Tommy the Sailor had the shakes so bad he had to slide his drink to the end of the bar, then, hoping not to spill any, clean and jerk it up to his mouth, followed by a quick swipe of the back of his hand and half a juice glass of Iron in a single gulp.

Looking at Tommy's lank hair, ruined face, and fading naval tattoo, Nig hated draping the older man's arm around his neck to help him home. Convinced that Nig never had enough to drink, Tommy muttered that Nig was too chicken to drink more. "Whatsa matter, kid," he'd slur, "ain'tcha got no balls?"

"Good boy," Jimmy O'Hara'd say when Nig came back, pulling a draft for the boy and sliding down the bowl of hard-boiled eggs and Tabasco sauce, "good boy. You're the best, Henry O'Donnell, and I'm just catching up."

Tommy the Sailor may have been charity, but it was a lot more than just a few hand-outs or errand jobs that Jimmy O'Hara managed. Bill Roland, as the new City Councilman, controlled patronage jobs, at least in his end of the city, and since Jimmy O'Hara was a major contributor he had a say there, too.

There were various companies beholden to Jimmy O'Hara for one reason or another—restaurant and uniform suppliers, trucking and construction firms, nite club operators, Forbes Field parking lots. And what fell off trucks as well.

Even the mills, for those who wanted to work there. Suffice it to say that if you were Irish, and you needed a job, you went to see Jimmy O'Hara. And if he liked you, or knew your family, you got one. It may not have been the job you wanted—that was your problem—but it was job enough to make a living. And for which you'd be grateful to Jimmy O'Hara.

Or should be.

At least you'd remember him at the end of every month.

Or he'd remember you, magically turning up at your door disguised as Regis Moran.

On the lighter side, Jimmy O'Hara always seemed to have tickets when anybody wanted them—for the Pirates, of course, but also for the Hornets, the Dukes, the fights, whatever football game was being played. They were always on the arm for friends, always with the vig for civilians.

For the Oakland Quartet, Jimmy O'Hara was their best hope for something good—better than the mills, at least. So they had to stay on his good side, to be judged stand-up guys who wouldn't make Jimmy O'Hara look bad, wouldn't make him lose face with *his* people. Because *his* people would just as soon dismiss him as a mick bartender who ran a few petty rackets and didn't know no better.

So Stash and Nig and Whitey—Mongol, too—were on their best behavior whether in the Emerald or playing pool upstairs or running errands at the Gaelic. If they took care of themselves, Jimmy O'Hara'd take care of them as well.

"Whatever you do, boys," Regis Moran told them one night, bleary-eyed and red-faced, but still sober enough to know which side of the line to drive on, "just don't fuck up *too* much."

They all agreed. But Nig—well, Nig couldn't leave well enough alone.

The funny thing about Nig was that even as he was chasing girls all over Oakland, he already regretted his life. More than any other member of the

Oakland Quartet, Nig always talked about true love, about finding Miss Right, about settling down to a regular life, a regular family. But we knew it would never happen. Not with Nig.

"Nig," Regis Moran'd say, after hours at the Gaelic, "Nig isn't a regular guy. And nothing regular is ever going to happen with his life. Some guys is like that, is all." Then he'd shrug. "Nig'll wind up in prison or dead—shot by some jealous husband. Nothin' we can do to stop it. It's the hand he was dealt." Then Regis Moran'd pause. "Or the dick. 'Cause that's all he thinks with."

That was the irony: it was Nig's sense of honor about women—something he sold to the other three—that changed their lives.

Nig gave it up for a girl he never slept with.

For the guy who prided himself as the world's most nimble at removing a young woman's underthings, Mary Margaret was the virginal little sister Nig'd never had.

Like the rest of us, Nig was a Catholic, or at least raised one, and far too young to have called himself lapsed. So, as a good acolyte of the Manichean Heresy, he had neatly divided the world, or at least all womanhood, into two Marys, Mother and Magdalene, virgin and whore-not-yet-redeemed. Even our own mothers were virgins, or so we wanted to believe. Because sex, *any* sex, even sex sanctified by the holy sacrament of marriage, with any of our mothers—no, it was simply impossible to imagine.

So Mary Margaret was his latter-day Virgin Mary, as holy an infant as God had ever created.

"She's a retard," Mongol snorted.

"She's no retard," Nig got red. "She's just a little slow is all."

Slow or not, Nig had adopted her, made her a kind of mascot. She was slender, and blonde, and spoke slowly, with a kind of stutter, and he simply adored her—the way you adore a little sister or a cute puppy.

Mary Margaret worked as a stock girl at Woolworth's, and Nig often hung around there just to see her. He'd walk her home after work, often buying her an Isaly's skyscraper cone to eat on the way.

Sometimes Nig carried her packages, or her groceries, ran errands for her, and generally treated her like royalty.

Because Nig did, everyone else did, too.

Maybe—just maybe—if she weren't so special to him then none of it would have happened. If Mary Margaret had been what he'd call "just another cooze not worth lookin' at"—their lives would have been very different.

Early summer morning, hazy, hot, and sulfurous. The sun, rising orange over Schenley Park, lit the dusky trees, turned the black streets iron-gray. With heat already rising from the sidewalks, song sparrows above the hillside past Dawson Street were marking their turf. Halket Street was quiet and empty, a brief pre-dawn rain having left the asphalt wet, already steaming.

For all his overnight activities, Nig was out early, waiting for Mary Margaret, waiting patiently, smoking Luckies he'd boosted from the Gaelic, ready to walk her to the streetcar. Watching the sun rise, feeling the sweat start to seep through his white T-shirt, Nig wondered what was keeping her. As the street traffic increased, and the men with work boots and lunch pails trudged south toward the great steel mill, toward Eliza, and the women in their housecoats began to call out to each other and hang wash, Nig wondered what was wrong. Mary Margaret was a good girl; like most challenged people, she kept rigorously to schedules, the foundation of her narrow life. Now she was late, noticeably late. Nig flipped a butt into the street and mounted the swaybacked wooden stairs to her mother's apartment.

The story came out quickly—Sally was all fists and red rage, and Mary Margaret's mother, wild-haired and Irish and understandably inconsolable, fumed about such a sweet girl, and who'd want to do such a thing?

Nig ran up the hill to see Mary Margaret in the hospital—the sun already raising beads of sweat on his back and thick, brown neck. Lying that he was a family member, he brushed past the rustle of the nurses' uniforms, the odd, hump-backed hospital beds, barely managing to control himself. In her room, smiling, telling her that everything would be all right, he kept looking at her broken, bandaged face, her shattered arm, the catheter, which, in his anguish, Nig couldn't bear to see.

Of course, he came back on fire. Finding the other three shooting pool, he was foaming, swearing revenge, that he'd find the son-of-bitch and kill him.

Calmly, nearly bemusedly, Stash asked who and what.

Weeping, Nig told the others of the beating and the rape. "Dragged her off the street into an alley," Nig said, "punched her in the face, threw her down, tore her panties off, stuffed them in her mouth, raped her, then left her, crying and bleeding. It was over in two minutes and, no, nobody heard nothin'.

"You gotta help me, guys," Nig cried. "We gotta kill that son-of-a-bitch."

Mongol, as you might imagine, ready to go right then, was already racking his cue and wiping his hands. Whitey, a bit dazed and bleary-eyed, looked over at Stash. After all, it was early in the day and he hadn't yet had an eye-opener.

At first, Stash counseled patience. "Let's see what the cops do," he said, tucking his shirt in his pants.

"They won't do a fuckin' thing," Nig objected.

Mongol mumbled his assent.

"Maybe so," Stash said, "but we have to wait. To see what they do."

Nig shook his head.

"You really don't want to get in their way," Stash said, then paused. "Then there's Jimmy O'Hara. If we don't get his permission, which he won't give, we'll have to find a way to do it so he won't ever know. Ever fucking know. Because if he does find out, well," Stash shrugged, "I'd rather deal with the cops."

Nig started to object.

"So the first thing," Stash looked right into his eyes, "is to shut up. Not say nothing to nobody. Nobody. Don't be promising nothing to Mary Margaret's family neither. Say nothing. See what happens. Then, if we have to do something, we have to think—think hard—before we do something really stupid."

Of course, Mary Margaret's family filed a police report, and two cops showed up in the hospital room—Tweedledum and Tweedledummer, Regis Moran called 'em—who stood around, red-faced and huffing, taking notes, shaking their heads. "It was dark," Mary Margaret stammered, "and I couldn't see too good. He hit me," she added, then started crying.

"Do we *have* to?" the red-eyed Mrs. Curran demanded.

"I'm afraid so," the smaller, rounder cop said. "Early memories are best."

"But can't you see the girl is—"

"We see very well," the taller, darker cop said. "Please let us do our job."

"Is there anything else you can tell us?" the smaller cop said, pencil poised over his notebook.

Weeping, Mary Margaret shook her head.

"Hey," Nig interjected, "can't you walk her around the neighborhood, see if she spots anybody, or have a line-up or something?"

"Son," the smaller cop said.

"Get Paddy out of here," the taller cop said, "before I have to knock him on his pimply Irish ass."

Of course, the cops made a big show of looking into it, going to the Halket Street site, poking around the garbage cans in the alley, asking people if they'd heard or seen anything, which of course they hadn't. Mary Margaret more or less described her attacker, but the cops said it wasn't enough to make an arrest. "I'm sure I'd know him," she said, but they let the matter drop—after all, the rape and beating of some poor, dim-witted little Irish girl didn't make all that big a stain on the police blotter. "One harp beatin' on another," Jimmy O'Hara heard them say. "Why should law-abiding taxpayers care? Let the fuckin' potato eaters deal with it themselves."

Of course, Jimmy O'Hara called Bill Roland, and of course Roland came around the neighborhood, new three-piece suit, full of himself, making a big show of everything. "We'll get to the bottom of this," he promised sententiously.

"The only thing he could get to the bottom of is his mother's privy," Regis Moran said. "Amazing how high an English pig can pile his own shit."

As Mary Margaret sat by the front window, twisting a small piece of cloth in her hands, her cousin Sally, muscles rippling in her arms and shoulders, told Nig to find him. "Kill him," she hissed. "Kill that son-of-a-bitch."

Nig didn't disagree.

For all his hotheadedness, Nig knew that the street has rules, all of them inviolable, all of them unwritten. The Man had his set, of course, but so did Jimmy O'Hara. And Regis Moran. Even Father Dave.

Nig understood the neighborhood code. This was more than a beating, more even than a rape. This was a point of honor. This was Mary Margaret. He had to stand up for her or he was nothing. *They*—the Oakland Quartet—were nothing.

And if they were nothing, then Jimmy O'Hara—all of Irish Oakland—were nothing.

And that could not be.

"No, no, no," Stash shook his head. "Let me think."

"Think about what?" Nig demanded. "We know what's right. We know what we have to do."

"Think about what Jimmy always says," Stash cautioned. "'You better be able to finish what you start,'" he warned. "'Otherwise, walk away.'"

"We can finish it," Nig protested. "We can. No sweat."

"I can," Mongol growled.

"Right," Whitey mumbled.

"I'm not so sure," Stash stubbed out his cigarette. "I don't think this thing is going to go right."

Of course, they didn't listen to him.

Quietly, carefully, Nig drove Mary Margaret around Oakland, slowing down every time they passed knots of men on the sidewalk. Passing groceries and pizza places, restaurants and bars, jewelry stores and newsstands, they saw the doors propped open, spicy smells mixing with trash and urine in the summer heat.

"No," she kept shaking her head. "No."

"Take your time," Nig told her. "There's no rush."

They kept it up for days, Nig driving the Dodge slowly, watching her carefully for any signs of recognition, Mary Margaret simpering and stammering and shaking her head. Blank look after blank look, she finally shuddered and looked away. Nig put his arms around her and Mary Margaret cried.

"See something?" Nig asked.

She nodded, shivering, afraid to speak.

"Where?" Nig asked.

"There," she pointed to a dark-skinned man in a button-down shirt. "That's him. I know it is."

"Got you, you bastard," Nig said, gripping the wheel tightly. "Got you."

Nig, sitting on the front fender of his '48 Dodge, smoking a Lucky and spitting on the sidewalk, thought about Jimmy O'Hara.

"Sooner or later," Jimmy O'Hara waggled a finger at an unrepentant Nig, "a man has to *choose*. Remember that."

"You got to give a man a chance," Jimmy O'Hara said. "*Then* you can crucify him."

"He had his fuckin' chance," Nig said, rising to his own occasion. "Now we're going to crucify him. That's *my* choice."

When Nig told them that later, they all nodded, even Whitey, who by that point in the day could barely hold his head up.

Stash may have nodded, but he still wasn't sure. It was one thing to mess around on the street. If things were right maybe even boost a car, take it to a chop shop, and make it disappear. But this? This was big casino. This was major leagues—and there was no bonus in it. They could never tell anyone. And if Jimmy O'Hara found out, there'd be hell to pay.

Not to mention the cops.

Whitey shrugged; he'd go along with anything. So would Mongol, as long as there was violence. As Nig pleaded his case, Mongol got visibly angrier.

But Stash still wasn't so sure.

Nig, who felt people's emotions as if they were vibrations coming through the floor, sensed Stash's hesitation.

"Come *on*," he said. "If we can't protect our own, we're nothin'. We're fuckin' sissies. We *got* to!"

There are any number of meetings you attend where you know that it's not majority rule—nothing of the kind. There's one vote in the room, the only vote that counts. Years later, when Bill Roland became Mayor, it would be his. Now, splitting a Lucky in the pool hall, with the fans barely stirring the smoke hanging in layers above the covered tables, it was Stash's.

He knew it was the wrong thing to do. That it could never turn out well. That somehow it would come out—and either Jimmy O'Hara or Regis Moran or the cops would beat the hell out of them.

But this was Nig, and they were the four musketeers. The Vikings who wanted to die with swords in their hands. They were the Oakland Quartet, the slickest infield the city had ever seen.

"All for one," he said, putting his hand out.

"And one for all," Nig answered eagerly, covering Stash's hand.

Whitey joined, then Mongol, who just smiled. "Kill a dago?" he glowered. "You don't have to ask me twice."

# CHAPTER THREE

▼

# MONGOL

They found him where he usually was, in the Medical Arts Barber Shop on Atwood Street, getting his hair cut, a fine crew cut, head shaved nearly like a marine. Dominic worked him over with chattering scissors, stropping the straight razor, brush and powder flying about like railroad dust, a hint of Old Spice at the end for the ladies. Peering in the window, they saw him, motioning. It was time for a good old fashioned War Council, and Mongol—Mongol the muscle—was central to the effort.

"They may be goddamn guineas," Mongol grinned, walking down Forbes Avenue, "but they sure as hell give good haircuts."

He got a shoe shine, too. "Get a shine," he'd say, "change your luck."

But not this time.

"Why don't we just hit him with a car?" Mongol asked. "Quick, easy, anonymous."

"Why don't we just shut up and think?" Stash said. "Before we do something really stupid."

After some back and forth, the Oakland Quartet decided to hold the War Council on the hillside beyond Dawson Street.

For them, Schenley Park was not the green world, not some version of the pastoral, but instead a yonic place—somewhere to hide, to drink stolen liquor, to bury themselves in wanton girls. While enclosed and cave-like, it was a place without boundaries, without rules. It was their demesne and their domain.

It was there that the Oakland Quartet felt invincible and invulnerable.

It was there, sitting in the dark, secluded in their secret place, they decided to have Billy Touhy steal a car, use the baseball bat that Gus Suhr had given Mongol's father, cold-cock the dago bastard, bring him to the park, finish the job if they had to, then bury him.

"Let's go," Mongol said, eager, ready.

"Let's think," Stash objected. "Let's smoke."

Nig, fetching a cribbed Lucky from behind his ear, lit it, inhaled, and passed it around. As the cigarette went from hand to hand, the burning tip illuminating their wan faces, they did not speak, considering the ritual smoke sealing the deed.

Finally, Nig took the butt and, scratching a shallow hole in the dirt, buried the Lucky Strike.

Wordlessly, the Oakland Quartet stood to go.


"Maybe," Whitey said a day later, a moment of weakness and sobriety upon him, "we should talk with Father Dave."

Stash didn't let the others respond, barely gave them time to think.

"Here's what I've learned from Jimmy O'Hara," he said, squirting catsup on his eggs. "Here's the difference between Father Dave and Father Jimmy."

Nig giggled.

"Father Dave lives in the world of *should*," Stash said. "Things *should* be this way. You boys *should* do that." He shook his head. "But we don't live in the world of *should*. We live in the world of *is*. That's Father Jimmy—what *is* and how you deal with it. This," he waved generally, and the Oakland Quartet knew what he meant, "is what is. This is what we have to deal with.

"So we can't trust Father Dave." Stash cut his eggs. "The poor Father'd be the first one to understand that. The first one to say we shouldn't."


That was the moment Stash could have stopped them. Why didn't he? Why did he go along with it? It was a question no one could answer. Not Jimmy O'Hara, who could only say that they were young, and that young people do stupid things. Not Regis Moran, who felt that Stash, for all his smarts, lacked good sense, lacked both the mental and physical toughness that makes a great leader. For Regis Moran, Stash's failure was as much about focus as it was about judgment. Not Father Dave, whose thoughts about Satan and temptation and sin were too overpowering for him to understand their actual failure.

I've always believed it was something else. Stash had no feel for the girl, as Nig did. He had no particular blood lust, as Mongol did. He didn't need to follow, as Whitey did. No, Stash was always his own man.

Some would look at all that and say perhaps it was nothing more than a hot summer night, getting on a riff, seeing how far they could go.

I say no. Instead, Stash, as a profound leader, understood where his mates *had* to go. To keep the Oakland Quartet together—to bind them permanently—they *had* to do this.

And so they did.

Mongol hoisted the scarred, stained Gus Suhr bat, sorry to see it go, happy that it was going to be used for an extraordinary purpose. Tossing it up, he caught it halfway up the barrel. Stash put his hand next to Mongol's, then Nig, finally, after a brief hesitation, Whitey. Then their left hands, until all eight hands were on the bat, the way they'd choose up sides in a sandlot game. "Blood brothers," Nig said. "This seals it."

"C'mon," Mongol said, wrenching the bat free. "Tomorrow night we go to Wopland. Tomorrow night we do this dago son-of-a-bitch."

That night, Nig tossed and turned, from the heat and the smoke, from uneasy dreams. He woke up sweating, breathing hard as if he'd run wind sprints.

That night, Stash sat in the small wooden chair in his room, chain-smoking Luckies, staring out the window without seeing anything.

That night, Whitey drank a half-bottle of Jumping Jack until he passed out, feeling nothing.

That night, Mongol enjoyed the sleep of the innocent.

While most people have switches that turn off their anger before it gets out of control, Mongol didn't. When he got angry, he just got more angry—until somebody was taken to the hospital. Or the morgue.

Not surprisingly, his role model was Regis Moran, a brawler, a puncher not a fighter. Regis Moran was good for a lot of things, not the least of which was keeping everybody in line for Jimmy O'Hara, who in turn kept the neighborhood in line for Bill Roland and the Mayor. After all, with fists the size of coal shovels, who'd want to fool with Regis Moran? In turn, Regis Moran stayed on the payroll. What was more important, Regis Moran got a place to hang his hat. "He's worth every nickel of the taxpayers' money that we chisel for him," Roland said, exuding wisdom far beyond his years.

How deserved was Regis Moran's reputation? He was big—six-foot-three and 260 pounds—with hulking broad shoulders and enormous hands. You'd call him a freak if he wouldn't push your face in for the insult. Regis Moran also had great leverage and an incredibly quick punch—a killer right—so that his fights never lasted long. One or two hits and it was over. After seeing him deck a couple of guys, not much of anybody, drunk or sober, wanted to get dusted by Regis Moran.

As Jimmy O'Hara put it, "there's no bonus fighting Regis Moran, which is how it ought to be."

That was the secret to being Regis Moran. It wasn't just that he was big—which he was, two trains running with a caboose to match. And it wasn't just that he was crazy—which he wasn't, not a bit of it. Because crazy men don't last. Sooner or later they do something that alters the balance with their fiends—or really scares their enemies. Then they become a liability, and one side or the other takes them out. As Jimmy O'Hara said, "a madman may have his day, but not his week."

No, Regis Moran's real power came from his unhesitating willingness to cold cock a man first, then ask questions, if questions were necessary.

Once that was understood on both sides of the line, then Oakland was peaceful. Oakland was fine.

So were the Emerald Lounge and the Gaelic Club. Consider the case of Marty Maguire, a charming gambler, a gentle, happy man who won all the time. One night, after clipping the Gaelic for a goodly cache of cash, Regis Moran figured Maguire was counting cards. "I can't spot how you're cheating," Regis Moran told Maguire that night, "but nobody's that lucky. So why don't you leave now before I have to heave you down the stairs?" Of course, it wasn't a question. "Believe me, under your own steam is a lot more dignified and a lot less painful."

Smiling, shrugging, Maguire marched to the door—and never returned.

"Take a minute," Regis Moran'd say, anticipating a brawl, "and always assess the situation—remembering that the situation is never something you ask for. Then always make sure there's no civilians in the line of fire. Then," he'd shrug.

Although he was married, Regis Moran didn't mind paying for sex—and didn't mind talking about it. "Look," he'd say, "it's nice, quiet, and peaceful. You have a drink or two, a bit of Irish whisky to warm the body and soothe the soul. Then you get together, two consenting adults. Afterward, there's no fault-finding, no debts to be paid or collected. She don't expect nothing else and neither do you. So where's the harm?"

Being Irish, Regis Moran was also a great story teller, and one of his favorites was about another local fighter, the Kid versus the Brown Bomber.

"It was a steamy night, June '41," he'd say, stretching out his long legs at the Gaelic, hoisting a Duke, chewing on a Lucky, winking at the Oakland Quartet. "Manhattan's Polo Grounds. Billy Conn's come to take the heavyweight title from mighty Joe Louis.

"He was tough, this Billy Conn, feisty. He'd battled his way up from high-school dropout to light heavyweight champ. Then the Flower of the Monongahela did something no one else had ever done, boys. He went heavyweight. And he did it to go after Joe Louis.

"Now the Bomber outweighed the Kid by 30 pounds, 199 to 169. But that don't stop the Kid. Not at all."

At this point, Regis Moran'd drain the bottle, nod for another, and for effect cast his gaze at everyone in the room.

"For 12 rounds the Kid bested the Champ. It was the Fight of the Century, boys, lemme tell ye. The Kid used that famous left, all jabs and hooks"—here Regis Moran assumed the stance and flailed away—"keeping away from the Bomber's right. That right," Regis Moran'd shake his head, "well, I never saw a better one. More impact than a 10-ton truck. That right made him Champ for a dozen years."

Another pause; another bottle of beer.

"For 12 rounds," Regis Moran said, "Billy Conn was the best heavyweight boxer in the world. Flat-out best.

"But it was a 15-round fight," Regis Moran shook his head. "All Sweet William had to do was hang on for three more rounds. Nine minutes, boys, that's all. Nine minutes. The Champ was tired, weary—everyone could see that."

Regis Moran paused; it seemed that the Oakland Quartet wasn't even breathing.

"But Billy, bein' *our* Billy, wouldn't take the title on points," Regis Moran said.

The Oakland Quartet nodded. Nobody around here ever backed into a title. Nobody. Never.

"Now here's what I didn't tell ye," Regis Moran set down his bottle. "Back home, back *here*, the Kid's poor, sainted mother was dying of cancer. And Billy'd promised her a knock out. A KO for mom. So in the 13$^{th}$ he went for it."

Regis Moran, up on his feet, danced around the room. "A step here, a feint there, and Louis saw his opening. A killer right to the jaw staggers the Kid. Then another, and a third. Counted out at 2:58, our Billy was two stinking seconds shy of the bell, six measly minutes from the heavyweight crown."

As Regis Moran hung his head, the Oakland Quartet breathed heavily. Mongol wanted to weep.

Finally, Nig said, "Hey, Regis, who's better, you or the Kid?"

"The Kid." Regis Moran never even hesitated. "I'm just a puncher. He's a great boxer. There's a difference. And don't you ever forget it."

If Regis Moran had one weakness, it was betting with his heart instead of his head. The Fighting Irish, the Boston Celtics—anything with a bit of the old sod in it, Regis Moran found irresistible. Long odds, short odds, it didn't matter.

Of course the bookies knew it. But, poor lad, he couldn't help himself.

Now and then, Regis Moran found himself away from the Gaelic laying down a bet or two. Sometimes they'd go the wrong way. That's when he'd call back to whoever it was tending bar—sometimes Stash, because they could trust him to get the count right—and ask, "how's the take tonight?"

Meaning, of course, that Regis Moran was deep into his bookie, and that should he need a quick cash reserve before the night was over, he would come back to the Gaelic and take a wee little non-interest-bearing loan.

And nobody, not even Jimmy O'Hara, would be none the wiser.

The Gaelic's unmarked door was on Atwood Street, next to an alley. On Saturday nights, that door, battered, scarred, painted blood-stain brown, was not locked—in Oakland in 1958 nobody ever walked through a door if they didn't know who or what was on the other side. This door opened to a steep set of stairs to the second floor, where there was a second door, this one guarded by a doorman. Occasionally, it was Regis Moran himself, but more often than not it was somebody from the neighborhood—big enough to make matters stick, if it came to that, but generally not looking for a fight.

"Remember this," Regis Moran told Mongol, "and tell it to your mates, Aloysius. Always duke the doorman. Always. 'Cause you never know when *you'll* be on the door one night, and what goes around comes around. And you never know when you'll need a friend in a fight." A wink and a nudge and a chew on his cigarette. "Remember that."

Mongol said he would.

"Like this," Regis Moran showed him, deftly folding a dollar bill in exact thirds. "Then you give it to him in a handshake, hidden like. On the QT, as if no one knows what's goin' on.

"Put 'er there!" he commanded, sticking out his right hand. Mongol complied, putting out his right hand, and Regis Moran shook it, nimbly depositing the folded bill.

"Pretty good," Mongol smiled, and held out the money.

"Nah," Regis Moran shook his head. "Keep it, Aloysius. You never know when you're going to need it. Remember, always a buck, a fin if you're feelin' real flush. Price of doing business."

Nodding, Mongol thanked Regis Moran and put the bill in his pocket.

The truth of it was that the two of them were kindred souls, and I think they both realized it. Although Regis Moran was calmer—well, a tornado is calmer than Mongol—and had a better sense of humor, they both were tough guys. Both born strong, both were used to having their own way.

And like a lot of tough guys, they were used to taking orders from someone smarter, Jimmy O'Hara, say, or Stash.

The stairs at the Gaelic were famous on their own. It was the 16 steps—"the Sweet Sixteen," Regis Moran'd laugh—you fell down if you were too drunk, or if Regis Moran decided that you had gotten out of line.

They led to a room where there were no windows, or at least none visible. No daylight or women allowed. (Except the occasional gangbang in the back room, but that was purely business, not social.) The cops never came in, and neither did Bill Roland, as Councilman or Mayor, but Jimmy O'Hara made certain that a percentage of the take got passed along anyway. "Another business cost," he'd grunt. "Price of maintaining our privacy. America," he'd add, tossing his dead cigar in the trash, "land of the free. Where you have to pay for everything. Even a little bit of peace and quiet and relaxation with your own kind."

Then Jimmy O'Hara'd get quiet for a moment. "For all the false nostalgia," he said, "Ireland's a poor, blighted place. 'The sow that eats her young,' Mr.

James Joyce called it. It's a good place to get away from. This is America. We got a deal here. Better than we could ever get back home."

At the door, Regis Moran heard him first, trudging up the narrow staircase to the Gaelic. A maintenance man at Forbes Field, short, squat Burt Shannon never married, lived with his mother, didn't smoke or drink. His chief vice, if he had one, was that he liked to hang around. As Jimmy O'Hara put it, the little round, bald man didn't have a mean bone in his body. At six in the morning, he came to mop the men's room floor, change the towels, wash the dishes.

"Always glad to see you," Regis Moran held out his enormous paw.

"Now why izzat?" Burt raised his shaggy eyebrows.

"Because I know it's time to go home."

It was after-hours at the Gaelic, which meant about five in the morning. After everyone had staggered out, the Oakland Quartet had to sweep up, clean the ashtrays, and carry the empties downstairs. Regis Moran stretched his long legs over three wooden folding chairs, used the table edge to knock the cap off a Duke, and lit a Lucky. Mongol, weary, eyes closed, barely kept from sleeping.

"I could have been a priest, you know, Aloysius," Regis Moran began, as if it were a topic they had been discussing all night. In truth, they hadn't said more than three words to each other, and had never discussed such things in the past.

"A monk, maybe," Regis Moran waved his Lucky. "Wearing the cassock. Maintaining a vow of silence. Contemplating life." He paused to consider it. "But, well, there's the street." He shrugged. "And of course there're women."

"A priest," Mongol said, eyes open now, incredulous. Regis Moran had never discussed anything religious, generally avoided Father Dave, and rarely, if ever, went to mass.

"Why not?" Regis Moran nodded. "With the bingo, the collection plate, and all those little envelopes passed to say a prayer for their poor sick old mother back in County Cork? Sweet Jesus! It's the Good Lord's own license to print money." Regis Moran laughed, and Mongol joined in. "Bein' a priest is almost as good as owning a tavern."

But owning a tavern wasn't without its difficulties that summer. Twisted and knotted like fishing line, even before the dago killing Jimmy O'Hara had so much trouble with his accounts that he actually considered closing down for a bit.

One night, a fight broke out at his pool hall: cues were broken, and windows, and the police had to be called to restore order—a major setback, to Jimmy O'Hara's way of thinking, because he always prided himself on taking care of his own business. Shaking his head piously, Bill Roland took his requisite gratuity so that the constabulary would conveniently forget to file charges—or look too closely at the kitchen.

Finally, at the Gaelic a couple of guys who knew better had a bit too much to drink, wound up calling the wrong people the wrong names, strongly objected to being put in their place, and found themselves beaten senseless in a nearby alley. Under orders, Regis Moran disappeared for a few days until it blew over.

Rumor was that he spent the entire time in the rack with a colored whore out in the mountains.

"It's every man for himself out there," Regis Moran said one afternoon after he returned, wiping down his face and neck. "You come into this world alone, and you go out alone," he said, signaling Jimmy O'Hara for a beer. "Ain't nobody gonna help you on Judgment Day." He took a long swig. "Now you got to be loyal to your own kind. But let fuckin' Barabbas take his own fuckin' rap. None of this 'far, far better' anything. None of this self-sacrifice shit." He drained his glass. "Don't fuckin' whine. Take it like a man. And don't have no regrets."

"Fuck no," Mongol said.

For all his bluster, Regis Moran wasn't without his tender moments. There was the time the Gaelic went completely out of character and sponsored a Mother's Day luncheon after mass. There was Regis—all six-foot-three of him—sober as Lloyd Waner (who, unlike his elbow-bending brother Paul, never touched a drop), hair slicked back, dressed in a suit and tie—"Christ on a crutch," he wailed, "I'm a fuckin' *civilian*, for shit's sake"—a tiny, quiet women, Mary Frances, his four-foot-eleven wife on his arm. The picture of sobriety and doting attention, Regis Moran served her poached eggs and toast as if she were Mamie Eisenhower herself.

"Regis," she'd say, hat, gloves, dress all perfect and shiny in their post-mass glow, speaking in the manner of a school marm, "would you pass the marmalade?"

"Certainly, m'dear," Regis Moran'd rumble, as if it were the most natural thing in the world.

It was all Stash could do, serving with the Oakland Quartet as waiters, to keep from laughing.

Later, Jimmy O'Hara remarked that it was the first—and last—time anyone remembered seeing Regis Moran and Mary Frances together since their wedding and the baptism of their two sons.

If he felt familiar with a fellow—friend, foe, it didn't matter—Regis Moran called him Aloysius. Could be he was about to buy the man the beer—or, in the intimacy of hand-to-hand combat, beat him bloody with his bare hands. (Regis Moran was notorious for not using—*never* using—anything other than his fists. As he himself said, they were more than enough.)

One time, Mongol asked him if he really called everyone Aloysius.

"On my good days," Regis Moran nodded, "I call my *wife* Aloysius."

Why Aloysius? Some people felt that Regis Moran was too stupid or lazy to remember people's names and so made one up. I don't think that was it. While Regis Moran himself never divulged the origin of the name—he was hardly a deep thinker, rarely talked about himself, and never answered a direct question about anything—three legends floated about the Gaelic and Emerald:

Version One, Aloysius was a real man, someone who served with Regis Moran in the army, and who—perhaps inadvertently—took a bullet for him.

Version Two, Aloysius was a real man, someone to whom a younger, less bellicose Regis Moran had taken the proverbial shine, and whose life Regis Moran had saved—dragged him away from enemy fire, or some such. Yes, this wars with Moran's oft-stated dictum, that "self-sacrifice is for saps," but it was war, and under fire we often do things without thinking. (Version B of Version Two is that Aloysius owed him money, and a dead GI can't pay off. That was the Regis Moran I knew.)

Version Three, Aloysius was a real man, someone whom Regis Moran beat to death in a basement boxing match. A right to the head that could have shattered armor plate, is the way some old-timers tell it, some who claimed to have been there. That moment forever forged the real Regis Moran—when he met himself face-to-face for the first time, when he knew himself, what he could do, and what his future was, the sum total of his life. It was a gift from a dead man named Aloysius, and in his memory Regis Moran, in way of Adam, renamed the world.

A somewhat different version of this, B of Three, one that also seemed to have gained some traction, dates back to Regis Moran's prize-fighting days. They were small-time, backyard affairs, go bare-knuckled, sell tickets, make book. The story here is that on a blistering Sunday afternoon Regis didn't know when to stop in the makeshift ring and beat a guy named Aloysius to death. Regis Moran quit boxing after that, but the experience left him scarred.

Take your pick.

Mongol first met Regis Moran when he was 10 years old, going down to the Gaelic on a Sunday to pick up a six-pack of beer for his father. Mongol despised and feared his father, hated running errands for him. But the beating he'd receive if he didn't do it, or did it wrong, was worse than the bile that rose in his throat, so he complied.

As he trudged up the long staircase to the second floor, Regis Moran stood at the top, the biggest man Mongol had ever seen. Regis Moran smiled at the boy, then, gently moving him aside, delivered summary justice, hurling a man—a bad card player, worse liar, and stone deadbeat—down the stairs. Winking at Mongol, Regis Moran went back inside the Gaelic.

Mongol thought he had caught a vision of the Heavenly Hosts. "That's the man," he thought. "That's the man I want to be."

"The trick," Regis Moran told Mongol, "is to be an ass kicker who's so tough he never has to kick asses. All he has to do is stand there." Regis Moran chewed his Lucky Strike and smiled. "It's all a matter of reputation. And when it's not," he shrugged, "you've got to know whose ass to kick, and when, and how."

Regis Moran showed Mongol an enormous fist, then relaxed his hand. "It helps people remember the way things are. It helps to keep people in line."

Mongol nodded, watching the men drink and play cards in the Gaelic.

"They're civilians," Regis Moran nodded at the men in the room. "They'll never understand."

"I get it," Mongol said.

"No," Regis Moran shook his head, "no, you don't, Aloysius, not yet. You don't know when to turn it on and when to turn it off. How to use it fast and how to use it slow. When to simply deck a guy and when to beat him silly." A shrug. "And when to make him disappear."

Mongol started to say something, but Regis Moran interrupted him.

"Stick around, Aloysius. Stick around. You will." Regis Moran nodded. "You're needed. You're *necessary*. You will."

No one could figure why Mongol had that kind of Asian cast to his face—sallow skin, high cheekbones, slightly slanted eyes. Neither one of his parents looked that way, nor his five brothers and sisters. No one made any jokes about his mother, not the way they did with Nig, not only because of Mongol's hellacious temper, but also because of who his mother was—maybe the most pious Irish Catholic lady in Oakland, maybe in the history of the world. When she wasn't caring for her frequently absent husband and hyperactive children, Rose Hannigan was in church, at mass or just saying her rosary. "She's there so much she could be a pew," Stash said, and everyone nodded.

Too bad his father wasn't like that; in fact, he was just the opposite. Of course, Rose had thrown him out years ago—not even she could stand his swearing and his beatings. Wherever he was, James Hannigan was angry and dirty and drunk—mean drunk. When he lived at home, and depending on who was around, and who got in his way, he beat everybody, Mongol's five brothers and sisters, but especially Mongol, the oldest, who caught most of the hell for crimes real and imagined. At first, like all children, Mongol blamed himself. Then, as he got a bit wiser, his self-loathing turned into seething anger—at his father, at the world.

The stories, even in his early teen years, were legion. Once, somebody—a stranger, a civilian—said something to him one day on Forbes Avenue. To this day nobody knows who, nobody knows what—and the Oakland Quartet had to drag him off the hapless guy, hustle him into Isaly's, give him a cold drink, and calm him down.

Another time, in the Briar Bowl, Mongol nearly put out his cigarette in some guy's eye because the guy accidentally jostled him.

And so on.

"He never met a tire iron he didn't like," Stash said one day after Mongol busted up somebody's car for some small, unstated infraction.

Once, under a late-night streetlight, Stash actually had to tackle Mongol, who was going after a skinny little kid.

"Great friend you have there," Father Dave said to Whitey, who wasn't sure if the padre meant Stash or Mongol.

The Oakland Quartet had the same teachers that Jimmy O'Hara and Regis Moran had at Central years before—"them nuns live forever," Regis Moran shook his head. "Havin' a closed-up snatch keeps 'em withered and warm."

One particular nemesis was their English teacher, Sister Agnes. Of indeterminate age, she was narrow-minded, ill-mannered, ill-tempered, and authoritarian. With all the pedagogical finesse of a tsunami, the Sister drilled Famous Quotes into her classes until they could barely breathe without reciting Shakespeare, Dickens, Lincoln, and the Good Lord, generally in that order.

If the quotes were often mangled, came up in the oddest places, and had obscene epithets added, no matter. Because in her own way, Sister Agnes had made an indelible impression on them, shaping the way they articulated their small, crabbed lives, and their dark, dull corner of Oakland. In the war that was Central education, it was some kind of victory.

She succeeded in other ways as well. Although reliable statistics are unavailable, Jimmy O'Hara credited Sister Agnes with causing more teenaged drop-outs than all the mill and mine accidents, military excursions, and economic necessities in history.

"A regular fuckin' Niagara Falls," he said.

Always fighting in school, always suspended, Mongol got in his first real punch-out at age 14, about the time his started to add man-muscle. There was some kind of commotion on the corner—somebody shoved somebody else, or insulted his girl, or his mother, somebody chucked a beer bottle, or swung on somebody else, and suddenly everybody on Bouquet Street was beating on each other.

Wading into the fray, Mongol started throwing uppercut rights hither and yon, knocking guys down, until the sirens started, and everybody scattered.

Afterward, strangely exhilarated, and daubing his few cuts with iodine, Mongol professed that he had found true love. "I was hittin' 'em like Billy Conn, Ma," Mongol told Wild Irish Rose, who was too busy with her Rosary to answer.

"Bip!" he swung in front of the mirror. "Bap!" a turn of the torso. "POW!"

Within two years Mongol had earned such a reputation as a free swinger that Regis Moran, of all people, had to sit him down and have a talk with him. "Fighting isn't about punching out everybody," Regis Moran said, looking into Mongol's eyes. "You got to pick your spots."

"Even you?" Mongol wondered.

"Even me," Regis Moran answered. In The Clock, eyeing Helen, he turned back to Mongol. "Especially me. 'Cause everybody's always gunnin' for me. What I learned is that you got to talk with a fellow first, if he'll listen.

You want to make him see it's not in his best interest to fight you. Then," a big, red-faced Irish shrug, "if he doesn't listen to reason, you can hurt him."

Mongol only smiled.

As he grew, the only thing that Mongol was good at, other than baseball and beatings, was pinball. He knew every machine in Oakland, how much you could jiggle each without tilting it. Although the one at Cozy's had the highest numbers and the loudest bells, he liked the Gottlieb *Score-Board* standing amid the tobacco and cut-rate paperback clutter at the Briar Bowl.

Of course, Mongol always needed a keeper when he played. Because if his beloved *Score-Board* dared to thwart him, he'd growl *pog mo thoin*. If things got out of hand, he'd yell *feis orts!* at the hapless machine. One of them, often Stash, would have to stop Mongol before he put his fist through the glass top.

Although he used tire irons for cars, metal on metal, for a while Mongol's flesh-mangling weapon-of-choice was the half-pool cue. Easy to hide, easy to heft, it was his knockout blow that kept the neighborhood trash, and any other interlopers, at bay. Regularly, for example, the two Erin brothers, short, squirrely scraggly-haired, not entirely all-present-or-accounted-for, were hassled—taunted, terrified, lunch money taken.

One night, Mongol decided to teach their antagonists—South Oakland mongrels in dirty blue jeans—some manners. Suffice it to say the Erin brothers were never bothered again.

Not that he needed such weapons, because brute force would generally do. And Mongol was the master of various kinds of killing blows, including the famed and feared rabbit punch, which, with the middle finger raised slightly into a wicked mallet, and delivered with overwhelming force, with purpose and alacrity in a key place—behind and slightly below the ear, say—would have the effect of dropping the fellow like a boulder hurled off a cliff. "Never fails," Mongol'd grunt.

Aside from baseball, Mongol's idea of sport was doing damage to parked cars. It'd be night, and someone else would drive—Billy the Car, say, who could handle a wheel with the best of them, parking cars on lawns during ballgames without so much as scratching a sidewall—and Mongol'd hang out shotgun, tire iron at the ready. As Billy inched past what Mongol indelicately called a

Wop Rod, he'd dig the tire iron into the finish, leaving a half-inch-deep gouge all the way down the side of the car.

Then there was the particular thrill of convertible tops—"so right," Mongol'd say, "for burnin.'" Driving by, he'd toss a lit gasoline-soaked rag on top. By the time anybody figured out what had happened, the top would be completely ruined—and Billy'd have Mongol safely north of Bates Street, safely back over the line.

"Slashing tires?" Whitey'd ask.

"Any fool can slash a tire," Mongol'd answer, exasperated at Whitey's besotted foolishness. "*You* can slash a tire. What I do takes *skill*, my man."

"Piss on him," Nig'd spit.

Stash'd just laugh and take another drag on the group smoke.

Jimmy O'Hara wanted to take Mongol on, despite his youthful inexperience and rough edges.

As much as he liked him, Regis Moran objected. "Too young," he said, biting on his Lucky Strike.

"Well," Jimmy O'Hara said, "he isn't going to get any younger, now, is he?"

Regis Moran conceded that the boss had a point.

"Find some things for him to do," Jimmy O'Hara said, "easy like, to start."

Regis Moran nodded.

"And," Jimmy O'Hara warned, "keep an eye on him."

"Will do, Boss," Regis Moran said, looking pious. "Cross me heart and hope to die. Will do."

So Mongol served a kind of apprenticeship—they all did, really, but Mongol's tasks were harder, required more physical strength, more strength of character, more mature judgments. "Let's see what he can do for us. Let's see what he's made of," Jimmy O'Hara said. "If he—if they—don't work out, we can always cut 'em loose. There's always the army. Or the mills." He shrugged. "It's 1958. There's always work somewhere."

To give him credit, Regis Moran was never quite sure. As time wore on, even he, who'd fight anybody, anywhere, anytime, for any reason, or for no reason, thought that Mongol was a few steps over the line. "Like half-a-mile," he'd say. "Too much caffeine," he'd shake his head, but that wasn't the problem.

"Like the mills," Regis Moran'd add, "the goal is to stay *out* of the clink."

After the dago killing, and after Regis Moran went away for it, Mongol did become Jimmy O'Hara's muscle for a time. It was then that Mongol stories began to echo all over Oakland, generally about cruelty and abandon. One of my favorites was about Mongol being hassled by a dago loan shark. Now the only reason Mongol had gone to this dago was that he was tapped out with Jimmy O'Hara, who had put the word out on Mongol. So one day this dago was giving Mongol a lot of shit about the money—the vig alone, the dago threatened, is outta sight. Uncharacteristically, Mongol nodded and listened, all docile like, like it's his mother bawlin' him out for comin' in late. Finally, Mongol said, "do you want to take a swing at me?"

The dago, who by that time was pretty fucking fed up with Mongol, shrugged and nodded.

"Go ahead," Mongol said.

The dago, old and wise enough to know better, belted him in the gut.

Mongol staggered then stood up. "You feel better now?" Mongol asked.

The dago nodded.

"Good," Mongol smiled. "'Cause after this, you won't."

Mongol took out his half-pool cue and crushed the dago's kneecap.

The dago crumpled, weeping in pain.

"A trick I learned from my cousin in Sinn Fein," Mongol said, then bent over the man lying on the ground and tapped the pool cue on his forehead. "Next time I hit you here. Crush your head like a fuckin' egg."

The way Jimmy O'Hara, and even Bill Roland if he'd admit it, looked at it, Mongol was as a comer, all right. If only he could control that temper.

"One day," Jimmy O'Hara said warily, "that lad is going to kill somebody—the wrong person in the wrong place at the wrong time. Maybe a bit of all three." He shook his head. "And that'll be the end of him. One side or the other will take care of him. There'll be nothing I—or anybody—can do for him then."

But Mongol couldn't, not then, not ever. My favorite Mongol story—everybody's favorite Mongol story, really—is one that no one can prove but everyone believes completely. It's the one they tell about his father, the one that happened about five years after Mary Margaret.

Before Wild Irish Rose threw him out, Mongol's father always rode Mongol pretty hard—which is a polite way of saying that Hannigan Sr. beat Mongol every chance he got. Mongol, like every good politician, never forgave and never forgot. No one knows why, but one day Mongol went looking for him. Found him, too, out in back of the Meyran Avenue house where his father was living. Seeing him tinkering with his car, Mongol cold-cocked his father with a piece of pipe, then choked him with barbed wire—must've hurt like a son-of-a-bitch—saying, "you think you're pretty fuckin' tough, know that? You feel fuckin' tough now? Do you?"

The old man, paralyzed with pain, was so scared he wet himself. "Not so fuckin' tough now, are you?" Mongol asked, tightening the wire like a turnbuckle. "Tell me, how fuckin' tough are you?"

Then, with his father bleeding and barely alive Mongol bound him with the barbed wire, tossed him in the back seat of the car, drove down to the Mon, where he had a little rowboat. Dragging him onto the boat, Mongol tied him to a cement block, rowed out into the middle of the river, dropped him in, watched the semi-conscious man wriggle for a moment then plummet straight to the river's murky bottom. Without a second look, Mongol rowed to shore.

I believe that story. So does Oakland.

Do we say that Mongol was a complete psycho? Or perhaps, as Garth Childress, Roland's little hawk-nosed shadow, later said, "not a complete psycho," he'd shrug. "A moderate psycho, maybe, but not a complete one."

So outrageous was Mongol's behavior that by the time he was 20, Mongol was the first stop for police questions about anything that went on in or around Oakland, or anything that might have Irish fingerprints on it.

Of course, no one could make anything stick. But that didn't prevent every cop on the force from asking questions.

Like the time Mongol thought some poor bastard waiting on a trolley had insulted him, and pushed the man's face through a men's clothing store window. The paper said it took 103 stitches to close up the wounds—and that one day he might regain the use of his right eye.

Or the time Mongol heaved a chunk of brick through the windshield of a passing car because he thought it was going too fast down Darragh Street.

"Can't help you," Jimmy O'Hara told Bill Roland, covering one too many times for Mongol, when the Councilman came looking to see what the hell was going on in the neighborhood. "Probably some guinea bastard out of control. Why don't you go south of the line and poke your stick around down there?"

Predictably, Mongol's after-story is simple. He was useful to them. He had no scruples, and no morals, except loyalty. He was intensely faithful to them like a son is, or should be, to a father.

One too many killings, one too many sets of fingerprints in the wrong places, and they cut him loose.

The last straw was supposed to have been an easy bit of business, a simple collection, Mongol along just in case the young fellow got frisky and needed to be shown the error of his ways. It turned out that the man—a nickel-a-week shy, living on Dawson Street, third-floor walk-up, in the rear facing the park—balked, and Mongol got a little rambunctious. All he had to do was remind the man that he owed some very impatient money some very long green. Well, the man said the wrong thing—perhaps insulted Mongol's lineage, perhaps not. Somehow a pipe wrench magically appeared—and *voila!*

"Have to do it," Jimmy O'Hara said. "Can't let him take down the ship."

"Regis Moran," Jimmy O'Hara drew a beer for Father Dave, "for all his mulishness, knew when to stop. For Regis Moran, beatings were a serious business. But it they were also a game. He had fun. He never lost his sense of proportion or his sense of humor."

Never one to be seen in church, Jimmy O'Hara used the Emerald as his confessional. It was late in the day, and Father Dave had stopped by to pay his respects. You never know when—or where—a man will try to save his soul, he reasoned.

And the padre never met a cold one he didn't like.

Jimmy O'Hara shook his head. "Mongol, well, to Mongol it's more even than blood sport. To Mongol, it's settling scores. To Mongol, it's life or death." He paused. "I think Mongol only feels alive when he is taking someone else's, as if he gains an extra life, an extra jolt out of the one he's taking." Jimmy O'Hara paused and shrugged heavily, regretfully. "I can't have that. Not in my business."

Father Dave said nothing. He was a good priest who had heard many confessions. He knew when to wait.

"There's a delicate balance here, Father," Jimmy O'Hara continued, holding out his hands palms down and moving them like a balance scale, "believe it or not a kind of gentleness."

Father Dave smiled in spite of himself, and Jimmy O'Hara did, too, and laughed.

"I know you don't think so, Father, but it's so. It's like running any institution. It's like running a church."

Father Dave raised his eyebrows.

"You've got to exact discipline. There has to be justice, Father, and punishment. But you can't overdo it. You can't drive people away. You can't scare them into not coming back. You can't make them *afraid*."

Father Dave nodded.

"You can use a hand for two things—to push people away or bring them close. Too many people push others away, especially down here," Jimmy O'Hara gestured. "You see that, don't you, Father? You can't be too hard on a soul in the confessional or he won't come back. And you have to offer the sinner salvation—or he'll desert your church."

Father Dave shrugged.

"And Mongol?" he asked.

"He's the left hand of God without the right," Jimmy O'Hara answered. "He's Justice without Forgiveness. Imagine your church if it were just one without the other."

"*Our* church, Jimmy," Father Dave said gently. "Our church."

"Right, Father," Jimmy O'Hara agreed. "Our church."

Mary Margaret was on their minds. Nig kept remembering her in the hospital, weeping, humiliated. He never let the Oakland Quartet forget that.

Those summer days were hot and humid, the wet air hanging on them like dying animals. At night, the mills burned orange and yellow at Oakland's southern edge, the sulfurous smoke blackening every pore, choking them, laying grit on their sweating faces.

The trick, they knew, was to catch the dago alone, and to do that the Oakland Quartet had to shadow him to know his moves. After a few days, they got it all. The man—Mario Gencorelli, 26, slender, slick hair, white shirt and skinny tie—took the streetcar Downtown at eight in the morning, came back at six. Went into a Dawson Street frame house owned by his mother, presumably for dinner, then came out, alone, went around the corner, presumably for a drink, and came back, sometimes with men, sometimes not. All they had to do was get a car.

And wait.

Billy Touhy was called Billy the Car for the obvious reason—a true gear head, he could steal anything on the road, get any car up and moving. And he would. Billy didn't necessarily like the money he made from stealing. He just liked cars, liked the movement of them. It was his natural environment, his milieu.

Like the Oakland Quartet, their centerfielder, Billy the Car—William NMI Touhy, Jr., pencil-thin, thick black hair, in dirty workpants and motorcycle boots—had other self-control issues. There was the night he came in drunk and tried to bust up the pool hall—and Regis Moran himself, reluctantly, because, as he put it, "this is one of the little minnows you throw back," had to teach him how to act. Billy wound up in the hospital with a busted-up face and a permanent limp.

Visiting him in Mercy Hospital, Father Dave wept then and later, much later, when Billy, working on a coughing, choking old Ford, forgot to ventilate the garage. While Billy didn't die from carbon monoxide poisoning, he did suffer permanent brain damage. A semi-invalid with no memory, he never drove again.

But that was years later, after the Oakland Quartet had been abandoned, one disappeared, one a hopeless drunk, two serving prison terms. Even Oakland itself had changed beyond recognition. No, that night, Billy the Car was still young, still fast, as nimble-fingered as a pastry chef. Nig wanted a car—nondescript, Nig said, one that wouldn't be spotted right away, one that he, or Billy, could ditch in a hurry.

"What for?" Billy demanded, more out of curiosity than belligerence.

"Better you don't know," Nig answered, and Billy wisely let the matter drop.

Billy the Car's chief attribute was his quickness—fastest kid anyone in Oakland had ever seen hotwire a car. In and out, five seconds flat. Or less.

He'd steal anything that rolled, anything on demand. By age 21 he'd serviced all the hot-car rings in the Mon Valley. By 25 he'd done time for grand-theft auto.

That murderously hot night, with Eliza thumping like a bitch in heat, her feminine sulfur smell filling the stale, humid air, Billy the Car went for a Chevy. "'Cause," the maestro himself said, "they got them sheath-thingies for the ignition. Like a cooze. Don't need no key. Don't need no screwdriver. Don't need no knife for the wires. Them ignitions is easier to pop than a clutch in second gear."

Easier to pop than a 14-year-old cherry, Nig thought.

Right on time, nine o'clock, corner of Oakland Avenue and Bates Street, Billy the Car rolled up in a two-year-old red Chevy sedan that he'd boosted in East Liberty a half-hour before.

"Perfect," Nig said. "We'll do our bit of business, then one of us can ditch the fuckin' thing 'fore anybody knows it's gone."

I'd love to say that it stormed that night, or some other great Romantic image—that the air was leaden, with the heat standing still the way it does before the wind picks up, and the thunder cracks, and the rain pours down in roiling sheets.

But it wasn't that way at all. It was just a normal summer night in Oakland, close and sticky, too many people outside talking, too many dogs barking, too many girls bent over trash cans in the alleys, too many radios playing too loudly, when the Oakland Quartet forever crossed the line. Rolling up next to Mario Gencorelli walking alone on Bates Street, Mongol jumped out the car, hit him with the Gus Suhr baseball bat, then dragged Gencorelli's limp body into the Chevy.

Mongol held the dago down in the back seat. Whitey, behind Nig driving, stared at the man's bloody head.

"Out cold," Mongol said.

Whitey felt like vomiting and, closing his eyes, turned his head out the window. He recognized Sarah Vaughan on the radio. Or was it Dinah Washington?

"Easy," Stash said, riding shotgun.

"I'm takin' it fuckin' easy," Nig protested.

"No, you're not," Stash said, cool as always. "You're going too fast, and you almost ran that stop sign. Now slow the fuck *down!*"

In back, Gencorelli began to moan.

Before anyone could say anything, Mongol punched him hard, shutting him up.

Stopping the car on Park Place, shutting off the engine and the lights, the Oakland Quartet hustled out of the car, Mongol dragging Gencorelli with them.

It *is* Sarah Vaughan, Whitey thought, Cole Porter's "Just One of Those Things," getting louder and louder, until he couldn't hear anything else.

Wordlessly, they tumbled down the path to their secret place, hidden by the hillside, a tiny grove of oaks and maples. Mongol, breathing heavily, threw Gencorelli on the ground.

Nig, barely able to control himself, kicked Gencorelli savagely. "This is for Mary Margaret, you dago son-of-a-bitch."

Whitey, the music pounding all around him, choking from Eliza's sulfurous stench, reeled back from the group.

Gencorelli, looking around in terror, began to get up. Before he could take a step, or cry out for help, Mongol cracked him in the ribs with the bat, and Gencorelli gagged, vomited, and crumpled to the ground.

"Give me that fuckin' thing," Nig commanded. Mongol, never taking his eyes off Gencorelli, handed it over, and Nig, aiming for his head, hit him hard on his right shoulder instead.

Groggy, Gencorelli looked up at the four of them. "Fuckin' harps," he said, then spit puke and blood.

Nig hit him again, this time a glancing blow on his face, causing his nose and mouth to split open and spurt blood.

Whitey turned away and vomited. Later, he swore he had heard Sarah Vaughan sing "Stardust," but Stash told him they were too far from Park Place to hear any music.

"Take the bat," Nig held it out it to Stash. "We all have to take a turn killing the bastard."

Looking down at Gencorelli, Stash hesitated.

"Kill the bastard!" Nig snarled. "Kill him!"

Stash took the bat and swung down as hard as he could, the barrel catching Gencorelli on the neck, causing his body to bounce off the ground, twitching. Another blow, this one to the head, stilled him.

"Whitey!" Nig commanded.

Whitey, his eyes closed and his back to them, did not respond.

Nig stepped over to him and turned him around. "We *all* got to do it," he commanded.

"I can't," Whitey wept.

"You *got* to," Nig repeated.

"Motherfucker!" Mongol said, grabbing Whitey, turning him around, and putting the bat in his hands. "You fuckin' candy-ass faggot. Do it!"

His eyes closed, Whitey, crying, dribbling vomit and snot, swung the bat down, at first missing, the barrel kicking up dust, then, in a humiliated rage, Whitey swung it again and again, hitting Gencorelli all over, his back, legs, finally his head.

Mongol grabbed the bat back, eyes wild, face frenzied and sweating, and began swinging the bat down, the sound like beating a thick carpet, until the dago was completely still in the dust.

"Is he?" Nig, breathing heavily, asked.

"Not sure," Mongol said and took one long, last swing at Gencorelli's head.

Whitey, crying and sniveling, couldn't hear anything, but Stash, curiously detached from it all, as if he were watching a movie, clearly heard Gencorelli's skull break, the sound somehow dull yet sharp, a shingle snapping under water.

Stash, one step ahead as always, started to clear a place to bury the body, battered and broken and oozing blood.

Stepping up behind him, Mongol used the knob end of the bat. Then Nig fell to his knees and began clawing at the dirt.

Whitey, weeping, sat down heavily on the ground. He heard nothing—not Sarah Vaughan, not the night-time shouting on Park Place, not even the distant thump of cars jouncing across Panther Hollow Bridge.

Nervous, wanting to be done with it, they tugged at the dirt, scrabbling with their hands, dirt under their nails and in their clothes, hurling clumps behind them as they dug, brown sweat-stains streaking down their faces and arms. When they'd finished digging the grave, Nig and Mongol rolled the body into it. "That's what you get for fucking with Mary Margaret," Nig said, then spat in the dead man's face. "Fuckin' dago jagoff."

Mongol raised the bat as if to hit him again, but Stash stopped him. "That's enough," he said quietly.

Tossing the bat in the grave, Mongol began to kick dirt in, the others following.

"Too bad about your bat," Stash said.

"Can't use it again," Mongol said, "with blood on it. But it was worth it."

"C'mon, Whitey," Stash tugged at his arm, "give us a hand."

"Or a foot," Nig said, then began to giggle.

Then they all laughed, even Whitey, who wiped his mouth, and his face, on his shirt and set to work with the rest of them, smoothing over the spot, tamping down the earth, covering it with scattered leaves and fallen branches until it seemed as if no one had ever been there.

"What the fuck was his name anyway?" Mongol asked as they climbed the hill out of the park.

"Who the fuck cares?" Nig answered. "We did what we had to do."

"Fuckin' right," Whitey mumbled, but Stash, peering out at the darkness of the park, and the pinpoint lights of distant cars, said nothing.

"Got to ditch the fuckin' car," Nig said.

"Fuck," Stash said. "Drive it over to Billy. He'll make it disappear."

"Fuckin' right," Nig said, and Mongol and Whitey nodded.

"Hands out," Stash said, standing by the car, and, dutifully, the Oakland Quartet held out their hands. Grasping them all, Stash said, "nobody talks about this, not to us, not to no one, not ever. Agreed?"

They all nodded.

"Let me hear you say it," Stash demanded.

"Agreed," the three said quietly.

"Good," Stash nodded. "Now let's get the fuck out of here."

Getting into the car, getting on with their lives, Nig eased the Chevy into gear, driving into a world that was changed forever.

# CHAPTER FOUR

▼

# WHITEY

When you push on the world, the world pushes back.

Two 10-year-old kids playing in the park—digging breastworks for a fort, Joshua Lawrence Chamberlain at Little Round Top, or some such—found the dago and the Gus Suhr baseball bat. They nearly didn't turn in the bat, figuring they could use it for games, or trade it for an air rifle, but one got worried and squeamish—it was covered in blood, after all.

Predictably, all hell broke loose. The area was cordoned off, police canvassed the neighborhood, asking if anyone had seen or heard anything, which of course they hadn't. They did background checks on the man—one Mario Gencorelli—and turned up nothing. Or so they said.

North of the line, the Oakland Quartet stayed in lock down, hoping the thing would blow over—some dago fight over a broad, Mongol said; that'd be about right, Nig answered. But the newsies wouldn't give it up. Then the Mayor weighed in, Roland, too, and the cops covered Oakland like soot on snow.

Like everybody else, Jimmy O'Hara didn't think much of it at first—dago killing, some amateur got all hot and bothered 'cause Giuseppe finger-fucked his sister, or some such. Them dagos just don't know how to act, he thought. They're worse than animals.

First time he got an inkling it might be somewhere more was when Bill Roland showed up, complaining more than usual. "We can't have this," he said. "Actually, the Mayor's saying 'we can't have this.'" Jimmy O'Hara had to bite his lip to keep from laughing: Roland did perhaps the world's worst imitation of the imperious Major Lawrence. "'We can't have dead bodies turning up in Mary Schenley's park.'"

"Let Davey Lawrence roast," Jimmy O'Hara drew Roland a Duke. "He wanted the damn job. Now he's got it. The heat's what he gets paid for."

"It's more than that," Roland shook his head. "The newsies aren't letting go of it. 'Menace in our Parks.' That kind of shit."

"They'll find the dago what did it," Jimmy O'Hara shrugged, "and it'll be yesterday's news right quick."

Roland hoisted his glass. "Hope so."

"Touch him up," Jimmy O'Hara nodded to Ed Delahanty, wiping down the bar with a rag. "Touch up that old harp at the end of the bar—and take one yourself."

Lithe and dark, Black Irish with an old polio limp and slick black hair combed straight back, Delahanty took a bottle of Four Roses, filled the shot glass at the old man's right and drew another draft for his left.

"Then cut him off," Jimmy O'Hara said, and Delahanty nodded.

The old man, Whitey Grogan, Sr., never looked up.

In Korea, Whitey's missing-in-action dad was thought to be dead—until he turned up shell-shocked so badly they sent him home. Back in Oakland, he lay in bed for two years until he could finally go peddle scrap. And drink. A lot.

At first, Whitey shadowed his dad, making sure he was all right, which he wasn't, but he was mobile and found his way home, so Whitey left him alone.

People called him Whitey, too, after his dad. Whitey, Jr., then just plain Whitey.

Not that he and his father didn't deserve it—they were both very fair, very blond, nearly albino white, with pink eyes and skin so translucent you could see the veins underneath.

Coal miner's tan, they called it.

Whitey's life's goal, he announced at an early age, was to get loaded.

The police were everywhere in Oakland, questioning everyone, poking in every alley, lifting every garbage can lid.

They were quickly followed by Mayor David L. Lawrence himself, huffing and puffing and promising a fast end, while Bill Roland stood, head bowed, silent and penitent by his side.

Jimmy O'Hara paid it no mind—why should he? It was a dead dago; could have been in the fuckin' Tuscan Hills for all it mattered to him.

As for the Oakland Quartet, they glanced among themselves, split their smokes, and said nothing.

In retrospect, I have to give Roland credit. He really tried to make it disappear, but he didn't have enough moxie—not yet, anyway. The DA was out for blood, and the DA was going to get it. Somebody was going to pay.

And the lower down the Irish food chain the better.

"Jimmy, my friend," Roland said, drinking his beer, dabbing his handkerchief on his mouth and then on his forehead, "you can't imagine the heat I'm getting Downtown about this."

"Why is that?" Jimmy O'Hara said, unconcerned. "You're not a cop. This isn't your problem."

"That's where you're wrong, my friend," Roland shook his head. "The Mayor's made it my problem. The Mayor's made it everybody's problem. Not only because the newsies won't let up on it"—he gestured in the direction of a discarded *Sun-Telegraph* in a far booth—"but because Oakland is my neighborhood. Somehow I'm supposed to keep everything quiet." A brief, tight smile. "And it's not very quiet."

"Other than beer and sympathy, the occasional hard-boiled egg and Slim Jim," Jimmy O'Hara shrugged, "how can I help you, Councilman?"

"You hear anything?" Roland asked.

"I hear it's a dago killing," Jimmy O'Hara said, "that's what I hear. Some dago got his head bashed in and got buried in the park. That's what I hear. I told you before: go find the dago what's done it."

"Well, that's reasonable," Roland agreed. "But that's not what old man Cicero is saying. Old man Cicero's all in a lather, telling the Mayor it's not one of his boys."

"And this is evidence that's going to stand up in a court of law?" Jimmy O'Hara nearly laughed. "One damn dago covering for another. There's a new twist."

"Trouble is," Roland countered, "the Mayor believes him. So does the DA. And the Chief. I wouldn't be surprised if Bishop Wright didn't believe him, too. Hanging it on a dago is one fine idea, Jimmy, my friend, but it won't stick. They can't find anybody they like for it."

"Seven thousand goddamn guineas and they can't find one?" Jimmy O'Hara nearly exploded. "Then let 'em find some nigger for it. Niggers are dumb enough to club somebody with a ball bat."

Roland exhaled. "You're not hearing me, Jimmy. They're making life difficult for me, and I'm here talking to you."

"And what am I supposed to do?" Jimmy O'Hara asked. "I'm only a poor Irish barkeep. You're acting as if I actually know something."

"No," Roland finished his beer and set the glass gently on the bar, as he always did. Fastidious son-of-a-bitch, Jimmy O'Hara thought. Probably a bed-wetter. "I don't think you do. But I think it would be in your best interest to keep your ears open. Ask a few discrete questions. See what you hear. Because you're going to be in for a lot of heat if something doesn't break with this goddamn thing soon. And, Jimmy, m'lad, I know that you're a fella that doesn't like a lot of light shining on you and what you do."

Jimmy O'Hara wanted to tell Roland that if tried leaning on him again he personally would shove Roland's head up his ass, but, as always when dealing with Roland, or anybody from Downtown, he thought better of it. To give this political hack the benefit of the doubt, he was under a lot of pressure—and was only the Mayor's messenger boy. They had nothing—*nothing*—or they wouldn't be sending a self-satisfied dimwit like Bill Roland around like this. So, having thought about it, Jimmy O'Hara decided it would be better to tell them exactly what they wanted to hear.

"I'll keep my ears open," Jimmy O'Hara said.

"That's the lad," Roland smiled, and stepped into the bright afternoon sun.

They called Whitey's Bouquet Street row house an Irish stew—because stuffed into it was Whitey's mother, Irish boarders of both genders, laundry all over the place, and more noise than a machine shop. Whitey's father—well, for the little he was there, he wasn't really there. Whitey's mother made no bones about it—she'd said for years that if the Church permitted divorce, she would've been rid of Michael Grogan, Sr., years ago.

People made fun of Whitey's father, and his family, but Whitey didn't seem to care, so they stopped. After all, what's the use of insulting someone's lineage if he won't rise to the bait?

If Mongol spent most of his time at Central in the Assistant Principal's office—a nasty, balding, hoarse-voiced fellow named Dietz who liked to dish out large dollops of corporal punishment—Whitey was perpetually bounced for being drunk in class. That, of course, was a much-admired talent—to show up soused at eight in the morning. It made him a legend.

"Untrustworthy," Jimmy O'Hara'd grunt when Stash tried to get Whitey on the payroll. "Can't even hold onto bus fare."

When we were 12, we all thought Whitey's drinking problem was funny. We'd be cleaning tables, sweeping floors, hauling trash at the Gaelic or church suppers, and Whitey'd be boosting beers, sometimes even bottles of Four Roses or Canadian Club. OK, sometimes he'd show up for practice loaded, or hung over, but we were kids, and it was all for laughs.

By the time he was 14, Whitey had guys buying him bottles of wine at the State Store and six-packs at the Emerald. His old man drank, too, so Whitey, Sr., never noticed. If he did, he didn't care.

It was after Korea and Oakland was full of drunks—Tommy the Sailor, with the messy black anchor tattooed on his forearm, Crazy Paddy, Whitey, Sr., and a bunch of others. They were older, veterans, and harmless. They were fat and slow and tired—they were going to die soon anyway. We were kids; we never thought any of us could turn out that way. Especially not somebody young; not somebody who played shortstop as well as Michael Grogan, Jr.

Jimmy O'Hara was exasperated. "It's a dead dago in the park," he tried once again to reason with Roland, which, Jimmy O'Hara understood, was like trying to tap dance on sand. "Let them hang it on some dago and be done with it."

"Trouble is," Roland answered, trying to sound reasonable, which he never did when he was presenting orders from Downtown, "it doesn't fit."

"Doesn't fit?" Jimmy O'Hara was incredulous. "With dagos?"

"They're all a bunch of rats, the dagos," Roland shrugged.

"Can't argue with you there," Jimmy O'Hara said. "I hate doing business with them cocksuckers. Niggers're better." He paused. "Not much, but better."

"Right," Roland agreed. "They do what they're told, and you don't get no beef. But this one—nobody's ratted nobody out. Usually they're lined up in the street to rat out cousin Dominic for something. Not this time," Roland shook his head. "The whole bunch of them are quiet. And mad."

"So some dago drove in from Cleveland and settled a score," Jimmy O'Hara said. "So what does this have to do with me? Other than serving you free beers."

"That's just it," Roland said. "According to the Chief, this guy, this Mario Gencorelli, didn't have any scores to settle. Clean. Honest. Hard-working."

"Balls," Jimmy O'Hara said, angry at himself for letting all this happy horseshit get to him. "Everybody has a score to settle, especially dagos. And still I ask you, The Right Honorable William F. Roland, City Councilman: what is all this to me?"

"He used a baseball bat."

"Does this look like a fucking sporting goods store?" Jimmy O'Hara couldn't believe it. "What does all this have to do with me?"

"You know any ballplayers?" Roland was unmoved.

"Because he used a baseball bat means that a baseball player did it? The only people who have baseball bats are ballplayers?" Jimmy O'Hara was nearly apoplectic. "Are you daft?"

"You know any ballplayers?" Roland repeated.

"I know plenty of ballplayers. Half the goddamn Pirates drink in here. You know that."

"They're looking for ballplayers," Roland said.

"Well, it's a dago killing," Jimmy O'Hara said. "There's plenty of dago ballplayers. Where the fuck is Joe DiMaggio?"

"Retired and living in San Francisco. You're not hearing me," Roland said.

"I heard you plenty, Bill," Jimmy O'Hara said. "For reasons known only to Sweet Jesus Himself, they're looking for ballplayers. Since you're here, I take it they're looking for *Irish* ballplayers. Irish ballplayers that might be known to me."

"Could be," Roland said.

"Now what motive might these imaginary Irish ballplayers have for killing some goddamn dago in Mary Schenley's Park?"

"They're not saying," Roland allowed. "If they had that, they'd have them."

"So they have nothing," Jimmy O'Hara said.

"They have the baseball bat," Roland reminded him.

"Is there a map of Ireland on it?" Jimmy O'Hara pressed. "Is this a joke?" Jimmy O'Hara took a step back, took his rag off his apron string, and began wiping down the bar. "They have nothing."

"I don't know," Roland said.

"Did they lift any prints off said bat?" Jimmy O'Hara prodded.

"All smudged," Roland shook his head.

"Tough titty. Any other identifying marks?"

"Gus Suhr model." Roland paused. "I'm doing you a favor here, Jimmy."

"I'm hard-pressed to see it, Bill, so why don't you tell me what that favor might be," Jimmy O'Hara said. "Because assuming I know anything about it all, which I don't, you wouldn't want me to roll over on any of my people, would you?"

"Of course not," Roland smiled. "It's just that in the interest of self-preservation, seeing everything that goes on around here—"

"Of which you take more than your fair share," Jimmy O'Hara interrupted, angry now and not caring if Roland knew it.

"And that doesn't buy you much, not on this one," Roland countered.

"Now you listen to me, Councilman," Jimmy O'Hara slapped down his rag and pointed his finger at Roland, "and you listen good. You've got a good thing going here. Don't ruin it. Don't you be threatening me over whispers and shadows. Neither one of them pays in the long run."

"If they turn themselves in, it might go easier on them. And you." Roland shrugged.

"Me?" Jimmy O'Hara nearly hit him. "I ought to run that fat English arse of yours out of here for good, Bill Roland. The police got nothing—other than some idiot idea that a baseball player did it because they found a ball bat. An *Irish* baseball player at that. Now you want some of my people to pin this on themselves to clear the case for Downtown—and make a name for you." Jimmy O'Hara spat on his own floor. "I'd hang first."

Roland cocked his head in amusement. "You're a smart man, Jimmy O'Hara," he smiled, "so know this. Everything is narrative. Everything is how it plays. It doesn't matter what a story is as long as everyone agrees to it." He paused. "Remember that, Jimmy."

Before Jimmy O'Hara could say another word, Roland took his leave. "I'll help you if I can, Jimmy. I give you my word on that."

"It's a good thing that St. Patrick drove the snakes from Ireland," an exasperated Jimmy O'Hara said later to Regis Moran. "Good for Ireland, but bad for us. He drove them all the way here, across the vast salt sea. And the Good Lord arranged that they should all make a living. He put them all to work on City Council."

It was after hours, and Jimmy O'Hara, apron off, cigar in hand, was leaning back in his office chair. Stash marveled at how much Jimmy O'Hara managed to stuff into the small, cramped space—his scarred wooden desk, mid-sized Mosler safe, ratty couch, and faded pictures of ballplayers and boxers and Ireland tacked to the dirty yellow plaster walls.

Jimmy O'Hara did not look happy, and that scared Stash, who had learned to read the older man's moods—and had learned when to duck. Trouble was, there was no one else around, and nowhere to hide.

It was the first time Stash had ever heard Jimmy O'Hara blaspheme. Sure, he knew all the bad words, and used them frequently, but never things that were irreligious. This time was different.

Somehow Jimmy O'Hara knew—Stash was certain of that. Somehow the police, as dumb and slow as they were, managed to put together one and one and come up with—not two, exactly, but something close enough. Maybe it was the dago and Mary Margaret and Nig. Maybe somebody knew that Mongol had that bat. Maybe somebody saw them. Stash didn't know—didn't want to know. But somehow, somebody had tipped Jimmy O'Hara to something, and he painted the rest of the picture.

"By the bleeding heart of Jesus," he said. "You dumb fuckin' mick." Jimmy O'Hara grabbed for air, then let his hands drop. "You really fucked up this time."

Stash looked down at the floor, and Jimmy O'Hara felt his anger subside.

"Look. I'm not saying you did it," Jimmy O'Hara began, and Stash knew what he was talking about. "But if you did, even if you had a good reason—and I'm not asking you, and I don't want to know *anything*—you need to know that's not what we do."

Stash started to protest, and Jimmy O'Hara held up a hand. "I'm doing the talking now," he said. "And I don't want to know *anything*. D'ye understand?"

Feeling the hairs rise on the back of his neck, Stash nodded.

"Whoever had that beef in the park, and brought all this heat into Oakland, didn't act the way we act. It was too wild, too messy. Left too many questions and too many loose ends." Jimmy O'Hara looked hard at Stash. "Whoever did made that mess ought to shut up and lay low."

Stash nodded.

"Whoever made that mess ought to think first next time, ask permission, follow orders, and do things the right way. Or whoever made that mess might find himself having a mess made of him. D'ye understand?"

Stash nodded.

"And while whoever made that mess is shutting up and laying low, we'll see what we can do to make that mess go away. D'ye understand?"

Very afraid now, Stash nodded.

"Good," Jimmy O'Hara nodded back. "Now get out of here, and don't come around again—all four of you—until I call you. D'ye understand?"

But Stash had already gone.

As he grew up in Oakland, more and more of Whitey's stories involved alcohol not baseball. Father Dave said that alcohol is a demon—either you control it, or it controls you. There's no middle way.

There wasn't with Whitey. "He really has to hate something in himself to want to kill it that badly," Father Dave said, hurt, hopeless, having no way to help.

Perhaps drinking starts as a social thing; I don't know. But for people in Oakland it quickly degenerated into something you did to take the pain away.

And there was a lot of pain in that life—heartaches to headaches to muscle aches. For all those myriad pains, alcohol was the working man's medicine. It was there, available without prescription, and cheap.

A lesson that Jimmy O'Hara learned and exploited early, and the Oakland Quartet learned the hard way, was that life never turned out the way you wanted it to. "That pain," he'd say, opening up in the morning, "might be the worst of all."

That's the pain Whitey felt the most.

Getting liquor was never a problem for Whitey. As far as the State Store went, he'd either get somebody to buy it for him, or, in his rare flush times, simply paid off the clerk. Aside from knowing every bartender in Oakland, and knowing who would serve him or not, and who locked the doors and let everybody drink 'til the morning light began to seep through the grimy windows, Whitey could always work the Gaelic and hook as many beers as he could. So staying loaded was never a problem for Whitey.

Which suited him just fine.

Standing in the alley behind the bar, where no one could hear him, arms folded across his chest, Jimmy O'Hara was saying something without saying it.

"Why are we out here, Jimmy?" Stash asked, smelling the sweet rotting odor of trash, and the greasy tang of fried fish sandwiches.

"Because the walls have ears," Jimmy O'Hara said, taking the cigar out of his mouth, looking at it, then jamming it back in the left corner.

"Even in your place?"

"*Especially* in my place," Jimmy O'Hara made a face. "Now shut up and listen. I thought you were smarter than that."

Looking down the alley at the greasy puddles and the trash cans with their lids askew, Stash found that he couldn't meet the older man's eyes. "We had to protect our own," he said.

"*I* do the protecting around here," Jimmy O'Hara said. "You know that."

Stash nodded.

"You made me look bad—with some very impatient people. Now I have to do something about it. Now I have to fix it."

"What do you want me to do?"

"You?" Jimmy O'Hara was incredulous. "Nothing right now. You've done enough damage already."

"Jimmy, I—"

"Just shut the fuck up and get out of here." Jimmy O'Hara paused, then his voice softened. "You did the right thing," he nodded, "and you did the wrong thing." He paused. "You see that, don't you?"

Stash nodded.

"Either way," Jimmy O'Hara said, taking his cigar out and tossing it down the alley, "there's a lot of heat from Downtown. It's my ass now."

"Sorry, Jimmy," Stash hung his head.

"It isn't going to be pretty." He put his hands on his hips. "Hell, Peter Andrew Kelly, you're supposed to be smarter than that."

"Jimmy," Stash began, "I—"

"Just shut the fuck up and get out of here," Jimmy O'Hara turned away.

They talked about it. No matter how much heat came down, Nig'd never talk. Mongol, either; he'd just laugh at them. Stash, well, he was too smart to get trapped into saying anything.

But Whitey, well, the White Man was another story. If anybody broke, it'd be Whitey; Whitey'd break first. Not that he'd want to. It's just that they'd trip him up, or his tongue would get all twisted. Or he'd really need a drink, and say so, and they'd promise him one just as soon as all this was over. Sooner or later he wouldn't be able to remember anything other than what happened, and would have to tell them.

Sooner or later, he'd give them all up.

Then his mother'd make a deal with the DA: her son would walk and the other three—"they're *really* guilty, your honor; they *made* my son come along"—would go to prison for life. Or worse.

The way the DA—and the Mayor—saw it, *somebody* had to go away. It really didn't matter who. It might as well be three Irish hoodlums. Might as well be Nig and Mongol and Stash.

Stash saw it all first. "We really got to do something about this," he said to Nig one steamy night as the two were splitting a beer behind the Emerald.

"Yeah," Nig agreed, "but what?"

"That's the 64-dollar question, isn't it?"

One Sunday, Whitey, along with his cousins Sean and Timothy, borrowed a rowboat with an outboard motor and went fishing down the Ohio. Loaded down with fishing tackle, wooden beer cases, and a Scotch cooler full of sandwiches, they started out from a dock just this side of the Point. Going about a mile or two past Downtown and the bridges, they dropped anchor where the houses stopped and the summer hills were so green and steep they seemed to fall right into the river's dark surface.

Dodging the bigger boats, and the endless black coal barges, diesel engines rumbling so loudly they drowned out all conversation, flat bottoms drawing enormous wakes, the three threw in for bass—and anything else they could snag.

However, since it was Whitey and his cousins, they mostly went to drink. So they'd fish, and drink, and fish, and drink, and drink some more, their beer bottles making a steady splashing tattoo on the river's muddy surface. Finally, it was time for lunch, so Whitey hauled out the Scotch cooler and handed out sandwiches wrapped in wax paper. Finished with his sandwich, Whitey went to throw the wax paper in the river. Thinking he'd flip it off the cooler top, Whitey, by then fairly loaded, accidentally tossed the top of the cooler in the river. Realizing what he had done, and that the cooler was now worthless, except perhaps as an umbrella stand, he stood up, muttered a drunken curse, and heaved the entire bucket into the Ohio, where, with a great slurping sound, it sank like a stone.

His cousins laughed so hard they nearly fell out of the boat. But Whitey didn't, because he knew his bitch mother would make him pay for the cooler.

Father Dave would say it's an article of faith that everyone can seek redemption, and achieve salvation, but that in order to do so he has to take advantage of his opportunities. Every man has to understand that he is given a moment—and he has to seize it.

About two weeks into the investigation, as Jimmy O'Hara started to think about the Oakland Quartet, one morning in The Clock, eggs over easy, wheat toast, and coffee, Nig salivating and Helen smirking, Father Dave stopped by, tall, slender, genial as ever. "Mind if I sit down?" he asked the Oakland Quartet.

"No," Stash said, speaking for all of them as usual. "Here, please."

Sliding over, they made room in the booth.

"I hear you boys are still the best," he smiled.

While Stash shrugged, Nig blurted out, "better," and Whitey and Mongol laughed.

"Atta boy, Henry," Father Dave laughed. "Never lose that humility."

"Aw, Father," Nig began.

"I know, I know," Father Dave smiled. "I was once a pretty fair centerfielder myself. I was no Max Carey, you understand. He was fast, noticeably fast. Took off after the ball as if he was on springs." Father Dave paused and smiled again. "But baseball is a young man's game."

The Oakland Quartet, especially Stash, wondered what was coming next.

"I also hear you boys may be in a spot of trouble," Father Dave said. "Or could be."

"We didn't do *nothin*'," Nig said, a little too angry, a little too fast.

"Well, maybe you did, and maybe you didn't. And maybe it's nothing the law can pin on you. Now you know there's nothing I can do for you there."

Almost involuntarily, the Oakland Quartet nodded.

"Right," Father Dave said. "But how about squaring it upstairs? That's where I have an in, you know."

They all knew that—but didn't care.

One Saturday morning, Whitey showed up early for infield practice—the Oakland Quartet always spent the first two hours on Saturday mornings whipping the ball around. Whitey, habitually, was never first. But that day, bright and sunny, he was out there, doing some ground work, chucking the ball into the backstop, practicing his pick-ups.

"'Sa'matter," Nig hollered when he saw Whitey, "they close the bars?"

Whitey stood upright. "A couple of drinks never hurt Paul Waner," he objected, then fired the ball at Nig, who caught it nimbly, and pivoted as if he were making the throw to first.

"Sure," Nig said, "but you're no Paul Waner."

"I know when I first fell in love," Whitey said.

Nig suppressed a giggle.

Stash took a pull on the cigarette and passed it to Mongol, who did the same.

"I was 10," Whitey said wistfully, leaning up against a late-model, two-tone Buick outside Stash's father's fix-it shop.

"Yeah?" Nig said, suddenly interested. "Who was she?"

"*She* was a cold bottle of Stoney's," Whitey smiled. "And, *man*, was she ever something."

Mongol flipped the butt into the street.

"Besides," Whitey said, "what good is baseball without a few training beers afterwards?" He paused. "Or before?"

"Got a point there," Stash shrugged.

But by then Nig had lost interest, and was moving after a girl carrying a grocery bag up the street.

Although Whitey never had anything approaching a career or a technical skill or even a trade, when he was sober his grease monkey work at a Boulevard of the Allies garage earned him a couple of bucks—which supplemented his major income source, cadging cash from his credulous mother's purse. When caught, Whitey always pleaded one thing or another and managed to get off the hook.

In later years various medical professionals and social workers tried to find a reason for his drinking, for his early descent into alcoholism. They wanted child abuse or a Celtic sense of tragic inevitability or some recessive gene—passed on by his father, no doubt. They wanted to make Whitey a case study, a journal article. But Whitey wasn't a case study. Whitey was just Whitey. Whitey just had a taste for drinking—and drinking had a real taste for him. Whitey just liked life loaded. To him, it may have been more sloppy, but it was also a lot more fun.

Although Whitey's boss at the garage was worried about Whitey's drinking, he thought Whitey might make a good mechanic, thought about sending him to trade school. But the Mary Margaret thing ended all that.

Whitey saw to that.

They kept thinking that Whitey would break, and that they'd have to do something about it, but during the first round of questioning he held firm. Sticking to the script like a pro, he kept saying they were hanging out that night, like a thousand other summer nights, nowhere in particular. Just another hot night in south Oakland, the famous Oakland Quartet just loafing.

The police tried every way to get him to slip—it'll go easier, it'll shame your mother, they knew what he did, Nig or Stash or Mongol had already ratted him out—but he held. *There stands Jackson like a stone wall*, Stash said, but no one knew what he was talking about. Maybe Whitey was too dumb to break, or more afraid of what Stash would say, and Mongol would do, but the cops couldn't shake his story.

After a couple of hours, the two cops—brainless, bull-headed guys, thick hair and heavy underbites—had to cut him loose.

"Don't leave town," the shorter, squatter one said.

"I live in Oakland," Whitey said. "I've never been anywhere else. Where would I go?"

*Fuckin' knucklehead jagoff cop*, he wanted to add.

But they weren't done with Whitey, or with any of them. Not by a long shot.

With a lot of pressure from Downtown to solve what the newsies kept calling "a senseless, brutal murder"—"senseless," Nig said one morning over breakfast, "only to them mugs what ain't got no sense"—the cops seemed to have camped out permanently in Oakland. While Stash seemed to take it all in stride—"*nothing* to worry about," he kept reassuring them—the rest of the Oakland Quartet weren't so sure anymore.

Nig seemed more nervous than usual, always spitting and looking around. Mongol was more jumpy, more willing to take offense, if such a thing were possible. Whitey took it particularly hard. Sullen, morose, he drank heavily, mumbled to himself about getting caught.

Even working out, their infield play slipped considerably from their early-summer try-out. Inexplicably dropping balls, the once-solid infield seemed as porous as a rusted steel shed. Unable to hold onto the ball, unable to make the double plays they once turned with ease, the Oakland Quartet began to bark and blame each other. Finally, when Mongol dropped a ball twice at third, then stood and glared it, the Oakland Quartet turned and strode wordlessly off the field.

They never played ball again.

Now if Regis Moran ever had a credo, which he decidedly didn't, it would have been something he said *sotto voce* from time to time. Some fool'd get his dick in a wringer, then come around begging favors, and sure enough Regis'd say, "a man holds his own." Then he'd pause. "You never take a fall for nobody."

"No quarter asked," Nig'd echo.

"None given," Mongol'd answer, punching his right fist into his left palm.

That bravado aside, Nig told Stash he wanted to meet for breakfast the next morning, just the two of them. So early, before Whitey and Mongol were awake, when the air was thick with dew and ozone, they went to The Clock. Eschewing his usual banter with Helen, waiting for coffee, Nig came right to the point.

"I'm afraid Whitey's going to break," he said, dipping his wheat toast into the runny eggs. "He's going to fuck us all up."

Stash shook his head. "I don't think so."

"C'mon, Stash," Nig objected, "we gotta do *something.*"

"No," Stash said slowly, "no, we don't. What we gotta do is just what Jimmy O'Hara would do. We gotta be calm. We gotta let this thing blow over. Sides," he shrugged, "they got nothin' on us. Nothin'. They can't tie us to the weapon or they would have already. They got no motive. They got no witnesses. So what do they got?"

"Cigarette butt?" Nig objected.

"Fuck," Stash said. "We're the only ones who ever smoked a Lucky Strike? Wake up and smell the coffee, Nig, will you?"

"No," Nig said, too loud, causing heads to turn, then spoke more softly. "*We've* got to control this thing. We've got to give them something—somebody—or they're coming right to us."

Stash wondered how he'd ever let himself get talked into doing it—and how he ever was going to square it with Jimmy O'Hara.

"See," Nig forked eggs and toast, "if they get Whitey to talk, then they've got all of us. He'll spill his guts in five fuckin' minutes."

"No," Stash shook his head, "he won't. But go ahead," he poured sugar into his coffee and stirred, "I want to see where you're going with this."

"Awright," Nig said, lowering his voice so that Stash could barely hear him over the sound of the traffic leaking through the door. "Why don't we blame it on Mongol? He's fuckin' crazy anyway. Once they have him, they won't come looking for the rest of us."

Stash stared and put his cup down. "I can't believe I'm hearing this."

Nig started to say it's the only way, but Stash held up his hand.

"There's two things I want you to think about, and then I want you to shut up and never bring up again. Do you understand?"

Nig, scared for the first time, stopped chewing and nodded.

"First, what's to prevent Mongol from ratting out the rest of us?"

"They'll never believe him," Nig blurted out. "Mongol's fuckin' nuts. Who the fuck'd believe *that* jagoff?"

"I said shut up," Stash put his finger in Nig's face.

Nig nodded.

"The other thing is we stand together. Do you understand that? We *don't* split apart. We *don't* give them one of us. We stand together. For all time. Now does your dumb little Nigger Lips ass understand that?"

Nig started to get out of his seat, but Stash grabbed his shirt and pulled him back down.

"Do you understand?"

Nig, the color draining out of his face, nodded.

"Good," Stash said, relaxing his grip. "Now finish your breakfast."

They were walking single file down a narrow trail in the park, a steep hillside to their right. "They could come for us," Mongol said, "and we'd shoot it out."

"Jesus," Nig said, but Stash just shook his head.

"It'd be the Earps and the Clantons," Mongol spread his hands, "at the OK Corral. It'd be the Vikings. *Odin!*"

"Shut the fuck up," Whitey said.

"Who woke him up?" Nig asked.

Roland took Jimmy O'Hara aside, behind the bar, and whispered to him.

"This comes right from the top, Jimmy," Roland said. "I wish it didn't, but it does. I tried to talk him, and the DA, into second-degree murder—a little too much drink, a little dust-up, you know. Hang out the obvious guy for it, have the others plead to accessory after the fact, get the judge to suspend the sentences."

Jimmy O'Hara nodded.

"I tried," Roland continued. "It might even be an easy case to plead if one of them stood up for the others." Roland shrugged. "But they weren't buying. They're hungry Downtown. They need a victory. And the case has been all over the papers—the bludgeoning. The burial. Malice aforethought. First degree murder. For all of them."

Jimmy O'Hara said nothing.

"Convictions mean re-elections," Roland shrugged.

"If they can tie up the package," Jimmy O'Hara said.

"Only a matter of time," Roland glanced around him, "the way I hear it. Either one more piece of physical evidence. Or sweat them until one breaks." Roland paused. "Thought you should know, Jimmy. Thought you should get a heads-up. Don't know what you can do with it, but I thought you should know."

Jimmy O'Hara stuck out his hand. "Pleasure doing business with you, Councilman."

Jimmy O'Hara wasn't so sure.

"I don't think they're done with you," he said to Stash that night after closing, not telling him about what Roland had said. "They have a hunch."

Stash said nothing.

I could be taking about the weather, Jimmy O'Hara thought, and I'd get the same reaction from him. This kid has ice in his veins.

"I also think they've tagged Whitey as your weak link," Jimmy O'Hara continued.

"He's not all here," Stash.

"Fuck," Jimmy O'Hara spat, exasperated. "What part of him *is* here?"

Stash shrugged. "You don't think Whitey'd turn rat, do you?"

"Anybody'd turn rat they turn the heat high enough," Jimmy O'Hara folded his arms and peered across the bar at Stash. "Anybody'd turn rat needs a drink that bad, like Whitey. Think about it, Peter Andrew Kelly. You got to watch him. Got to. And *you* got to take care of him."

"Jimmy," Stash began, but Jimmy O'Hara wasn't listening.

"Because the last thing you want is for your friend Whitey to become the White Rat. Oh, that shyster Dennehy probably has the moxie to make the whole thing go away, but I wouldn't want to bet on that. Besides, it would be all over the newspapers—you and your mates. Me. Even Roland." Jimmy O'Hara shook his head. "Christ on the Cross! We don't want that lot all over us. It'd be the end of everything." He leveled a finger at Stash. "You dumb fuckin' mick knucklehead. All of you! Even if you do skate, you'll be finished. Done. No power in heaven or on earth will be able to save you." He paused. "Me, too."

Stash exhaled.

"Right," Jimmy O'Hara answered, "main force."

Reaching under the bar, he pulled out the Colt Python, gleaming dully in the bar's dim light. "Take it," he gestured.

Stash hesitated, picked up the gun, opened the cylinder to see if it was loaded, then put it back down. It sat on the bar, a vile, repulsive religious relic.

"It's a bit like Korea," Jimmy O'Hara said, putting both hands firmly on the bar. "Those fighter pilots who ditched into the ocean. The water froze their balls into cocktail nuts. They could survive it once 'cause they didn't know what was coming. Twice? No fuckin' way.

"That's your friend Whitey. He won't be able to stand up to another grilling. They'll come at him harder this time. They'll break him.

"So you're going to have to take care of it," he nudged the gun toward Stash. "If they come anywhere near him again, you've got to use this."

"Why me?" Stash nearly whimpered. "Why not Mongol?"

"Because you're the smart one. You, you stupid mick, you should have stopped it before it ever got started. Mongol doesn't have the brains he was born with. Nig? He'd be off gettin' his weasel greased. This is *your* punishment for letting that little cunt brain do your thinking. You're going to take care of Whitey."

Stash looked at the floor.

"It's your ass or his, boyo," Jimmy O'Hara said with sudden vehemence. "And mine, too. Because Dennehy or no Dennehy they'll wind up hanging this on me, one way or another. And I'm too old to start from nothing."

Stash began to say something, but Jimmy O'Hara didn't pause.

"Even if they have *nothing* on me, which is what they have, they're going to blame me for having you around. You four are part of my crew, which means you're part of *me*. Everybody knows that. I've stood up for you with Roland. I might as well have taken out an ad in the goddamn newspaper. So if you go, I go, too. Accessory before or after the fact. Some such shit. Doesn't fuckin' matter. Even if *nothing* sticks, it's meant to teach me a lesson. And warn everybody else in the city. That's how the game is played. So if it comes to it, you *better* take care of this."

Stash just stared.

"Let me put this another way," Jimmy O'Hara said. "You—you and your whole fuckin' knucklehead crew. You wanted to grow up fast. You wanted to be men. Well, it's time for you to become men. It's time for you to take care of this before this takes care of you. And me. And the others."

Stash didn't move.

"He'll skate on you—you know that. Sure as the day is hot and long, and the air smells like shit, and Mr. John Jameson makes some fine Irish whiskey, he'll skate. He'll flip faster than a beetle on a summer sidewalk. Meanwhile, you'll be all righteous—until the minute they strap you down in the gas chamber. So take the Python, Peter Andrew Kelly. Or spend the rest of your life in prison. If they don't hang you."

Stash picked up the Python, put it in the waistband of his trousers, and walked out of the Emerald.

Stash had convinced the other three to keep their mouths shut, even to Duffy, especially to Duffy, who'd sell out his own sainted grandmother Rose McMahon to get a leg up in his career.

But Stash needed counsel. Of course, he couldn't go back to Jimmy O'Hara. Instead, he went to the one man whom he knew would say nothing. Even if he didn't know what to do, he'd honor the code of silence.

If anybody could help him, it was Regis Moran.

"Jesus, Joseph, and Mary," Regis Moran chewed on his cigarette. Sitting in the dark Gaelic on a humid Thursday afternoon, staring into the gloom, he just shook his head. "Jesus, Aloysius, even I never fucked up that bad."

"I want all of them here," he told Stash a day later, "tomorrow afternoon. Jimmy O'Hara, too. That's all. No civilians."

Stash began to ask what Regis Moran was thinking.

"Tomorrow," Regis Moran said, and turned away.

"You're in a jackpot, all right," Regis Moran said to the Oakland Quartet, spread out before him on folding chairs.

"What a sorry bunch of fuck-ups," Jimmy O'Hara shook his head.

"Maybe it just happened," Mongol shrugged.

It the maddest they ever saw Jimmy O'Hara. "Nothing just happens," he said, face all red. "Not now. Not ever. Not nothing.

"You got the whole city calling for your heads. And they'll get your heads, or somebody's. I ought to turn you in myself. For being stupid. And for making me look bad. You know how much this is going to cost me?"

Before Stash could stop him, Nig blurted out they had nothing on them.

"Get this idiot out of here before I drill him another arsehole," he said to Stash. "Nothing on you? Aside from 100 people ready to testify that you were foaming at the mouth about killing this guy? That's nothing? And another 100 who'll put that goddamn bat in your hands? Nothing? Besides, you know how it works—and if you don't, you will now. They don't *need* anything. All they need is you—and they'll fill in the blanks."

The Oakland Quartet sat silent.

"Your fucking jackpot. And I'm going to have to the pay the freight."

Turning with what seemed like infinite sadness, Regis Moran asked Jimmy O'Hara to save his remarks until he was finished. "Don't make this any harder than it already is," Regis Moran said.

Shrugging, Jimmy O'Hara sat back, arms folded.

"I may not have gone to church as often as I should have," Regis Moran began, and to a man the Oakland Quartet wondered where he was going with this, Whitey especially, who always thought of Regis Moran as a puncher and nothing else. "And I may have given Father Dave a lot of shit about it." A brief, tight smile. "You know how that is, boys."

Involuntarily, the Oakland Quartet nodded and smiled back.

"But I always took the stories to heart," Regis Moran said, exhaling smoke. "Especially the story of Jesus taking Barabbas' place on the Cross."

The Gaelic, murky in the afternoon, dust motes floating in the dim light, was silent. Whitey could barely hear the traffic on Fifth Avenue. Even the trolleys had seemed to stop running.

"Something you don't know," Regis Moran smiled, "not even you, Jimmy. I've got lung cancer. The docs gave me six months. Maybe a little more."

Of course, Jimmy O'Hara and the Oakland Quartet blurted out protests, but Regis Moran waved them away. "I hid it pretty good," he said, "but I got spots on my lungs. I got all the signs."

"It ain't right," Whitey protested.

"It's what it is," Regis Moran shrugged.

Jimmy O'Hara started to stand up.

"Let me cut to the chase," Regis Moran said. "I think they want you," he nodded to at the Oakland Quartet, who looked at the floor, "and if they want you, they'll get you."

Jimmy O'Hara sat down and nodded. He had Dennehy in his back pocket, but figured he'd wait out Regis Moran. He thought he knew where Regis Moran was going, but Jimmy O'Hara was wrong.

"I'm dying—you're the first to know it. I'm dying. And you guys are young. Stupid—really fucking stupid. I can't say what you did is right. But, given what that dago son-of-a-bitch did to poor Mary Margaret, I can't say what you did is wrong, either."

Nodding, Nig looked around.

"Somebody had to set things right, somebody had to send a message to those goddamn dagos that they can't cross the line. You know that, Jimmy."

Reluctantly, Jimmy O'Hara nodded.

"Now you've got your whole lives ahead of you. I don't." Regis Moran paused to light another Lucky Strike. "Another nail," he shrugged. "So I'll take your place on the cross. I'll give myself up. I'll cop to the crime."

Led by Jimmy O'Hara, the Oakland Quartet started to protest.

"Let me finish," Regis Moran waved them down. "They may not believe me, not at first. But if I stick to my story—hothead, fighter, dago took a swing at me, et cetera—they'll understand they can make their case standing up. They'll have their conviction. The newsies'll be happy—and off to something else. David Leo Lawrence will be happy, the self-satisfied little prick. That asshole Bill Roland, too. It'll make them all look good. That's all they care about."

Regis Moran paused; nobody said anything.

"I'll even let that shit-for-brains Bill Roland take the credit for bringing me in," Regis Moran actually shuddered, "if that'll help you, Jimmy."

For once, Jimmy O'Hara was speechless, then gestured to Whitey, "give us all a drink here, boyo. I think we need one."

That may have been the plan, but timing is everything. And if they got Whitey first, it would fall apart.

So Stash still kept watch on Whitey, watched him closely. Nothing seemed out of the ordinary, meaning that Whitey was drinking three times as much as the rest of them.

Meanwhile, as Regis Moran briefed old man Dennehy, the newsies didn't give up on the story. DAY TWENTY-FIVE NO BREAK IN CASE ran the *Sun-Tele*'s banner head. What the paper didn't say was that the police decided to go after the Oakland Quartet. "Nothing more than a hunch," the Chief told Roland, "but my hunches are generally pretty good. A lot of people've seen those kids with that bat." Out of courtesy, and because there was something in it for him, Roland passed it on to Jimmy O'Hara.

Stopping their unmarked white-and-gold '57 Dodge at Whitey's Bouquet Street house, two detectives—new ones, slender, in new suits; Stash had never seen them before—began to get out.

Nauseated, thinking of what he'd have to do, Stash figured that even if Whitey spilled his guts, they'd release him, and, tightening his hand around the Python, he could take care of it then.

Who knew they'd show up so fast? he thought.

Before they could close the car doors, their radio began to crackle. One ducked back in to take the call.

"Get back in," he said to the second man, "we're going back Downtown. Somebody just copped to the killing."

"Anybody we know?"

"Would you believe it? I'd give you 20 questions, but you'd blow them all. Regis Moran."

"Regis Moran? You're shittin' me."

"Nah," he smiled. "Gave it up in a minute. Just like that."

"Christ. I always knew we'd get that big dumb mick for *something*. Never figured it would be this."

The first man slammed the door. "OK, let's go."

Standing alone in the Emerald, rag in his hand, Jimmy O'Hara shook his head. "Lucky sons of bitches," he muttered. "Luckiest sons of bitches alive."

It was quite the scene, staged perfectly for maximum effect. Out from his two-story Atwood Street house—not the Emerald, *not* the Gaelic; that was part of the deal with Roland—strode Regis Moran. Hands cuffed, held triumphantly aloft like a victorious boxer, grin big enough to fit around an entire blueberry pie, Regis Moran, accompanied by two burly, uniformed officers, posed for the newsies. It was a huge public relations victory for the Mayor, who, being the Mayor, never shared anything with anybody, unless they had more money than he did.

Quickly, it became the region's biggest news story, with all the appropriate mutterings, people from the Mayor to the Man in the Street musing on the end of "this dreadful threat to brave, hardworking men and women all across our great city," and so on. And there he was, happy, grinning, Regis Moran brandishing his hammer-sized fists, posing for photographers, holding down the front page, a place he had scrupulously avoided his entire life.

I still have the clippings.

It was hard not to laugh, but I'm certain that Bill Roland did—and filed away the lesson for the time, not too distant, he hoped, when he would ascend and take Lawrence's place.

They had all said it: Regis Moran was a stand-up guy.

With Regis Moran's well documented history of violence, no one in his right mind doubted the veracity of his confession. Here was a well known walloping tough willing to admit to the crime. Here was a conviction on the proverbial silver platter. Forget that it was all a little too pat. Those were black-and-white times, and this was a black-and-white case. It's all narrative anyway. "It doesn't matter what our story is," Roland famously said, then and many times afterward, "as long as we all agree to it." So they took Regis Moran at face value, struck the set, and moved the morality play somewhere else.

To give him credit, Regis Moran played his part perfectly. A model defendant, he was cooperative, penitent, discursive—funny, even. No matter how much his lawyer—old man Dennehy himself, all wire-rimmed glasses and wattles over his too-tight collar—tried to excuse him, Regis Moran, acting the rube, managed to make the charge stick for good.

The newsies had their story—Mad Mick Murders Mario. And *voila!* everyone else—Lawrence and Roland, Jimmy O'Hara and the Oakland Quartet—was conveniently off the hook.

There would be closure. Oakland could heal and move on.

No, the prosecution couldn't introduce his extensive rap sheet, or his priors, but he was the legendary Regis Moran, and everybody already knew him. In the present case, although old man Dennehy fought on motive, trying to knock down the charge to second-degree murder because they agreed to fight, or so Regis Moran claimed, the prosecutor—some pinch-faced zealot named Souici—managed to seat with the jury the idea that Regis Moran didn't need any more motive than a good street brawl, which the two men decided to finish in the park. And that trip to park was sufficient malice aforethought to qualify as Murder One.

The weapon? "Me?" Moran nearly laughed, brandishing a DeSoto-sized fist. "I don't need no ball bat to bash a guy's head in. That dumb dago brought it, took a swing at me. I took it from him and did the honors, just to teach him a lesson." He paused. "Lesson stuck, too, huh, judge?"

Of course, the spectators wept with laughter, and the judge—a stuffy fellow named Charleston—was *not* amused and threatened to clear the courtroom. By the time he gave his charge about "this heinous crime, this public disgrace," the damage was done. Regis Moran, suddenly docile, just sat and took his trip to the woodshed like the trooper he was.

Of course, no one around the Emerald could understand it, and Jimmy O'Hara just lied and shrugged and shook his head. "I don't have any better answer than you do," he allowed.

It took the jury all of about 35 seconds to decide: first-degree murder, because Regis Moran *intended* to murder, Western Penitentiary, 25-to-life.

All Regis Moran did was smile.

Regis Moran, as jovial as ever, greeted Father Dave in Western's gray, institutional visitors room.

"Hiya, Father," he said expansively. "Tell you what. I want to confess."

"Well," Father Dave said, surprised. "There's a first time for everything. How long's it been since your last confession?"

"You mean the confession I never had?" Regis Moran laughed. "Well, there's a last time for everything, too, Father. And this isn't a real one anyway. None of that hocus-pocus stuff. But I want you to know the truth."

"Thank the Lord for that," Father Dave said.

"You're a kind and decent man, Father," Regis Moran said, "and a good one. You're on the side of the angels, assuming there are angels, and assuming they take sides."

"There are," Father Dave assured him, "and they do. Thank you for the confidence. Now what is it that you want to tell me?"

"I copped to the deed," Regis Moran began, "to take the heat off the boys. I'm dying of cancer, Father. And they have their whole lives ahead of them. So I took the rap. I wanted you to know. I wanted you to know that I did listen to all that Jesus and Barabbas shit."

Hiding his surprise, Father Dave nodded sagely.

"Now I want something in return," Regis Moran demanded.

"And what might that be?" Over the years, Father Dave had learned not to be surprised—and not to antagonize anyone who wanted a quiet moment with him. So he waited.

"As long as I'm alive, I want to know how they're doing. And I want to know that you'll look after them, huh? See that they're stayin' out of trouble, Father. That they're not fucking up. That they're not turning out like me."

"Well," Father Dave smiled, "I can't promise outcomes, Regis. But I can promise I can make those reports. As far as how they turn out, I'll do what I can."

"Thanks, Father," Regis Moran, extending a hand. "A man can't ask no more'n that."

"Hey, Regis," Father Dave smiled as Regis Moran stood to leave the visitors room. "How do you make holy water?"

Old drunks spend their days and retirement checks in the shadowland of gin mills. Taverns, beer gardens, tap rooms, after-hours clubs—these were holy places to Whitey, where the beer had so soaked into the worn wooden floors that the odor would never dissipate.

Father Dave said that everyone seeks salvation, but that poor Whitey was selling his soul cheaply at the bottom of a glass.

If liquor mellowed out Whitey—made him docile, peaceful—it made Mongol, always angry to begin with, seriously twisted. But while Mongol could take liquor or leave it, Whitey felt the edge more and more—felt how hard life had become after Mary Margaret, how depressing, how oppressive. He needed liquor, one drink, then two, then four, until no one—not Jimmy O'Hara, not the Oakland Quartet—could help him anymore. "He needs a minder," Jimmy O'Hara shook his head, meaning that he was officially banished from Eden.

In one of his few remaining cogent thoughts, Whitey knew that visiting Father Dave made his mother feel good. For his part, Whitey felt Father Dave was sufficiently harmless so as not to affect badly the equilibrium of his life, alcoholic as it was. Father Dave's quarters—awash in the standard musty church smell, ameliorated by the heavy odor of old wood and melting wax—were pleasant enough, and, besides, Father Dave always had plenty of cigs he was more than willing to share.

For all his smiles, there was no hiding the fact that Father Dave was possessed of a *weltanschauung* that mediated between the twin poles of Tragic

Inevitability and the Postlapsarian Fall of Man. Of course, he believed in Redemption and Salvation, believed that it could be achieved by anyone. It was just that in Man's Fallen State, he was generally too lazy or foolish or short-sighted to pursue Salvation with much alacrity.

Such a dark view of the human cosmos, however, while causing undue stress to the good padre, and no doubt hastening his relatively early demise, did not prevent him from trying to save as many souls as he could. Including, or especially, Whitey's.

Whitey was basically good—Father Dave knew that. "But when someone feels that life is that bleak," Father Dave shook his head, "he tends to do one of two things, or one thing, really, in one of two directions. To stop the searing pain of living, he either turns to violence, hoping to staunch his own wound by inflicting pain on others. Or he kills himself. There's never any middle ground."

In Whitey's case—a child who saw his father perpetually drunk and mother pinned beneath the wheel—he was anesthetizing himself to the point of *thanatos*, to the point of death itself. "I can't do much for him," Father Dave said in his own confession one bright December morning. "He's like a terminal case in the hospital. Maybe all I can do is hold his hand.

"I'm afraid he's already lost this world and the next."

Truth be told, they were more alike than not, Whitey and Father Dave, with their guilt-encrusted lives, but as Whitey sank deeper into the abyss, Father Dave stretched his hand farther and farther to try to help.

Until Whitey was too far gone for anyone.

Panhandling, caging meals, visiting old watering holes, Whitey stumbled around Oakland. He slept in bars, on floors, in chairs. His hair grew long, and beard scruffy, and every so often someone—a friend of Jimmy O'Hara's, generally—got him cleaned up. That would last for a week or so, and then he'd be back to it.

Stash didn't find it funny, but others did, taking bets on where Whitey'd turn up. Strand Theater. Behind the counter at the Briar Bowl. Anywhere but Gus Miller's. Old Gus didn't want any part of Whitey, would throw him out before he was even in the door, even before he could take out a couple of greasy quarters for some smokes.

For a time—a pitifully brief time—Whitey sobered up, and, with Jimmy O'Hara's help, got a job driving a bread truck. Making decent money, keeping regular—albeit early—hours, Whitey seemed to have turned his life around. No one knows what happened, but one day he didn't show up for work.

Two weeks later they found him asleep in a chair in an Oakland insurance office. By that time, he'd become an urban legend, and the befuddled insurance agent called the Emerald. Two beefy young men—polite, well dressed—came and took Whitey away.

The beginning of the end came when Whitey couldn't control himself anymore—really couldn't control himself. Somehow he had scraped together a few bucks, laid them on the bar of an after-hours joint that wouldn't run him a tab, and was drinking Imp 'n' Arn—shots of Imperial whiskey chased by Iron City beer. As the evening wore on, and Whitey went farther and farther into the bag, he'd stagger to the gents—little more than a hole in the wall in the far right-hand corner. Weaving, barely able to see, he aimed for the toilet but couldn't stand up straight. Spraying the floor and the walls, he stumbled out, somehow finding the entire exercise excrutiatingly funny.

It was amusing, if only to Whitey himself. The next time, however, he simply forgot to make it to the commode, and simply wet himself, the stain spreading down his pants legs. "That's enough," the bartender—an immense dago whom everybody called Fat Eddie—said, and had Whitey tossed onto the sidewalk, where he proceeded to vomit up all his boilermakers.

"Did a huey," two kids, sitting on a parked car on the opposite side of the street, pointed and laughed. Too drunk to protest, Whitey tried unsuccessfully to roll away from the puddle of yellow vomit.

*"Huey!"* they yelled, laughed, and flipped cigarette butts at him.

Whitey, passing out in the brisk autumn air, was too paralyzed to protest.

It was a quiet night in the Emerald. The Pirates, on the corner TV, were winning, as they did with some regularity in those days. Relenting, Jimmy O'Hara had permitted Whitey to return—conditionally. Fumbling for a cigarette, Whitey searched his pockets for matches—slowly, methodically, a man under water.

"Fire," he mumbled. "Need some fire."

Everyone ignored him.

"Fire," he said, louder. "Gimme some fire."

Now everyone looked up.

"Fire," he said, waving his unlit cigarette around. "I need some fire. Where's some fire?"

Whitey began tossing things out of his way—napkins, coasters, ashtrays, all the while shouting, "Fire! Fire!"

While it might have been funny in another context, it wasn't in Jimmy O'Hara's place. Not when Jimmy O'Hara's patience with a self-indulgent drunk had gone past the breaking point.

"We can't have that kind of racket here," he shook his head. "Stash, Mongol, take care of this. Take him out of here. And don't bring him back."

Without a word, or even an indication that they had heard him, the two put their hands under Whitey's arms, picked him up, and more or less carried him out the door, down the block, and around the corner to his home.

Sure, Whitey came around the next day, all hang-dog and apologetic, but Jimmy O'Hara wasn't having any of it.

"Better stay away for a while," Nig said, sweeping out the place.

"Yeah," Mongol added, "like the next 15,000 years."

"At least until Jimmy O'Hara cools down," Stash said quietly. "I'll let you know," he nodded, walking Whitey out the door and away from the Emerald, for what Whitey hoped wouldn't be the last time.


He's a troubled soul, Father Dave thought. Troubled and troubling. Then he paused and considered Whitey's mates. They're *all* troubled souls.

Taking stock of his own small, stunted life, he shrugged. Well, so am I.

"Whitey," he said the name aloud. Troubled. Tortured. Was he damned from birth? Is that heresy? It's like he was kissed by the Evil One himself.

Better not go there, Father Dave shook his head, drained his ration of Jameson, and contemplated God's wondrous gift, His creation of spirits.

A favorite of the Oakland Quartet—all the Central boys, really—Father Dave was always easy with absolution. As he admitted to close friends over a late-night Miller High Life, he had such a dour view of their lives, and their souls, and their salvation, that anything that brought these wayward souls into church, and brought them back, was worth it. If an easy absolution did it, fine. There was time enough for stronger medicine—good, stiff doses of hellfire, brimstone, and damnation—later.

Always smiling, always smelling of lilac vegetal, Father Dave encouraged the boys to be boys. Certainly in the eyes of the Church they were men, but not in their own eyes, and not in the eyes of society. So he encouraged them, and their games, especially baseball, where so few of them came home hurt.

"Time will catch up soon enough with these fellas," he'd say. "There's a last time for everything, including baseball."

Father Dave also knew that the boys came from bad, broken homes. He saw the welts on their faces and arms. He knew the kind of violence and abuse they suffered. So aside from easy absolution, he acted *in loco parentis*, taking the boys to doctors or emergency rooms or truant officers or court appearances, serving as a character witness, speaking about a boy's sterling attributes. When asked by a surly priest how he could lie like that, Father Dave's face reddened. "I am *not* lying," he answered the taunt. "I am testifying about the boy's *potential*, about his pure and holy soul. With our help he will find the right path, achieve that potential, and fill the mouths of the naysayers with ashes."

Although Father Dave tried not to interfere in the boys' lives, when he felt that a particular boy needed a little more parenting, he often reached out to the boy, inviting him to the parish house for a chat, taking him out for an Isaly's ice cream cone, giving him tickets to a Pirate game. "I do what I can," he shrugged one night, explaining his m.o. to Bishop Wright.

"Father," the Bishop answered, "you do a great deal."

So it was with great sorrow that he found the Oakland Quartet avoiding him. They didn't go to church; if they saw him on the street, they scattered. Finally, they couldn't avoid him. Coming out of the alley behind the Gaelic, they turned onto Atwood Street and there he was—tall, regal even, short hair, smiling at them. Face to face, he looked at them—until the Oakland Quartet could no longer bear it. Hanging their heads, all of them, even Stash, the brightest and most brazen of them all, walked away.

In the normal process of things people focus on mistakes or regrets, and grind on them for entire lives.

Not the Oakland Quartet. They grew into adulthood believing they were impervious, invulnerable to the normal working of things. That they literally could get away with murder.

Further, that not being punished, or even called to account, actually washed away their sin.

It didn't, of course. It just made it worse.

Stash and Nig believed that no matter what they did somehow the authorities wouldn't find them. If they did, there would always be a Regis Moran to play Jesus to their Barabbas, Sidney Carton to their Charles Darnay, taking their places on the cross or the guillotine.

For Mongol, success incited his near-insane taste for blood; he re-created himself as a man who felt most alive only when he was hurting another.

Before Prozac and Percocet, Whitey's medicine was American rye.

Success, simply stated, gave the idea to the Oakland Quartet that they lived charmed lives to which no harm could ever come. "No man of woman born," is how Stash remembered it from *Macbeth*, from the Shakespeare that the forbidding Sister Agnes—in black-and-white wimple and steel spectacles—drilled into them. "No man of woman born can ever hurt the Oakland Quartet."

How wrong he was.

# EPILOGUE

▼

# DUFFY

Whitey wasn't much over 60 when he died—liver shot, body emaciated and dehydrated, by the end there wasn't much left.

As a charity case, it seemed for a time that he wouldn't have a funeral and instead simply be put in a pauper's grave. But for some reason Duffy, who didn't have a sentimental bone in his overpaid body, sprang for the funeral. It was the minimum, but at least there was a viewing, a wake of sorts, a proper send-off.

It was Spartan—utilitarian, small, quick—and Catholic. Held in a tiny Oakland chapel, a handful of people came—some nuns Whitey had known at the Little Sisters of the Poor, a few fellow rummies, and the surviving, non-incarcerated members of the Oakland Quartet.

What was even more surprising, Duffy had tried to spring Mongol for the occasion—to give him credit, Duffy even claimed that Whitey was Mongol's half-brother—but the state wouldn't hear about it. In solitary most of the time—Mongol had nearly killed one inmate in the chow line, another in the yard—there was no way they were going to let him out, even chained to two DOC marshals.

The other two did come, though. Nervous, glaze-eyed, jumpy, Stash showed up in his chauffeur's uniform. Never signing the book, he sat by himself in the back, left before it was over. Although he did bend his knee and cross himself, he offered no words of condolence, never looked anyone in the eye. Head bowed, he stood as silent as their blighted history, and wept.

When wizened little Nig approached Duffy with his hand out, asking how he was and offering to shake, Duffy simply ignored Nig's outstretched hand, said, "better for not having spoken to you for the last 25 years," and walked away.

A young, long-haired priest, Father Tom Clark, spoke about some pretty high-fallutin' things, including the idea that youth, life's glorious, golden moment, feels itself impervious to all harm. Nothing can intrude—not sickness, depression, war. We will all emerge victorious.

Yet, the young father added, there is an architect hereabouts who designs perfectly normal buildings then thrusts a red wedge into them, startlingly—dramatically—dissecting their mid-sections.

By chance or choice, Father Clark added, life does just that. Is there tragic inevitably or merely choice and the consequence of choice? Is life nothing more than you broke it, you bought it?

While Father Clark predictably discussed redemption and salvation, I wondered what he would say about Whitey. Was Whitey set up to be a drunk? And die relatively young? Was there tragic inevitability about his small, stunted life? Or did Whitey—having peered into the abyss of the world, and his own life, and his crime—choose to die early and anesthetized? Proud of it, in his own way, triumphant, victorious, like Regis Moran?

"We are here," Father Clark summed up, "to ask God's forgiveness for the sad, conflicted soul of Michael "Whitey" Grogan, may he rest in peace."

"Amen," murmured the small crowd as if it were one organism, nodding, weeping, looking at the floor.

"Nice little depressing sermon, Father," Duffy mumbled. "Way to send off Whitey."

Father Clark lit a candle and prayed for the souls of all sinners, imploring them to avoid eternal damnation and the unbearable fires of hell.

The eulogy over, people rose, some to thank the father, others to slink out into the gray, late-autumn afternoon. I'm a social worker, not a theologian. I make sure people get their benefits; I don't get to answer the big questions.

I stopped by to pay my respects. Peering down at the artificially pink-cheeked, unrecognizable former shortstop, I said to my former battery mate, "you know what, Duffy? I could use a drink."

Duffy shrugged. "So could Whitey."

The burial in Calvary seemed to take a whole 10 seconds—about as fast as a hurried Hail Mary—then back to work. "He was a ghost for so long," Duffy said, "it's like he was never here."

After Regis Moran took a dive for the Oakland Quartet I missed a lot of what happened next—and had to piece it together over the years.

After Central, I went into army intelligence, spending the better part of two years listening to a radio in Germany. Mustered out in time to miss the Cuban Missile Crisis, I moved away, wildcatting for oil in Texas and Louisiana, wrangling horses in Florida, working as a foreman in Indian River farms, sod-busting in Nebraska. Following a brunette with loose hair and looser morals, I hammered nails in Colorado and Wyoming. When the wind blew farther west, I wound up washing dishes in Alaska. Nothing seemed to stick.

Finally, my knees caught up with me. I came home, to bury my mother, to take a social work degree, to get a job as a case worker. I learned how systems work and how people do—or don't—fit. I learned how neighborhoods like Oakland affect people, the delicate balance between nature and nurture. Did the Oakland Quartet create themselves? Or were they creations of Oakland as real and brick-solid as Eliza and the Emerald?

By the time I returned to Oakland, the Oakland Quartet—like the mills they had tried so hard to avoid—had disappeared.

If I've learned nothing else as a social worker, it's that every person, like every culture, has a narrative—*has* to have one, has to have a story line, something that makes sense of, makes order out of, the chaos. For Jimmy O'Hara, for example, the operative thesis included being part of a beset minority. The Irish were never going to be fully accepted here—No Irish Need Apply and all—so he bent the intrinsically unfair rules, greased the proverbial wheels, made sure every Irish soul was taken care of. For this he received a finder's fee, of course, but who could begrudge him that?

Every story begins, and every story ends. Every story. Even if the person falls off the edge of the world and disappears, that, too, is an ending, a conclusion.

Jimmy O'Hara barely lasted another decade. A lifetime of bad eating and worse hours gave him esophageal cancer, and by 1965 he was too sick to run the Emerald. He, and it, went lights out three years later.

By then, the world had changed. Neighborhoods. Oakland. People went to college and filled out forms; they didn't need protectors like Jimmy

O'Hara. Maybe that's why he could never find an heir to his throne. Jimmy O'Hara's own sons wanted nothing to do with it, or him, or Oakland, for that matter. They moved west and disappeared. For a while, Nig was being fitted for the purple, but after Mary Margaret, and all that skirt-chasing—no, not even a sick and wilting Jimmy O'Hara could see his way to naming Nig his next-in-line.

I'll admit that I miss the Emerald, even miss Jimmy O'Hara, although I was never one of his guys. People say I live too much in the past. We all have a moment, and perhaps that moment is, or seems, perfect, then ethereal, then fades—as fast as a will-of-the-wisp it's gone. Replaced by others, certainly, some sweeter, some better, perhaps, but as soon as that perfect moment is there, it's gone.

For me, the tale of the Oakland Quartet illustrates the one immutable fact of life is loss. Oakland itself was once glorious, golden, perfect—or so it seemed when I caught for Central. We were young. We bowled all night. We played ball until it was too dark to see. We smoked and drank. Nothing ached, inside or out. Nothing hurt.

That's all changed now, all gone. Quinque's and The Clock. The Fort Pitt Tavern and Forbes Field. Even Frankie Gustine's, where the man himself would tell you about being a very young ballplayer and rooming with a very old Paul Waner—or with his luggage, at least. They're all gone.

So is the Emerald Lounge. So is Forbes Field, where the Oakland Quartet so badly wanted to be, and Eliza, where they didn't.

So are Jimmy O'Hara and Regis Moran.

The Gaelic Club has closed, and Cantor's, and Cicero's. Even the Park Schenley, where all the swells went, which was so grand, and seemed so impervious to tastes and trends, is gone. "Failed to read the tea leaves," Bill Roland himself said before he died. My mother, elderly, Irish, and sadly sentimental, who saved her pennies to eat there every year on her birthday, wept when she heard the news.

David Lawrence died, and Old Bill Roland after him. And that Viking funeral they gave Roland—what a piece of wit. Seems that somebody stole Roland's body from the funeral home, put it on a barge on the Mon, then set it on fire. By the time the city fire boat arrived, the barge—and Roland on it—had burned to the water line. "Old Bill Roland a crispy critter," Nig said very solemnly, then laughed so hard I thought he would have a stroke. They never caught whoever did it. Maybe they didn't want to. Good for them.

Pie Traynor. Father Dave. Everyone close to the Oakland Quartet, one way or another, all gone.

Even Mary Margaret, Nig's perfect little angel. Not dead, but might as well be. Grew up and moved away. Nobody, not even Nig, knew where.

No, their world, and the men who made them, written out of existence. But one thing was for certain. The Oakland Quartet were scarred, irrevocably, by that single act on a hot night in 1958. In saving one life, or so they thought, they had ruined four others. Their own.

To no one's surprise, Nig continued wild and profligate. He came close to getting married twice, but they were wild girls, too, and he backed off. Wisely.

Against all sense and better judgment, Mongol got married—busty, big-hipped nurse who was going to change him. Sure, she would. He beat her up—once—and she had the marriage annulled. Or her father did, someone with enough pull with the bishop to make it come out right. Mercifully, their brief union produced no progeny.

For this part, Whitey floated in and out of two marriages, the poor creatures trying to play Wendy to his Peter Pan, trying to dry him out, pitying him, relenting, giving him money for strong drink. Even saints would have tired of his constant recidivism, and these two washerwomen were hardly otherworldly. Tired of trying to keep the incorrigible—and incorrigibly addicted—Whitey away from their grocery money, they cut him loose. Unshaven, unbathed, unkempt, looking years older than his age, Whitey ended up as he knew he would—alone.

Stash did right well for himself, for a while, at least. The job that Roland got him with the city allowed him to buy a big old Park Place house and to get married—to a nice girl named Mary Haney. Sweet, slender, demure, she was right out of the convent school and a Duquesne nursing degree.

She wasn't shanty Irish, either, but lace curtain all the way. The daughter of a very respectable insurance broker with an office on Oakland Avenue, he gave out turkeys at holiday time and posted pictures of the Central baseball team in his window every spring. An usher at St. Paul's when that meant something, Mr. Haney never touched a drop, never crossed the threshold of the Gaelic. "A man doesn't need liquor to find his courage," he liked to say, crossing his arms across his ample chest. "And he doesn't need card playing to make his fortune."

By that time Stash was so connected with Roland—it was Mayor Roland then—that Bishop Wright himself celebrated mass for the wedding.

It was a grand affair, too, the men all in morning coats, the women in white gowns like the bride, who wore what looked to Nig like 300 yards of lace.

It was the only time anybody ever remembered seeing Roland in a hat—an old fashioned homburg, which he wore cocked to one side as if he himself were the one getting married.

There was Stash, settled down to be a model citizen.

Or so it seemed.

If time has taught me nothing else, it's that sooner or later things catch up with you. The late nights. The liquor. The women. Breaking the rules. Maybe not the first time—maybe you get lucky. Maybe you skate, the way the Oakland Quartet did. Maybe not the second or the third. But sooner or later. You lose your edge. You forego your promise.

It's what I learned playing baseball. It's one step. It's a half-step. And then you're gone. The game has passed you by.

Life, too.

You can't play infield any longer.

Nothing lasts.

Oakland is a different place, now, all genteel and prettified. They don't have the dust-ups that we used to, when we measured Saturday nights by how many dagos 'n' darkies we sent to the hospital. Those days are long gone.

But I don't know if Oakland's a better place. It's lost its loyalties, that's for sure. The new generation is All-American and apolitical. They no longer vote ethnic—if they vote at all.

They no longer have places for Jimmy O'Hara and Bill Roland.

Maybe it was better back then, better when four boys on the make, four boys like the Oakland Quartet, roamed the streets, looking out for the common weal, looking to become, if not ballplayers, then men, taking their rightful place in the daily tussle of neighborhood life.

I don't know. I'm not the one to make that call.

I do know that they all believed in their narrative, their story line—they had done a terrible thing to do something good, to save a young girl. The ends, to them, justified the means, even if it meant taking a human life.

"Is that so different from what Duffy does every day," Stash demanded, "making sure that some very bad guys wriggle through the system?" He gestured impotently. "Just because somebody else says the means are OK, Duffy gets hooligans out on the street. He makes good money, and he gets fucking initials after his name. No hauling trash for Duffy, like his old man did. Duffy takes care of things. So did we. What the fuck's the difference?"

If it was better, it was also a tough time in a tough neighborhood. People wound up dead—and if they didn't, it wasn't for lack of trying. While the life term in prison didn't kill Mongol, the gun set off in his ear nearly did. Should have, in fact, but for the fact that he flinched at the last second. That little dust-up—a dago just about as angry as he was, if such a thing were possible—left Mongol deaf in that ear for the rest of his life.

So, too, the Oakland Quartet woke up one morning no longer young, no longer forgiven their minor mistakes and puny peccadilloes.

They woke up one morning to the world of consequences.

As predicted, Regis Moran didn't live very long inside. First, there were some old beefs that followed him. He got in a fight in the County Jail, and two in Western, one bad, the other worse, and wound up in solitary, which was just plain awful. While Regis Moran was far too tough to bend over for that, it was cancer that trimmed him. Coughing up blood, x-rays showed spots on his lungs. Six months later, six months nearly to the day after he walked into Western, he was dead.

There were other odd, unsettling endings. Stash, who had fallen in love early and hard with the vig, finally got nailed for it. Sure, he had dodged a bullet on the dago killing, and was so far up Bill Roland's ass that Stash thought extracting him for running a major kickback scheme out of the Mayor's Office meant also taking Roland down. Therefore, Stash always believed Roland would protect him—to save himself.

Roland may have—up to a point. "There's a little bit of larceny in all of us," he often said, shrugging and looking the other way when his people ladled themselves a little extra soup. "The price of the people's business," Roland smiled. Had proportions been observed, had Stash managed to control himself, he would have been fine. After all, a lot of guys do very well with over- and under-the-line accounting.

But Stash, being Stash, ran one too many hustles—and it's always the last one that queers the deal. By the time the feds got done with him, they had him signed, sealed, and delivered for bid-rigging, embezzling, kickbacking, macing, and two or three other things that didn't make the papers.

At first, they really did try not to nail him for all that—the same party was in the White House, and it would make Mayor Roland, a staunch political ally, look very, very bad if one of his prime lieutenants was bilking the taxpayers that heartily. "What are we going to do with you?" Roland finally asked Stash a week after the livid Mayor calmed down.

Stash hung his head, chagrined that he'd been sufficiently stupid—or arrogant—to get caught.

"We could just make you disappear," Roland mused. "If we let your old friend Mongol loose he'd have no problem doing that, would he?"

Stash knew better than to say anything—or even look up.

"But what we really need to do is have you humiliated, not dead."

Head still down, Stash nodded.

"You're damn fucking right," Roland banged his hand on his desk. "You better fucking take it."

Stash didn't move. From long experience he knew that Roland's anger was like pine branches, fast burning, fast out.

Calm now, Roland said, "and you were like a son to me."

"And a father to me," Stash whispered.

"Fucking knucklehead mick jagoff," Roland shook his head. "I should've cut you loose after that killing. Fucking Jimmy O'Hara. Fucking Father Dave. Fuck all you micks. I let myself get talked into it."

Roland paused.

"I should've cut your fucking balls off. Maybe I'll do it now."

Stash began to hope he'd survive long enough to get into prison.

Duffy defended him, and those who were there said it was his finest hour, a true work of art. With enough charges to send Stash away for life-plus-tax, Duffy bargained, cajoled, argued away most of them. When the proceedings ground to a halt, Stash caught a mere five-spot in Lewisburg for his myriad crimes—"all fine political pursuits," Duffy said mildly, "but not if you're caught on the wrong side of the table."

Of course Stash claimed he was left holding the bag, just taking his little slice, maintaining that everybody else Downtown made the big money. "Somebody had to go down for it," he said bitterly. "They made sure it was me."

That's when Duffy told him to shut up. "You're lucky it's only a nickel," he said. "We damn near had to plead you were the sole support of your mother."

That was in private. Publicly, Stash was always smart and loyal, always seeing his way through to the end of the deal, always a stand-up guy. Stash could always invent a good story, and he could always make that story stick. Sure, he pissed and moaned about it, but he took the heat away from everybody else.

Still, life has consequences, the more unforeseen, the more painful. Stash found out all about that.

By the time Stash went on trial, Mary had filled out a little bit, brushed her hair straight back, came to court every day. Sitting unfazed, a perfect cigar-store Indian, she displaying no emotion whatsoever. The newsies dubbed her Oakland's Maureen Dean, after the Watergate wife, and the resemblance was sufficiently strong to warrant the comparison. When the trial was over, she kissed Stash goodbye, watched him being led away, tried to cope, then finally disappeared.

Of course, her family gave her hell, but she could have withstood that—even withstood his perpetual lies to her. "Men do that," she reasoned.

But how their three children dealt with it was more than she could take. Teased unmercifully about it at school—*your father's a jailbird, your father takes it up the ass*—they pretended that they didn't have a father. When Mary forced them to visit him in County, they hated it—the clammy off-white walls, sticky furniture, and broken toys—and pretended they didn't know him, answering questions mechanically, kissing him with no more interest or passion than their kisses on the Mother of Sorrows statue at school.

After Stash went to Lewisburg, Mary divorced him, moved away with the kids, left no forwarding address. She never even said goodbye.

The rumor—and it was a pretty good one, given who Mary was and the tenor of the times—was that she lied about her past, re-married, changed all their names. For their part, the kids were happy to tell their new step-dad that their real dad had died many years ago.

"We never really knew him," the oldest, Al, said, and little Mikey and Petey shook their heads sadly.

For his part, Stash never spoke about her. He simply let her go.

As you might imagine, in my line of work I've known a lot of guys who've done time, and the one thing I can say is that being inside the joint is like being with a woman—everybody does it a little differently.

Of course, the first issue is turf. Right away, first day in Lewisburg, Stash had to fight some huge Hispanic dude who wanted to play grab-ass. After Stash decked him, everybody left Stash alone.

Which is how Stash wanted it: he did his time by retreating into himself. He never answered letters. He never made phone calls; in fact, he traded all his talk time for commissary scrip. He never went to see the chaplain, either the prison priest, a tall, well groomed man named Father Besserer, or Father Dave, who made the drive once, and, rebuffed, never returned. Stash never went to confession or mass. He never played ball, or cards, or checkers. He never had visitors—never even made out a visitors list, so if people ever came, they would not be allowed to see him. Not even his mother, who wept when Stash was sentenced. "Don't come to see me there," he told her. "I'll see you back here." Nodding, she never said a word. Drying her eyes, she walked out of the room, ignored the newsies barking at her, and caught a bus back to Oakland.

Shutting himself off completely, Stash took his trip to the woodshed like a man, never speaking about it, before, during, or after.

Still, in prison nothing ever stays still for very long. There are favors to be given and debts to be paid. Outside, the lingering heat made life difficult for Bill Roland, and he felt that Stash's account of good will was overdrawn. Roland had very long arms, and, as threatened, decided he wasn't done with Stash. Two years into his sentence Roland made sure Stash did hard time—very hard time.

"Payback's a bitch," Roland liked to say, leaning back in his chair, lacing his fingers across his ample belly, "isn't it?"

Calling in a few markers, Roland sent Garth Childress, his nasty little *aide-de-guerre*, out to Lewisburg, out to see the warden, a friend of a friend named John Trench. Childress' instructions: make sure Stash was introduced to some very bad men who'd make sure he learned his lesson. Many times over.

Why didn't Roland simply have him killed? "That wouldn't have taught anybody a lesson," Duffy told me over drinks one night. "Better to have a beaten-down Stash walking around as living testimony to what happens to anyone who crosses Bill Roland."

Duffy laughed, draining his Bushmill's. "Stash is going to be paying dividends to Bill Roland until they bury him."

By the time Stash got out three years later, he wasn't walking so tall no more. Couldn't get a stool in any Irish bar in Oakland. Couldn't get into the Gaelic Club—Regis Moran's nephew had taken over the door when his uncle went away, and in many ways junior was worse than the old man.

For Stash, what made matters worse was that he couldn't get a job anywhere near anybody else's money.

"He ain't squaring his shoulders now," Nig crowed, Nig, always jealous of Stash's obvious intelligence and undeniable leadership. "He ain't hitchin' up them fuckin' pants. Jagoff ain't struttin' 'round like he fuckin' owns Oakland—or the whole fuckin' world. He ain't so fuckin' regal no more, is he?"

Now Jimmy O'Hara promised he'd take care of Stash if he ever got in trouble. But Jimmy O'Hara couldn't—probably wouldn't—but no matter. By the time Stash was back on the street, Jimmy O'Hara was long gone—cancer took him down to 85 pounds, full morphine drip, full hospice. Oakland had changed; there was no one around to honor Jimmy O'Hara's promises. A man named Giuseppe Albanese—courtly, white-haired; a European who preferred sitting *al fresco*, sipping espresso—ran Oakland, or what was left of it. As Albanese liked to say, he'd be the last man on earth to honor any commitment made by some lowlife barkeep, much less a shanty Irish hoodlum.

Stash couldn't go back to the City purchasing office—that was obviously off the table. Roland blackballed him, rightfully claiming that Stash had nearly brought him and the entire Party down. While that last bit was something of a stretch, in Roland's world, A) they never forgive, B) they never forget, and C) they never admit any fault. They get the credit, *all* the credit, while somebody else—it doesn't matter if he had anything to do with it or not—somebody, *anybody* gets the blame, all the blame. So Roland made the charges stick, and Stash, a once-favored son, could barely get a job parking cars, a real Oakland legacy. What goes around comes around.

Never trusted again, by anybody, Stash tried every small-time hustle and get-rich scheme imaginable. Some worked; most didn't.

They grind exceeding small, and by inches Stash was being worn to the nub. Sometimes he lived well, other times he lived on friend's couches or in their basements. Sometimes he could afford women, sometimes he couldn't.

Living in a one-room apartment on Meyran Avenue, one night Stash drank too much Guinness and bragged to me that "I had a second career. Made a pretty good living at it. Got a bunch of broads pregnant, then took a piece of every welfare check. Pretty good gig, as long you can keep it up."

He blew a large, languid smoke ring, then laughed at his own double entendre.

"We were young, Beef. We were going to live forever."

Stash shook his head.

"When I was a kid," he said, "watchin' my old man, I always wondered if I'd ever learn how to smoke and drink. Well, I learned how to smoke and drink. And *damn!* it caught up with me.

"You hang around long enough, Beef," he started to weep, "you see how you fucked up. You see how bein' a jagoff makes you lose everything."

A year or two after that, Stash sucked it up. Sobered up. Got himself a chauffeur's license, and one of those nasty little caps. Slumped over, with deep sacks under his eyes, calling everyone "sir" and "ma'am," Stash drove a limo to rich people's home and parties.

Predictably, he hated it.

Although Nig had always dismissed the possibility that his father had Negro blood, he secretly feared it, feared that if he ever had children they'd be black as Joe Louis, as he put it one night over too many Dukes. Although he came close twice, Nig never married, never had children. Because *if* it were true, he wouldn't have been able to face it.

Having skated on the murder charge—two murder charges, really, the Iroquois husband and the dago in the park—Nig's taste for women, especially other people's women, made him more than suspect in Jimmy O'Hara's eyes. Sure, Jimmy O'Hara ran whores, and staged the occasional gang-bang, but, like any good Irish Catholic, he liked all things, including vices, in moderation. Whitey may have been the exception that proved Jimmy O'Hara's rule—while he hated sloppy drunks, for some reason he tolerated Whitey. But in general, Jimmy O'Hara hated all things slovenly. And Nig epitomized that, in his thinking, in his proclivities. Chasing skirts a little too much—OK, way too much—meant that one way or another he got too many people upset.

After much thought and vacillation, after one too many stories about the ladies, and with the memory of the dago killing hanging in the air like meat smoke, Jimmy O'Hara decided he had no further use for Nig. "Good boy," he said to no one in particular, washing glasses, wiping down the bar, "very good boy. But I can't have a boy around who can't control himself. Never know what he's going to do next when there's a skirt around. And when he gets up a head of steam," Jimmy O'Hara just shook his head. "The world needs a steady hand, clear thinking, temperate judgments. So, no. I've got to get rid of him."

Jimmy O'Hara cited the general case—"bad for business"—and banished Nig for life.

It was the end of Nig's world, the end of his dreams.

Jimmy O'Hara was heartbroken, too; everyone could see it. Nig had become family to him, especially after Jimmy's brother Frank, convicted for that armed robbery gone awry, went to Western on that 10-year bit. Especially after Jimmy O'Hara's own sons wanted nothing to do with his business. So while Jimmy O'Hara had had great hopes for the undersized, dark-skinned Nig, he also knew that Nig's wildness, even allowing points for youthful enthusiasm, would sink him one day. And, sinking, could pull down the entire temple around them.

"A man needs judgment," Jimmy O'Hara finally said to Nig one night, taking out his keys to lock the Emerald. "You're smart, Henry. God knows you're smart. And you work hard. But you have no judgment. So I can't have you. And that's the all of it."

Nig started to speak, but Jimmy O'Hara waved him off.

"I've got to cut you loose," Jimmy O'Hara shook his head. "I wish I didn't have to, Henry," he added, laying a heavy hand on Nig's shoulder, "and I wish you Godspeed. But I can't turn my back on you. I can't trust you to do the right thing every time. And that's how you survive in this business. By getting it right."

"Cut me loose?" Nig was incredulous. "Cut me loose? After everything I've done? After everything I've seen?"

"You saw *nothing*," Jimmy O'Hara said so swiftly that Nig shuddered as if he'd been slapped. "If you *think* you saw something, you'll find yourself in the river." Jimmy O'Hara paused to let the blood drain from his own face. "So count your blessings, you fuckin' knucklehead, and walk out on your own two feet. While you still can."

Bereft of his patron, Nig had to make his way in the wide world.

First, he hustled pool. But it was Oakland, and after a while nobody would play him. Enjoined to travel, Nig couldn't. He couldn't leave Oakland, even if it meant hanging up his stick—in his case, selling it to a Homewood pawn shop.

In a world chock-a-block with ironies, Nig wound up not running a tavern, not running the neighborhood like his mentor Jimmy O'Hara, but instead taking Jimmy O'Hara's cover job, tending bar. Not in Oakland, where most of the neighborhood taverns had been replaced by coffee shops—and coeds toking reefer—but north, in Lawrenceville, where all the watering holes had migrated. On Sundays, he'd fill in for red-jacketed guys at country clubs. "Lotta good cooze out there," he said.

But nobody likes a barkeep who keeps hitting on the guests. Bounced from one job after another, Nig did odd jobs, drove a cab, worked in the produce yards. Perpetually broke, perpetually running after one woman or another, he stayed away from everyone. The only one he kept in touch with was Stash.

Everybody asked, did he leave town? Get pneumonia—or AIDS—and die? Was he shot by some jealous boyfriend-spouse-lover-all of the above and dumped down an abandoned mineshaft? No one knew. When told about it shortly before his death, all the ailing Jimmy O'Hara did was shrug. "I don't know him," he said. "And if I did ever know him, good riddance. He was a man who saw all the stop signs—and ran every one of them."

"I think it was worse than that," Father Dave added, having a snort with me in the waning hours before the Emerald, tired and unwashed and shopworn, closed for good. "If you don't mind me saying so, Beef, because I know he was your friend. Nig was a lad who invited Satan to the feast—then found what many do, that he couldn't be rid of him. He faced his demons—and lost. Then carried the knowledge of what's inside him for the rest of his life.

"All his life," Father Dave added, "the person he most avoided was himself."

Where Nig was, or what he had done, no one knew—save for Stash. But there he was, at Whitey's funeral, as if he'd been in Oakland all along and Oakland just couldn't see him anymore.

Truth was, Nig had never left. He'd just become restless, moving from place to place. He'd have half a sub and a beer at Quinque's, shoot pool for money on Forbes Avenue, con Frankie Gustine out of a beer—and never forget to laugh at Frankie's story about rooming with Paul Waner's luggage. When Nig could afford a cheap hooker, he'd be in the back room of the Fort Pitt Tavern, beers lined up, TV on, the woman bouncing on his lap. "Oakland," he'd say, "is the greatest place in the world. You got everything you want right here."

As he got older, Nig developed a taste for strippers. It got so that if Stash wanted to find Nig in a public place, he'd either be beating somebody at pool or sitting at one of the local titty bars. Acrobats to anorexics—bodies scarred and wasted and black-and-blue from bad drugs and worse needles, their hip bones and rib cages bursting out of their translucent skin—Nig loved 'em all.

He nearly married a couple of them—at different times, of course—but boyfriends, managers, and the odd bout of clear thinking dissuaded him.

Killing that husband at the Iroquois nearly did him in. Sure, Duffy got Nig off that murder rap—Nig shot that woman's husband, shot him twice, then twice more, even though the man was unarmed and not dangerous.

Facing the jury, Duffy said that "while you and I would never approve of carrying on the way this man did, you are not here to judge him for that. Instead, you sit here today to judge whether he was in mortal fear for his life. I submit to you that he was."

Of course, Nig had lied to Duffy, lied to everybody about everything, and when Duffy found out he was furious. While he was afraid—rightfully so—that he would disbarred for falsifying evidence, nothing ever came of it. But as soon as Nig was found innocent, Duffy told him that they would be parting company for the rest of recorded time and two eternities beyond that.

Before Nig could say anything, Duffy walked away.

Predictably, the dago killing engendered in Mongol a taste for blood, a real taste for it, the way Whitey had a taste for liquor, Nig for women, Stash for money. Put another way, there's a lot of pain in the world, and Mongol tried to inflict all of it.

Despite his real trepidations, Jimmy O'Hara made use of Mongol—anyone with those huge muscles, and that tiny conscience, would never be out of work very long. A natural enforcer, after Regis Moran's abrupt departure Mongol collected bad debts, kept order, and meted out roughly a beating a year, not only to punish miscreants, but to keep everyone else in line. It worked beautifully.

Until it didn't.

As time wore on, even Jimmy O'Hara found Mongol uncontrollable. "He's like Regis Moran," Jimmy O'Hara said, "but without any smarts."

"Without restraint," Bill Roland added, shaking his head.

It was too much of this, and too much of that, and, finally, when Mongol beat a guy to death with a pipe wrench, Jimmy O'Hara said he could no longer afford him and gave him up. Turned him loose, sure, but everybody was surprised that it was Jimmy O'Hara who dropped the dime on Mongol. Couldn't do him for his father's murder—who knows where the river took that body?—or the dago in the park, so it was his most recent bit. "Can't have it," Jimmy O'Hara said to Roland, who nodded. "Can't have guys who don't know when to stop. Christ on the cross, Bill. This is a business. We're not here to punish sinners."

Mongol, who of course never knew that it was Jimmy O'Hara who ratted him out, never complained, never cursed his luck or his fate—or his employer.

Why not? Many people have theories, but I think that finally getting caught, and going to prison, was a relief for him. Finally, it was a way to keep him away from his own worst impulses.

Duffy, who, out of the DA's office, and, having switched sides to represent the same guys he'd so gleefully put away, defended Mongol. As he did with Stash, Duffy did a great job. Everybody said so. Duffy did just enough so that Mongol cheated the hangman but was never going to get out for the rest of his natural life. And 99 years after that.

"Try to visit him in Western once in a while, would you, counselor?" Jimmy O'Hara asked Duffy before Mongol went away. "Make sure he's keepin' his nose clean. And his mouth shut. We don't need any trouble from inside, do we?"

Duffy said he would.

And he did—but his visits were entirely unnecessary. Mongol never squawked, not once. He smiled, and kept his temper, and never admitted anything.

Like the others, Jimmy O'Hara never had anything to do with Mongol again. He hadn't gone to the trial, never visited him in prison, never acknowledged they had ever met. If someone mentioned Mongol, Jimmy O'Hara either ignored the fellow or changed the subject. That was Jimmy O'Hara—once he cut someone out of his life, he stayed out, as if he had never existed.

That's the way it had to be. Because to be Jimmy O'Hara meant that a certain percentage of people were shrugged off as breakage. Simply abandoned, dropped by the roadside, cast off and left for dead.

It was the way west. It was America.


He hated being shackled like an animal, and when they were taken off him in Western Mongol thought about decking the guard, *two* guards, really, but there were too many steel doors, and more guards around the corner, so he swallowed his bile.

Ensconced in Western, after a month in the intake unit, and two weeks in the hole, Mongol tried to get Regis Moran's old cell, but the CO—a runty little guy named Hawkshaw, his white shirt stretched tight across his bony chest—just laughed at him. "You think this is a fuckin' hotel, Hannigan? You're such a fuckin' freak you're lucky we don't lock you in the hole for the rest of your miserable fuckin' life." Hawkshaw spat, right there on the floor. "We would, too, 'cept we don't want a lot of shit from the ACLU or some other candy-ass prisoners rights group if they find out you're there too long. Just be happy you're in B Block, 'cause over in A Block they'd really fuck your ass."

Mongol wanted to snap Hawkshaw's wretched little neck like a pencil, and would have, too, except he hated the hole, with its stench and its mildew, even more than he hated Hawkshaw, so he didn't. He just stood there, hands in his pockets, nodding docilely, a child told that he'd have to wait for his hall pass.

Approached by the Aryan Brotherhood, Mongol turned them down. Typically Mongol, he trusted only his kind, and these weren't.

Did the Brotherhood plan some kind of payback for new meat as comeuppance? Not known, because before they could do anything a naive young non-Aryan foolishly annoyed Mongol in the weight room. Not thinking twice about it, Mongol simply broke the man's neck. Sure, he got the hole for it, but when Mongol came out he had earned a great deal of respect—the respect that meant that everybody left him alone, including the guards. "It doesn't hurt," Duffy said, "that he's built like an ox—and that he's just fucking nuts."

Against all odds and predictions, Mongol thrived in Western. For as sullen as he was on the outside, inside Mongol talked to everyone who came to see him, seemed genuinely glad to have visitors. For someone who had no use for the clergy outside, as a lifer he gave Father Dave as much time as the padre wanted. OK, according to Mongol there was no Heaven, no Hell, no reward, no punishment, Mongol playing his hand straight out. But at least he was friendly—even affable—about it.

In a light blue shirt and dark blue slacks, Mongol smiled and shook the priest's hand. For his part, Father Dave wasn't certain whether Mongol was simply calm—or had been over-beaten or over-medicated. He's controlled, Father Dave thought, in a controlled environment. Perhaps for the first time in his life.

"Is there anything I can get you?" Father Dave asked. "Is there anything I can do for you?"

"Nah, Father," Mongol shrugged. "They treat me pretty square in here."

Father Dave waited, hands folded and legs crossed.

"I'm glad you don't talk about my sins, Father," Mongol smiled.

"There's not much in that, is there, Jerry?" Father Dave smiled back. "Besides, with my own sins being so great, talking of yours would only lead the Good Lord to more closely to examine mine. And that Heavenly Eye my poor soul can do without." Father Dave smiled again. "So let's just keep the card game friendly, shall we?"

Truth be told, it was trying for Father Dave to visit Mongol in prison. Because Mongol, in his way, and Whitey, in his, confirmed the Father's essential pessimism about life. Certainly, there was salvation available to all, but a soul had to *want* to be saved. For whatever reason, for whatever demons tortured Mongol and Whitey—Nig and Stash, too, that whole legendary infield—they simply wouldn't reach out their hands. "Talking to those cement heads," he muttered to himself, brushing back his thinning hair, "is like talking to a wall." Then he shook his head. "I'd swear the walls are more responsive."

Still, Father Dave went every week, across the Allegheny River, down through Manchester, to Western Penitentiary, through the main gate, through the inside doors, to the visiting room. Mongol, ever-present buzz cut, was always waiting for him. Always restive, eyes always darting about as if looking for danger, he nevertheless welcomed the priest.

"How is it here, son?" Father Dave began, smiling, as he always did, speaking to Mongol's good ear.

"You know, father," Mongol shifted and shrugged. "Same old same old. Trying to stay out of trouble. Got a long time to be here."

The boy doesn't see the tunnel, Father Dave thought, much less the light. Although, he considered, it had been more than three years since Mongol had gotten into a fight—or been written up for any infraction. Docile, Father Dave thought. Well, maybe not docile. Controlled. Perhaps inwardly afraid of Western's notoriously severe punishments. Reprisals, really, from both the authorities and the inmates. A man caged is a man reborn, Father Dave considered, then asked: reborn into what?

"Eternity's a much longer time," the priest gently reminded him.

Mongol shifted away.

"Does that kind of talk make you uncomfortable, Jerry?" Father Dave asked. Father Dave had always used the Oakland Quartet's real names, considering their nicknames to be demeaning, regardless of how much they themselves used them.

"Nah, father," Mongol shrugged. "Just don't mean nothin' to me is all."

"Maybe you should think about it," Father Dave pressed.

"Father," Mongol began.

"Just a little," the priest smiled.

Silent, Mongol looked away.

"Do you want to try confessing, son?" Father Dave prodded.

Certainly, there was a lot there, the priest reasoned, if all that he had heard were true. Even his own father's murder. The Italian in the park. Sure, Regis Moran stood up for that, but nobody much believed it—ball bats weren't his style. And to be so calm and gentle, go like a little lamb with Little Bo Peep. There were a lot of other snippets, things he had heard here and there, none of which he discounted, not with Jimmy O'Hara to guide him, and Jerry Hannigan and his world-class temper.

"Nah," Mongol shrugged without looking.

"You're deep in the count, son," Father Dave tried one more time, "and you can't bunt your way on."

"Look, Father," Mongol looked at the priest. "Confession's for saps. I'm doin' my bit standin' up, and that's the end of it."

"Jerry," Father Dave said gently, his heart sinking as Mongol re-confirmed his worst fears about unredeemed humanity.

"Beggin' your pardon, Father," Mongol said, standing, motioning to the guard that he was ready to go.

Defeated, deflated, the priest watched Mongol's broad blue back step through the door, then shuddered involuntarily as its snapped shut behind the troubled young man.

He'd visit now and again, both men speaking gently to each other, for all the world like a couple of long-lost cousins. In the visitors room—hard plastic chairs, dirty toys for children—an inmate in braids was berating his wife and child. Father Dave wanted to stop the man, but understand that it wasn't his business.

Mongol, too, was distracted, and the priest gently put his hand on his arm.

"Have you thought about your immortal soul?" Father Dave pressed.

Mongol shrugged.

"It's not too late," Father Dave said, "and it's not too hard."

Mongol stood up, stretching his back like a giant lizard, and moved toward the guard. "Thanks for comin', Father," he said, "but I know where I stand with the Man Upstairs." Mongol shrugged. "And it ain't good."

"Jerry," Father Dave remonstrated, "you have it all wrong."

"Goodbye, Father," Mongol said, stepping inside the steel door, assuming a boxing stance. "Don't forget to keep your left up."

Inside, Mongol never broke faith with Regis Moran. Never said a word about his own father, all wrapped up in barbed wire and tied to a cement bock at the bottom of the Monongahela. And never, *never*, not even in his sleep, mentioned the damn dumb dago they'd bludgeoned to death so many years ago.

Mongol and Stash weren't in County at the same time. And they did their bits at different prisons. So they never saw each other inside.

But one guy that Mongol saw all the time was Billy the Car. Resale, chop-shopping, Billy was the slickest car booster in the world, or at least in Oakland. Could get into anything, alarm, no alarm, it didn't matter. Flying entirely under the radar, Billy was so good, so well valued by the hot-car trade, that the police had never even heard of him.

Until, of course, they did.

One night, Billy took a Mercedes out of Schenley Farms—in it and down the road—in about three seconds. The owner, a dour corporate type, saw it go and objected mightily to losing his car. So he called the police, who usually yawned their way through reports of stolen cars. "I've got two hundred dollars cash," he said, "that's two crisp new C-notes for the officer who returns my car. No questions asked."

Thus having their fire lit, the City's Finest found his car—a little dinged perhaps, but all in one piece, and with the john's mistress' vital information still in the glove box—and returned it by first light.

By the time they were done with Billy, he was happy to take his three years in Western standing up.

"Whitey?" a tall, blond, broad-shouldered young man drawing drafts said to me in the refurbished Emerald Lounge, re-cast and renamed as the decidedly non-ethnic Broken Bottle. "Why, there he is." Pointing to a sad, sodden old man sitting in the far corner, propped up by the wall, "Look at him," he said. "He's a sack of spoiled potatoes. There's nothing left."

There wasn't. Before he died, time had carved deep crevices in Whitey's face. Skin as pale as gin itself, watery eyes, tremor in his hands, Whitey was an old drunk barely holding it together.

It seemed that everybody in Oakland had a Whitey story. Even drunk, it was said, he still folded his bills in half, put them neatly in his money clip.

One vignette had Whitey cutting a deal with the bar keep at a joint up Oakland Avenue: a crumpled dollar and change for a juice glass of dago red with a slug of Imperial whiskey in it. Those were the days when Whitey loafed with other heavy juicers down on their luck—horses that didn't make it, women that ran out on them, scams that went sour. Sooner or later, all heavy juicers get down on their luck. Comes with the territory.

Not long after, Whitey's prodigious appetite pickled his brains. Slinking back to his mother's house, to a little apartment she made up for him in the basement, he sat in a threadbare chair, worn baseball glove on his left hand, watching the Pirates on television, announcing the plays.

After Whitey's mother died, Stash kept him for a bit, served him, let him sleep it off in his front room. "Better here," he'd say, "than with strangers. Better this medicine than some other stuff that'll kill him." Stash'd pause and look away. "I'm taking care of people no one else will."

Sober for a bit, Stash and Nig figured that Whitey'd be better off outside of Oakland. Less triggers for the sauce, maybe. So they took him to the Little Sisters of the Poor. Figuring that since he'd taken the cure, sooner or later he'd die peacefully—and since the Sisters were on the North Side, he'd die far away from his old friends who'd had enough of him. Predictably, Whitey hated it—all those dried up, wizened old women, the musty smell, the heavy quiet. "Place gives me the creeps," he complained one afternoon to Nig, who came to make sure he was all right.

"Best place for you," Nig forced a smile. "You know that, Whitey. You know you can't take care of yourself. So let the Sisters do it. They're good people."

"Don't want 'em fuckin' touchin' me," Whitey said, looking around to make sure he wasn't overheard. "Fuckin' jagoff nuns."

Nig looked, too, at the heavy, overstuffed furniture in the visitors room. The statues, the color portraits—no, it was too much. No wonder Whitey hates it, Nig thought. But as long as he's here he's not my problem.

"They got fuckin' bugs on 'em," Whitey whispered. "You hear that, Nigger Lips? Fuckin' bugs! And they're gonna fuckin' give 'em to me."

"Take it easy, Whitey," Nig spread out his hands. "Ain't no bugs here. Ain't nobody gonna hurt you."

Whitey, convinced otherwise, decided to take action. Once an alky—alky, ex-alky, they're all the same—gets something into his head, sooner or later it's going to happen. So it wasn't too long until Whitey simply upped and ran off. The Sisters called Nig—who had signed as next of kin—who didn't know anything. What's more, he wasn't about to go trolling all over the city for a broken-down albino shortstop, so he just let it go.

"They'll find him," he said to Stash. "Sooner or later, they'll find him. Face down in the gutter."

"You done all you could," Stash shrugged. "If he wants to be found, he knows where we are. We ain't moved out of this neighborhood in 50 years."

Sure enough, two weeks later, clothes soiled and tattered, shoes torn, back on the sauce, worse for the wear, Whitey showed up at the Broken Bottle, sat in his corner, wiped his mouth with the back of a dirty hand, and waited for someone to serve him his usual, Imp 'n' Arn as if he'd never been away.

There was talk of letting Whitey sleep behind the bar, but the incredulous owner would have none of it. "He'd drink the place dry inside of a week," Tim McManna shook his head. Young, college-educated, well read, he was everything the old Oakland wasn't. Having re-opened the bar as a post-undergraduate lark, he had none of Jimmy O'Hara's loyalties to people or place. "Fuckin' fern bar could be anywhere," Nig complained. "Just happens to be here."

Not mentioning the obvious, that Whitey was perhaps the least trustworthy person on the planet—from not locking the door at night to giving stuff away—McManna said the liability was too great. "He dies drunk in here," McManna said, "somebody'll sue me for everything I have. Then start in on my wife. So, no, can't have it." To end the conversation, he turned his back and walked away.

With a little help from one or two of Nig's girlfriends, they found Whitey a third-floor walk-up room where he could sleep, even take a bath, which he did with great irregularity. But at least it gave him some dignity. At least it was his.

When he worked, which was rarely, it was in a gas station. Most of the time, though, Whitey was drunk, or getting there, or coming back.

Whitey ran a few errands for people until he could no longer be trusted to keep anything straight. Drowning in bottle after bottle, Whitey went on public assistance, was watched over by Nig and his ladies, who served him drinks, kept him in his place, and made sure he was reasonably neat and clean.

When Nig more or less disappeared, the women, their hearts brimming with pity, continued to care for Whitey, who was generally too loaded to notice.

On Whitey's bad days, they cleaned up his vomit, saw him through the DTs, took him to the clinic at St. Francis. By the end, when the sky turned black and Whitey was ruled by his hallucinations, he'd become a complete wreck, sallow, unshaven, toothless. The two women, sad, lonely, overweight divorcees, never knew what dago he was talking about, or talking to, which was all to the good.

Some hurts never heal; some scars run too deep.

Institutionalized, he had no idea who he was. When a young priest came to administer the last rites, Whitey was too far gone to answer. The young fellow—a lanky, long-haired man named Father Tom Clark—left with tears in his eyes.

Finally, Whitey's liver simply gave out. "Surprised he lasted that long," Duffy said, taking care of the death certificate. Then, after a pause, "poor bastard. We all like to take a drink, more or less, but this," he shook his head. "Poor bastard."

There's an end to every story. Whether we like it or not, however pretty or ugly, even if someone has fallen off the edge of the Earth, there's an end.

Helen, the object of Nig's desire, the belle of the ball, had her pick of all the men who lusted after her. Marrying a middle-aged man who owned real estate, she watched him smoke, drink, and cheat on her, enjoying what passed for the high life in Oakland. Like a dutiful '50s wife, she ignored it. But the first time he hit her, Helen divorced him, soaked him good, and moved into genteel retirement at the Fairfax, down Fifth Avenue. There, while necessarily discrete, she took lovers, younger and younger as the years wore on. Eventually losing her looks, she suffered the early onset of Alzheimer's. Helen, the beautiful, sexy goddess, wound up in a locked unit, distracted, disheveled, barking like a dog.

Like a bitch in heat, Nig would say, ever the gentle soul.

Like me, Duffy never had any pretentions of being a ballplayer. "Rag arm," he used to shrug about himself. "Best I could do is pitch batting practice. And pick up bottles after the game."

But for all of his dour faces and dire predictions, all his talk about college, Duffy actually got a farther shot than we had imagined. Unbeknownst to us, he'd worked out with weights, added some muscle, worked on his curve and control. To our surprised, Duffy was invited to an Indians tryout camp, where he showed 'em decent heat, and better breaking stuff, and got taken into the low minors—short-season single A, some two-stick town with a general store/post office and plenty of farmers' daughters.

We never knew he was that good or wanted it that much—well, Duffy was never much on showing his cards until he had to. One theory was that he did it just to show up the Oakland Quartet—that he could do it and they couldn't. Another theory, one which I liked better, was that he was proving that he had two ways out of Oakland—and they had none.

Well, Ol' Duff was doin' jes' fahn, as they say, 'til one day he broke off one sweet curveball. Then Ol' Duff picked up his elbow off third base and went home.

Having to make a living at something legal, more or less, and deciding, like the Oakland Quartet, that he didn't want to lift things, he chose law, criminal law, in part because of the neighborhood. "With the guys I know," Duffy'd say to his law-school study group, thinking of Jimmy O'Hara and Regis Moran and the Oakland Quartet, "I'll never run out of clients."

His study group—a bunch of button-downed Ivy League types, all crew cuts, blue blazers, rep ties, penny loafers, and horn-rimmed glasses—laughed.

Duffy didn't.

While Duffy didn't exactly set the world on fire in college or in law school, he didn't need to. No dean's list, no law review, nothing. But he persevered. He made it through. Because he knew that if he stayed in Oakland, he had a ready-made client base and a guaranteed income.

Truth be told, while Jimmy O'Hara didn't much care for Duffy—"the little mick thinks he's lace-curtain," Jimmy O'Hara liked to say, "thinks he's never stepped in shit like the rest of us"—he did want one of his own as legal counsel.

"Pretentious," Stash pronounced Duffy.

"The lad," Jimmy O'Hara said, "is wondrously obnoxious." Then he paused. "But before you tie him in a sack and drown him in the river"—a nod here to Mongol, who was too dim-witted to be embarrassed by the jibe—"remember, he's one of us. No matter how different he thinks he is, he's got skills that none of you potato-eatin' paddies have. You never know when you'll need him. You never know when you'll want him. So think about that before throwing his sorry ass off a bridge.

"Now get out of here," he waved. "Find some trouble to stay out of."

Jimmy O'Hara liked to mete out punishment for offenses real or imagined, and Duffy had a way of pushing his buttons.

"To make an omelet," Jimmy O'Hara'd shrug, "you have to break eggs. But Duffy, well, he's different."

"Because he's a lawyer," a new recruit named Kennedy said.

"Because I know his mother," Jimmy O'Hara corrected him. "Because I don't want to be going to his wake on account of anything having to do with us. So I don't want anything happening to him." A pause. "Understood?"

Jimmy O'Hara did trust Duffy to follow orders, never overreach, and, most of all, keep his mouth shut. "Despite all appearances," Jimmy O'Hara told Bill Roland one night after hours, "he knows how to be loyal."

"To himself," Roland grunted.

"Never fault a man for lookin' out for himself," Jimmy O'Hara reminded Roland. "In so doing, William, Duffy'll be looking after you, too."

With Roland so converted he helped Duffy land a job as an assistant DA, the young man proving to be focused, hard-working, and utterly ruthless. A striver born to the task, he rose on the backs of the people he'd sent to prison. "Too bad," he was known to say over late-night drinks at the courthouse watering hole, "that we don't have Old Sparky any more. Then I'd really have a kill rate."

As a rising young attorney taking the bus every day out of Oakland, Duffy discovered other ideas, other agendas. In order to get up in the world, he had to prove to Bill Roland that he no longer had any loyalties other than to the Mayor. There was no neighborhood. There were no boyhood friends. There was never a time he'd pitched in front of the Oakland Quartet, the slickest infield the neighborhood had ever seen.

To be a made guy Downtown, Duffy had to leave Oakland behind. He didn't flinch.

One of his more notorious cases was the murder trial of one Donald "Dirty Dino" Scafetta. Used as an enforcer by Bobby I and his successors in the dago rackets, it seems that one night ol' Dino exceeded his brief by just a tad. "Maybe he wanted to get caught," Duffy said, "who knows?" In any case, Dino got mad—madder than usual—and, having shot some mutt in the head, Dino then soaked the corpse in gasoline and set it on fire. "Dino," Duffy told his boss, a red-faced, short-tenured, highly phlegmatic DA named Schmidt, "is good at his work and likes it. Too bad he was spotted by an unimpeachable witness and left his fingerprints all over the place. Not like him. Usually, he's more careful than that."

"You'll make your bones on this one," the DA predicted, hands laced behind his neck, and he was right.

For Duffy, who never went anywhere but for the throat, the case against Dino was a slam dunk. It was 25-to-life before the jury left the box—and Duffy, certain of the outcome, started giving interviews before the verdict, the way a pitcher hangs a curve and *knows* it's going in the seats.

By the time Duffy was finished, people were surprised that the dago wasn't summarily executed, strung up next to the Courthouse fountain.

After one of the most gruesome and celebrated cases in city history William "Duffy" McGinnis became a household name, and his political career seemed assured.

"Wouldn't be the first prosecutor to use this as a stepping stone to higher office. Might even be governor one day," Bill Roland predicted, "if the nasty little mick doesn't fuck up." Roland cocked his ear as if listening to a distant voice. "Three-to-two against. Any takers?"

Of course, there weren't. Nobody else around the Courthouse much liked Duffy, either, and knew that he didn't have the temperament for an electoral campaign. "Only if they're electing the guy you'd *least* trust to guard the public coffers," one old hand said.

Years later, after Roland finally calmed down about Stash, one night over his favorite drink, VO neat, in the privacy of his inner office—leather couch, antique desk, secure phone, framed photos of Franklin D. Roosevelt and David L. Lawrence—the Mayor breathed heavily, mumbled something unintelligible, then reminisced about his early days in Oakland. "Jimmy O'Hara," he said to Garth Childress, his sawed-off amanuensis and alter ego, "was father to them all."

"Who better?" Childress sipped his whiskey.

"I can see him still," Roland smiled, jiggling the cut-glass tumbler, "big shoulders, big belly, big belligerence."

"He was a good man," Childress shrugged.

"He was a useful man," Roland corrected him. "He was also a dinosaur. He died 20 years too late."

"Along with his jailbird brother Frank," Childress smirked.

"Leave it to you," Roland reached for the bottle, "to remember every miscreant who ever crawled out from under a rock."

"That's what you pay me for, boss," Childress raised his glass.

"Don't call me—" Roland began, snorted, raised his glass back.

"Jimmy taught them well," Roland said after a moment's reflection, "too well. That bar, the Emerald Lounge, where everything flowed in and out." Roland made a waving motion with his hand. "The hustles. The rackets. The vig. Jesus." He shook his head. "No wonder none of them ever got life right. They were terrific ballplayers—I remember that, very clearly. Just terrific. Great hands, all of them." He stopped to drink. "But what a sorry mess."

"Amen to that," Childress said.

"Sure, we sent up Regis Moran for that Gencorelli killing—he was dying, perfect for the part, and got to go out a hero. It made for a wonderfully clean case. The value-added was that it dead-ended what would have been a war in Oakland. But the four of them—they did it, we knew they did it, and they knew we knew they did it—walked. And it ruined them. It ruined every one of them for life. They would have been better off going up for it—or at least hanging it on Mongol and being done with it. Instead," he shrugged.

A last bit from the bottle before Roland set it in the bottom desk drawer.

"Duffy," he said. "That smarmy, self-righteous, shanty Irish piece of shit."

"You forgot sanctimonious," Childress said, setting his glass on the edge of Roland's desk.

Duffy could have stayed in the DA's office forever—it wasn't much money, but it was regular and guaranteed, and the work was hardly heavy lifting. But he was bored, and so after the death of old man Dennehy, who had handled all of Jimmy O'Hara's legal work, Duffy went into private practice. Of course, he maintained a relationship with Downtown, but more important, or more lucrative, he handled all of Dennehy's immigration work, labor agreements, real estate transfers, and wills. Then there were the troubles that the late Jimmy O'Hara's old crew got into, which, for a time, were passing large indeed.

In military intelligence they taught me to watch for little things, small details that indicate loyalties and comradeship—or betrayal. Figures of speech, cuff links—anything that shows where people stand. "Birds of a feather," my captain used to say sententiously.

I looked at the newspaper photos. When Duffy defended Jimmy O'Hara's crew, I couldn't help but notice that, like Bill Roland, he was a guy on the make—new suit, shoes shined, snappy briefcase. Clearly, Duffy wanted it all—and whatever broke along the way didn't matter.

He did have his loyal moments, I'll have to give him that. Defending Nig on that murder charge, for example, Duffy never charged him, never dunned Nig's family, never even submitted an invoice to Jimmy O'Hara for services rendered. When Duffy's Dickensian, high-strung partner pressed him on it, Duffy simply said, "we don't bill family," and never mentioned it again.

Of course, the fix was in with Mongol—everybody but Mongol knew it. Mustering his best defense, Duffy rolled out the nature v. nurture speech. Making it look like he was trying to spring Mongol, Duffy made sure Mongol was sent away for life.

"At least I kept him alive," Duffy said.

"Yeah," Nig answered. "Alive for what?"

I've often thought about it. Maybe Duffy was so good at his job because of his early training. As young 'uns, the McGinnis children were seen and not heard. They literally had to fight their way to the big table, where an outraged, vociferous conversation always seemed to be taking place—politics, sports, money. To sit there, to stay there, you had to hold your own. You had to mix it up with the best of them, lest you be judged a sissy, a mere child, and be told to sit back down with the wee shavers. To his credit, once Duffy moved up, nobody moved him out of his seat. Ever.

He played it by the rules, and he prospered. Nice house, nice family. Didn't want to be known for his scruffy background, the frayed collars and torn cuffs of the shanty Irish.

By then, he was William F. McGinnis, Esquire.

Times change, as do neighborhoods. In Oakland, the Irish intermarried and moved away. Finally, even Duffy moved out of the neighborhood—Atwood Street wasn't good enough for him any longer. Heading north across the river to Fox Chapel, he found old houses and even older money. He sent his kids to private schools.

After Whitey's death, every one of the Oakland Quartet lived unhappily—unfulfilled, unfinished. I wonder if Duffy'll go the same way—the gnawing feeling that nothing, not the big house across the river, the trophy wife, the thousand-dollar suits, could ameliorate or erase the idea that he was a *poseur*, that he was still one of us, a ragged kid from Irish Oakland, playing ball, hoping for a break.

If so, he never let on. Duffy became a self-righteous, self-satisfied success—and dreadfully dull.

They always are. Failures are far more interesting—at least to a social worker.

Funny thing was, they would've beaten the rap—twice.

With Jimmy O'Hara's help, they would have won the battle—despite witnesses (weak), despite evidence (tenuous), despite Whitey's presumed confession (which the police would have managed to get—and which old man Dennehy would have gotten quashed as the ravings of an alcoholic with a habitually guilty mind.)

Sure, Jimmy O'Hara had sent Stash to take care of the problem, and Jimmy O'Hara presumed that Good Soldier Stash would have. But Jimmy O'Hara being Jimmy O'Hara, and knowing human frailty as well as, if not better than Father Dave, he had a back-up plan—for Stash, for the gun, for Whitey, for everything. Dennehy to the rescue! As it was, he had to use none of them.

As it was, even Jimmy O'Hara was surprised. As surprised as Father Dave, if not more so. Regis Moran taking a dive? For *anyone*? Couldn't be.

We all knew that Jimmy O'Hara would have won because he wanted it that way. "They may be knuckleheads," Jimmy O'Hara would've told Bill Roland, "but they're *my* knuckleheads, and I want them out and walking around."

But they didn't need all that firepower. By the time Regis Moran got done with the cops and the DA, they had a better confession, a tighter case, a guy really made for the part.

That was good for Jimmy O'Hara, too. Who knew when or where the loose cannon that was Regis Moran would go off? It saved Jimmy O'Hara's crew, got rid of Regis Moran, and got Bill Roland off his back. That easy conviction was win/win/win all the way around.

Maybe not. The Oakland Quartet was barely 20. They had the rest of their lives to live with it.

And they couldn't.

The crossover into murder ate at them like the cancer that shredded Jimmy O'Hara.

The Oakland Quartet may have dodged John Law, but they dealt with a far greater, more powerful one—the law of unintended consequences. Immutable, inviolable, a law of nature as puissant and powerful as any of Newton's. It didn't matter if you had malice aforethought. It didn't matter if it was malfeasance or misfeasance or no damn feasance at all. You owned it. And punishment was always meted out, inevitably in ways you did not intend or expect. Often, punishment came at the worst possible time and in the worst possible way.

Put a different way, perhaps the way Father Dave would have it, there are places where you receive absolution. And places you don't. Oakland, on the street, in the hearts of four young miscreants, were all places that you didn't get off the hook.

Not then.

Not ever.

I get up early, hit the street early every morning.

Walking down Oakland Avenue, I skirt a line of vomit on the sidewalk.

Perhaps it's the time, or the day, but I see their story everywhere. We all have lines in life, lines that you cross and you can't come back. That was the Oakland Quartet.

I wander broken back alleys, past buckled porches and broken stairs, rusted fire escapes and overflowing dumpsters. There are lights across the park, on hills, reflected in the river. It's a dark, restive scene, and I can't rest.

Oakland is a winter dawn, a landscape in shadow, black and gray and brown. I walk past the hand-lettered Java and Jesus signs, past fountains chained shut for winter, past curio shops and comics stores. I hide in doorways, away from the wind.

Across the street, two flags snap smartly. Beneath them a long-haired man in a cloth cap smokes a cigarette. He is like the past; he does not see me.

I follow him into a coffee shop, sit behind him. He admits to a friend, an unshaven man in a ragged yellow sweatshirt, that he is worried. He is at a crossroads. He's done enough, doesn't have to prove anything. He eats a sandwich. He is 66, he says, and can't see a future. His wife is much younger. He needs money.

He is what Oakland has become, anxious, querulous. He skitters in the wind like a scrap of paper.

Like Duffy, forgetting who he was, and who he wanted to be.

It's five years since Whitey's funeral.

More, I think.

Yes, more.

I think of time past, of time passing. Of loss, of elegy. Oakland, 1958, is as foreign today as the Chartres Cathedral is to contemporary Paris.

As changed as it is, Oakland is the one place I can't leave.

The question still haunts me. Why did they do it? Four young men who never cared for anything other than themselves?

Sometimes these things have a life of their own—but I don't like that answer. Or the answer that we all like the wild motorcycle ride—to push the limits and see what happens, to go through the looking glass and see who we are when we come out on the other side.

I don't like that, either.

Instead, I think that, sooner or later, we all are loyal to someone. Even Silas Marner had his foundling, Scrooge his Tiny Tim. I don't know that the Oakland Quartet's loyalty was any more quixotic than anyone else's.

Life has a way of taking odd turns.

Maybe if they were more talented.

Maybe if Pie Traynor had seen something more.

They changed irrevocably when they killed that man.

In their own way, I think they sought absolution—and failed. Their crime was too great, their personalities too strong, their streets too powerful.

They all wanted to go home. Except they couldn't. It no longer exists—either inside or outside. Oakland, and the Oakland Quartet, are gone.

Neighborhood is fate.

There's a point in our lives when time stops. When we don't get any older, at least on the inside, when things 40 years ago seem like yesterday. So after all that's happened, after my own battered career and ruined knees, after death and prison and disappearance, the Oakland Quartet seems as young and perfect and glorious as they did that sunny morning in 1958 when, happy and full of promise, they worked out for Pie Traynor at Forbes Field, each hoping for a shot at the Major Leagues.

Of course, Duffy, the last man standing, is always available to rain on anybody's parade. Remembering the old Philadelphia Athletics, somebody—likely it was Stash—dubbed the Oakland Quartet the $100,000 infield.

"$100,000 infield?" Duffy snorted. "More like the $100 infield. And *you* put up the C-note."

Somehow it's always the Duffys of this world who inherit it. The guys who get the last word. The guys who play by the rules, keep their noses relatively clean, find some generally decent way to make a living, don't dissipate.

I'll make it, too, bad knees and all.

You don't intend to get old. You just hang around long enough and it happens. You're not smart, necessarily, or strong; it's just that you've survived.

They survived, at least for a while. But that summer haunted them the rest of their lives.

They never discussed it. Never drank to curse old times. Never told how they saved one girl, but lost the world entire.

Sure, they held it together for Whitey's funeral, but just barely. Stash fell apart—eyes dim, memory shot, libido non-existent. For a decade, he haunted the shadows in Oakland, the college kids seeing him as a harmless old fool.

At last report, he's in some down-at-the-heels senior center, a place to die.

Half-deaf, defeated by life, Mongol will never get out of prison. Old and getting older, having made many enemies inside, one day long-dead enmities are likely to spring to life—and hurl Mongol off a cell block's top tier, if they don't plant an ice pick in his back first.

Nig, who surfaced for the funeral, is in permanent rehab—an amphetamine addiction, I believe, but it doesn't pay to ask too many questions. He thought junk could keep him going during his sex marathons, and it ended up eating him alive.

Odds are he'll simply collapse one day, unremarked, unremembered, a man with talent and drive who wasted his life.

As they all did.

They were the best infield Oakland ever saw.

They were kids.

They were criminals.

They got away with murder.

And they paid with their lives.

# AFTERWORD

▼

# LOST OAKLAND

When I was much younger, and had living grandparents, they talked about life in Europe and 19<sup>th</sup>-century New York City as if they were worlds that no longer existed. I thought about that as I started writing about the Oakland of 1958, which I missed by seven years. Still, in 1965, when I first encountered it, Oakland was much the same, fading, certainly, but still the vibrant, self-contained city neighborhood that it had been for decades.

Now, with Forbes Field and the steel mills gone, and the section of the neighborhood I write about almost entirely eaten by the university and its medical center, Oakland—its pool halls, neighborhood taverns, mom 'n' pop stores, and independent restaurants (all places I loved and haunted)—like pre-War Europe no longer exists. Entirely different, Oakland has changed not for the better, I believe, but who is one man to stand against progress?

Although most of my Oakland only exists in memory, one of the reasons I still treasure it is that the neighborhood had a wonderfully compact, city feel to it. Something more than bricks and mortar—it was something alive, something only those people, and the institutions they created, could forge.

Truth be told, everyone loved places like Oakland, before times became more genteel, before air conditioning drove everyone indoors, before urban renewal ate up land and put working-class joints out of business. Oakland, and its thousand cognates across America, was a place where a fellow could enjoy a bite and a beer, play pinball or pool, bowl all night or sit in the movies, and feel an integral part of the streetscape.

Those days, when people drank lightheartedly and stayed out all night, are long gone. Now we have iPods and WiFi and Blackberries. Today, polite conversation has sadly been replaced by surly silence, self-absorbed people hunched over coldly glowing computer screens. The little left of street life has dissolved into tattoos and tank tops Oakland, like so many other American places, now stands as a piece of urban archeology, chain stores layered over an earlier, more vital time, one populated by more earthy people, good and bad. When I walk through Oakland today it feels unreal, a theme park or movie set. I can't see it without comparing it to the old days—and finding the contemporary version wanting in every particular. Living in this 3-D pentimento, I felt compelled to write about Lost Oakland—and the kinds of people who once lived there. I felt compelled to remember them even—or especially—if no one else in Oakland could or would.

If my *Ghost Dancer* is a book of stories where, in some cases, the plots take one small step beyond the probable, then *The Oakland Quartet* is super-real—one giant leap back into the past. And if *Ghost Dancer* features stories past the edge of remembrance, then *The Oakland Quartet* is firmly rooted in memory, the bedrock of place and time. As such, it's more elegiac, more cognizant of passing time, more akin to my *End of the Road.*

There are links across the board, of course, as there are in much of my fiction. Bill Roland is part of the action here, younger, somewhat more slender, certainly less powerful than he is in *Ghost Dancer,* where he pops up a few times, in "Lefty," a very political story, and "My Brother Bobby," another bit of betrayal. The streets here are as mean, if a bit less psychedelic, as they are in "Magazine Street," where he's mentioned, or "The Fire at the Chinatown Inn," where he makes a cameo appearance. Having said that, and despite the obvious parallels, this Oakland stands alone in my *oeuvre.* Mercifully, too, the Mayor's amanuensis, the relentless and often entirely ruthless Garth Childress, barely steps on stage here.

Except for a brief mention or two, Garth takes a powder here because he exists entirely for politics, whereas the protagonists in *The Oakland Quartet* don't. Along with its forthcoming companion novel, *Kings Point,* this book is about potential—paradise, if you will, and paradise lost. Here, and in *Kings Point,* we witness all that glorious youthful potential—and what happens to it.

Writing *The Oakland Quartet* I thought about that old literary line, that the English write about good and bad while the Americans write about good and evil: *Bleak House* versus *Moby Dick, Middlemarch* versus *The Scarlet Letter*. England, as the older sister, understands the Gray Scale, while America, being the babe in the family, sees the world mainly in stark black and white.

Willie Stark, in Robert Penn Warren's *All the King's Men*: hardly an accident there.

While that certainly might have been true in the 19th Century—although we could argue the point, for while Silas Marner is an old softie, Bill Sykes is evil, no?—we grew up fast on the left side of the Atlantic, and after the First World War, it seems to me that one can easily see the nuanced, English-style narrative in *Gatsby*, even in *A Farewell to Arms*. And so on.

One could argue further that Mongol is a true American throwback, truly evil; perhaps he is, perhaps not. Are the others? The crime they commit is evil, certainly, even horrific, but do we separate one from the other, the actor from the act? It's hard to say. I'm a storyteller; I try not to judge.

It's a question right out of my *Paradise Boys*, another fictional account of arrested development: are they bad boys or merely confused? And does that confusion, or that crime, fester in them forever? Did their lack of moral role models affect these boys as badly as their own wrongheadedness? These are difficult things to state with surety.

Of course, no fiction is woven entirely of whole cloth; invention, certainly, is paramount, but it must start somewhere. The distant models for this book were all hot young ballplayers who grew up to deal with prison sentences, alcoholism, busted families, disgrace. All these morally impoverished characters are people whose lives have slipped one way or another, cars on an icy road.

The Oakland Quartet was inspired, too, by my own volunteer prison work, visiting inmates in various institutions. Certainly, as one woman told me of a man who had committed a particularly heinous crime, but who inside was the picture of docility, he is controlled in a controlled environment. They all are, more or less. Otherwise as normal as you or I, for some reason they—and many like them—went down the wrong path. As with the Oakland Quartet, who knows if the right encouragement might have helped? I can't help but think that it might have saved these four fellows. And their victim.

My late mother always preached supervision of children, although I didn't realize just how important it was until I was much older. I realized then, too, that I was enormously blessed to have the right mentors at the right time in my life, some of them tough, street-wise people who boxed my ears and sent me home more than once. Otherwise, *quien sabe*?

To tell the story of the Oakland Quartet, I used any number of real people and places. David Lawrence was indeed the city's mayor in 1958, impatient and imperious, one of the last of the big-city bosses. Gus Greenlee did indeed run numbers, and various other enterprises, including the great Crawfords, although by 1958 he had died. Harold "Pie" Traynor was indeed a retired Hall-of-Fame baseball player, a polite, gentle man, a highly visible fixture in Oakland at that time. Of course, all his dialogue, including his baseball pronouncements, are my own invention.

Forbes Field was real. As was its polar opposite, at least in this narrative, Eliza. Both were Oakland monuments for decades. Both met the wrecking ball, discarded as the unusable husks of an earlier age.

Although I frequented many an Oakland neighborhood tavern in my drinking days, and some are mentioned here by name, Jimmy O'Hara's Emerald Lounge is entirely fabricated.

I knew no priests in Oakland, although there was a real Father Dave in my life. A close reader of some of my writings might discern that I, too, was a troubled youth, or perhaps just a youth in trouble. Father David Reddy was a wonderful man who was very different from the fellow described in these pages. Befriended by Father Dave at a key time in my life, I have never forgotten his many kindnesses. I pay him homage here by shamelessly stealing his name, for which I'm certain, from his present perch in Heaven, he forgives me.

Early readers complained—all my early readers complain—that there are an insufficient number of women in the book. Those that are here, they sigh, are either nearly invisible mothers, fleeting sirens, or slow-witted urchins. Or slatterns who merely stand in the shadows.

That's all true. But my early readers don't realize how wrong are their objections. The year 1958 was a Dark Time for women. Barely seen, never heard, they were barefoot, pregnant, and invisible. As but a single indication of this phenomenon, a few years back I took a trip to Alaska. One ubiquitous photo is the celebration of statehood—just a year after *The Oakland Quartet* takes place. Despite the real diversity of our nation's 49th and largest state, everyone in the photo was a white male.

While one simply cannot imagine that kind of photo—that kind of naked power brokering—anymore, that was the world in 1959. That is the world reflected here, especially for the very male members of the Oakland Quartet.

Parenthetically, Nig's attitude and behavior find contemporary cognates in professional athletics, where women continue to play secondary, supporting roles. Women on the road are seen as necessary evils—and are treated as such, as mere camp followers. Wives, barred from traveling with their husbands on extended trips, are often relegated to the status of old-time political unions, conveniently absent, bearing children to continue the line. Despite a bit of dressing up in the front offices, the near-misogyny which had women more or less barred from Toots Shor's legendary watering hole, and other like hangouts, is still quite prevalent today.

The sports world, like the one of 1958, appears to have things very clear. The older we get, however, the more slippery the ground becomes. Back then, the *terra* was more *firma*—or at least seemed to be.

Yet we know, or should, that things have infinite possibilities, and any action can have enormous consequences. Life is indeed far simpler when we don't consider the next logical step—as it seemed to be for the Oakland Quartet.

Perhaps it's the historian in all of us to try to understand such things. Because it takes time to sort out life; it's hard to grasp a moment, and all its import, when it's before us. Events in the present are too fresh; only after time sets the pot to boiling do important things rise to the surface (or tumble to the bottom.)

I tell my writing students that one must believe the reality of a story in order to write it. As the great French pantomimist Marcel Marceau demonstrated, one has to believe the physicality of what is *not* there. It has taken me some time to do that. Now, the story of these boys is as real to me as if it had happened—their youth, deadly innocence, bad choices, crime, and aftermath. I hope this has been your experience as well.

Two final points: some readers asked me what I know of these people, of this culture. On the one hand, I was raised with a lot of folks like the ones here, and lived and worked with many of them over the years. As a youngster, with my fair, freckled skin, curly hair, and blue eyes, I was often mistaken for Irish. (At one point, a fellow named Patty Mumford could've passed as my twin brother.) When I went out for high school football, Coach Casey was convinced I was Irish—until I told him my name. Later, my entire Explorer post was Irish Catholic—and some of those long-ago names edged their way in here, too.

In addition, I believe that all story tellers are empaths. Recently, I found myself telling a story of a particular urban renewal project-cum-political squabble—money and neighborhoods, history and architecture, power and race. It was a tale fraught with high emotions, far too much brio, hellish political betrayals, and a lot of angry people, people angry for 50 years and more.

I have known this story, and many of the principals, and have written about them many times. As I told the story to out-of-town guests, stating the cases from various sides, my story-telling became somewhat spirited.

In the midst of my recitative, a cousin, somewhat alarmed by my performance, asked if I had a vested interest in the story. I was certainly emotional about it, she said, but she couldn't tell which side I was on.

I told her that I'm not on either side—I have no personal feelings one way or another, that it wasn't my fight, and, besides, there's plenty of right and wrong to go around. What I found myself channeling was all their anger, their varied emotions that have welled up decades.

That's a bit of what goes on in *The Oakland Quartet*. I know these people, know how they act, how they fail, how they try to redeem themselves. I didn't have to live it. Instead, I saw it, channeled it, wrote it.

If that's not as high-fallutin' as the writer's art, it's certainly the writer's craft, and I trust I have not dishonored them, their lives, or their neighborhood with my version of their lives and what happened to them.

Abby Mendelson
August 2012